UNSKILLED

A. SKODA

A. Skoda

This novel is dedicated to so many people.
My children who witnessed my time in retail and who were often forced to be patient with my availability.
My husband who listened to me lament for countless hours about the conditions of my job.
This novel is dedicated to my family who sat beside me as I tried to figure out if food or sanity was more important.

Lastly, this novel is dedicated to the people who work in any service industry that feel as if their voices are not being heard. You are heard, and your experiences are real.

Author's Note

Instead of creating a memoir, this novel is largely based on events and stories I have personally experienced throughout my career in retail as well as the experiences of the people I have met along the way. I wrote this book to shine a light on the industry rather than throwing a single company in the limelight. If you ever found yourself in retail, no matter what company you worked for, chances are you have experienced something similar. Knowing that the stories you are about to read are commonplace beyond the companies I had been involved with, it was important to me to give a voice to the millions of people who are working in retail while protecting those companies that hired me and the people who worked with me.

Oftentimes, service industry workers are considered unskilled. They are belittled, berated, and find themselves in situations that no college course could prepare them for. These people are skilled beyond the confines of any lesson. Despite being looked over by most of the community, these workers are strapped with a skillset that is both transferable and necessary.

They stock shelves so that we can lazily pick the food we want to eat. They stock clothing racks so that we can flaunt the newest fashion trends. They are the people who are holding our communities up by the products they offer. Sometimes, they are the unnamed friends we confide in. Sometimes, they are our punching bags. Sometimes, they are our pillars of stability. However, they are rarely seen as human, rarely recognized for their hard work, and are often scrutinized for their profession. But they have stories that are worth being told. Their voices deserve to be heard.

So, dear reader, here is Lennox's story.

ONE

Welfare Central

I t was hard to tell who the desperate one was. Was it the multimillion dollar company who hired the pregnant teen on the spot? Or, was it me willingly accepting a role after answering a few simple questions such as *How do you handle an angry customer?* Considering I had been dealing with the insults of strangers hurling towards me since my pregnant belly began to swell, it was a no brainer how to answer. I simply told the hiring manager to not take their insults personally and explained I had bigger fish to fry than to worry about someone else's opinion.

It was then that my soon to be boss in khaki pants extended his hand towards me and told me I had landed the job as a cashier. As long as I passed their drug test I could start with the next round of orientation. This was my path towards stability and I was ready for it.

When Orientation Day rolled around, I was terrified yet thrilled to be embarking on my new adventure. The training was to be taking place in a converted break room. The air was fresh with curiosity and a little bit of nervousness. Between the glances and the body language of my new coworkers, I realized that the training we were entering into was going to drone on longer than necessary.

Because this was my first job, I soaked every moment in. The crinkle of snack bags opening, the smell of morning breath, and the slight buzz of the fluorescent lights filled the air. Our cafeteria-style tables created an odd seating arrangement. None of us knew exactly what wall to face and we squirmed awkwardly at the round tables waiting for our shifts to begin. They rolled in a T.V. that brought me back to my elementary school days. The training Leader popped in a VHS and the screen flicked on. We were greeted with a bright blue and white logo bouncing around happily welcoming us to their vast company. It suggested that we were part of a family- a very dysfunctional and cryptic family.

There were the typical nuances of new hire videos. The CEO greeted us from his million-dollar office, his veneers shined brightly between his lips as he spoke. His voice meandered through the history of his company often overlapping black and white pictures displayed to show us their humble beginnings. A few hours of this passed by. The talking points bounced between safety protocols, clocking in and clocking out, where you can and cannot have your breaks (you could enjoy your break in your car or the breakroom), where you can park, how to address concerns to Human Resources, and most importantly, how the pay structure is set up as well as how they evaluated your job performance. Eventually, he began talking about his intended topic. He loves us, and he cares about our well-being.

For that reason, he wanted to take the time to tell us that he understands how hard it is to provide for our families. The mood became intense as his next few sentences sputtered out. Competitive wages were never addressed. Affordable health insurance was not mentioned. Instead, he knew of a better way to help us provide for our families. Welfare.

He then passed the torch to another person that oversaw every store in the state I resided in. They wanted to get the information as accurate as possible so that we could get the help we needed. Our regional director began explaining that the paperwork to apply for social services was located in the Human Resources office. They were ready to help when we needed it. Over the course of 30 minutes, the CEO Helper went into grave detail on how to properly fill out the paperwork. We went over food stamps, cash assistance, childcare, and most importantly state health insurance.

Pictures of the forms with written notes began fluttering on the screen. The whole point of this job for me was to get off of Welfare. How to apply was old news to me. But my new comrades were watching intently. Their eyes were glued to the TV. Were we all experiencing the same amount of thoughts racing through our head as we grappled with the idea our new company was well aware of their meager wages. Was this really happening right now? Some smiles began to perk up onto their faces. They seemed relieved to know they can receive help applying for help. Slowly, I swiveled in my chair just to make sure I was still alive and coherent.

Our CEO reminded us again that he loved each and every one of us, which is why he is helping us get state assistance. It was clear every one of us would need to fill out this form to survive.

When the video was over, not only did we have all of the tools to apply for state assistance, the training Leader asked if we had any questions. The floor was open for discussion. Nobody dared to ask why they wouldn't just pay us a livable wage. Instead, meek hands crept upwards. Questions about if employees could drop the paperwork off here at the store began to filter through timid mouths. It was quickly revealed the company just provided the paperwork but it was up to us employees to drop off the forms at the midtown offices. My new coworker's face fell, the bus didn't come up this far north and it would be near impossible to get his form to the mid town office.

When asked why they provided us with this information, the Human Resources Bot answered by avoiding the question. Their only solid talking point was how the middle class was dwindling due to the political climate and inflation thanks to our president. In other words, the employees worked for poverty wages so the company could be praised for its low prices and affordability.

TWO

Size, It Matters

R egardless if the company's target audience was
low income or the snooty privileged, they all
understood that love is always in the air. Whether the
condoms were made of latex or lambskin, the awkward-
ness of the customer purchasing their rubber of choice
was always the same.

It was easy to see when they were getting ready to
buy them. Waiting to go through the line, men (or
teenage boys) would refuse to look my way. They
couldn't make eye contact for fear of being guilty of
experiencing pleasure. They would either bury the box
of promised fun under a pile of energy drinks, sweatshirts, and Hot Cheetos or discretely hand them over.

When they handed it over it was always in a gentle
manner as if they were afraid my eyes could pierce holes
into the thin barriers. Their precious cargo was as fragile
as a snowflake. And if they were mishandled, I was to be
the one responsible when they failed.

The contrast between when men would buy these
sheath protectors and when women would purchase

them was laughable. Men clearly don't buy pregnancy tests enough to realize there are far more personal things you can purchase. Most guys wouldn't make eye contact with me and I was tasked with keeping up small talk when there wasn't much to say besides I hope you enjoy getting laid.

Women were the only ones that would buy these suckers with pride. They would hold their head up high as the box gets rung through. Usually, they would buy some sort of pre-made coffee to accompany the rubbers. Evolution hasn't caught up with the modern world and condoms are always treated like a trophy for "earning" a man. They have protection, they have a hunter, they are better than you.

As my teen bopping pregnant belly swelled with defiance, customers would become more and more uncertain going through my line. Teen boys that were scrawny and short would come through my register all the time. Their baby soft skin glistened and impatiently waited for their facial hair to grow. They never bought normal sized condoms. It was always boxes of XL, or even XXL wrappers. Stifling my laughter became a daily task.

It became a game for me to see how uncomfortable I could make the teenagers when they bought their condoms. Most of them looked like they didn't even have a driver's license. I barely had my own but it was still fun to evaluate my eager sex addicts. My imagination would run wild as to where they were actually having sex if they couldn't do it in a car. Horny teenagers driving into abandonded parks tucking themselves into the anonymity of night to fuck the night away was the easy route. It brought a whole other meaning to a stick shift. So where would they even slink off to enjoy their new tricks without a vehicle?

A memorable trio of 15 year old males came through the line one day. Each had their box of 100 count XXL condoms (ribbed for her pleasure) and they each had a Redbull, a Monster, and Takis. Their clothes smelled like lilac- the mark of their mothers lingered wherever they went. They were just a few inches taller than me, if the boys were proportional to their height and gait, those condoms would slip right off. Nervous giggling began to slip from their mouths. As a very pregnant teenage cashier, it wasn't abnormal to see shaky hands, sweat beading on foreheads, and the occasional sigh emanating from men as they purchased their products. But giggling? That was a new one.

"Hi! How are you boys today?" Watching them squirm added some quality entertainment to my day.

"Uhm, hi…" The baby alpha's voice cracked revealing his journey through puberty. All three of them looked down. "Just tell me the total." Baby Alpha tried to demand as they all gathered their items and began counting their crinkled dollars and change. I can't say much about this because I paid for my pregnancy test in dimes. Yep. Dimes. Still, his cockiness (maybe the pun was intended here) bothered me. Let's blame that on the hormones.

"It's too bad you're buying these ones." My response pulsated out of my mouth before I could filter it. If they were real grown-ups they could read the total blaring in neon green.

"Wh-what do you mean?" Baby Alpha stammered, unable to understand where the conversation was going.

"Those are the exact ones we used." A smile tried to force itself on my face. Alpha Boy's fear started wafting towards me. The other two boys began to sweat and fidget with their oversized sweatshirts. "Size matters, too big? They fail. Trust me, I know." I patted my belly as if I was remorseful. Without a word, the boys slinked back to the aisle filled with condoms abandoning their original choices.

My register was within view of the pleasure promising aisle and their faces grew long as they realized the pregnancy tests were right next to the rubber shields. It has always given me a good laugh as to where the tests were placed. Did the condom break? Well... here's the tests ready and available for ya!

After a few minutes, for an unknown reason, the boys crept back up into my line. There were a few other cashiers they could have gone to, self checkout was also a contender to avoid any more harassment but maybe they liked the mockery. This time, they held boxes filled with S/M wrappers. The boys finished their transaction in silence.

THREE

First to Know

B efore women plan their intense and over the top pregnancy reveal they need to find out officially if they are indeed pregnant(who even started that shit anyways, early pregnancy is miserable and nobody needs an extra thing to think about). They need to know if it is the real deal, food poisoning, or a bad hangover. To do that, they must buy a pregnancy test, and guess who sees it? Cashiers. We see everything before your partner even has a clue.

It has happened countless times. Prospective mothers would hide the tests between gobs of ginger and bags of lemons. Usually, tea would be nestled in the mix trying to settle their seasick stomachs. Their mother's ancient remedies clogged up the conveyor belt as they desperately sought out relief. These remedies never do anything from what I hear but many women insist on drinking that God awful medieval concoction. Every now and then there would be Miralax or FiberOne thrown into the mix to try to help with the never talked about constipation.

Us cashiers have experienced it all. Tests have been thrown at me, shoved under the register as if it were part of a drug deal, and proudly placed at my station waiting to tell the world about the possibility of pregnancy. The pee sticks bring out whole new personas out of people and when one was flung near me I knew to tread lightly. There were always side glances from the potential mothers as if they were worried I would say anything. The prideful wanna-be moms would always try to coax me to say things to them. Maybe a pre-congratulations salute is what they wanted. I would never. It wasn't my job to congratulate or conceal. According to many people, it was never my business in the first place.

When I was 17 and purchasing my test I felt the same way. The cashier's emotions were muddled as she scanned the cheap test that was being purchased. She began to furrow her brows as the realization of my tender age came to fruition. When my friend and I began to pay for the test in a medley of dimes, she stayed silent as she flung newly found disdain at my nervous body. Embarrassment and guilt washed over me as I silently walked away from her register. Because of this, everytime a potential mom brought a test to my line, I allowed them freedom from my own opinions. I would never remark, never allow my face to change, and I swallowed every bit of word vomit that threatened to spill. Their secret stayed with me.

Time would explain to me how hard this promise would be to keep. One woman was straddled by her three young children as they approached my register. From my perspective it looked like they were all under 4, two still in diapers. The kids all looked like Irish twins and their mom was barely holding it together. Her messy hair don't care attitude shone brightly under the fluorescent lights. The bags under her eyes were just as poofy as her Ugg boots. She donned sweatpants that were clearly hand-me-downs from her husbands' high school days. Her vibe was that of a woman who believed her glory days were behind her.

She piled her children's clothes on top of the register belt hastily. They were screaming and hitting each other and their referee was desperate to leave the store quickly. A cold snap had swept through the desert and she was desperate to buy her children suitable clothes for this anomaly- but just as interested in leaving.

"Shit." She said, looking me up and down when I started ringing up her order. Her face went white as she studied my underage gestating body. It wasn't abnormal for people to become uncomfortable looking at me. I had become the teen with the Scarlet Letter for getting knocked up.

But, when my hand touched the box under the pile of clothes, it all clicked. Hate to break it to you sweetheart but… your husband's pull-out game could use some improvement. My thoughts almost spurted out but at this point I almost felt bad for her. She was trapped in a cycle that she didn't seem to understand how to fix.

Taking pity on her, the box was scanned and thrown into a bag discreetly. It was clearly important that the pee stick was well hidden so into the pile of clothes it went. Something told me that she wouldn't mind the clothes being thrown into the bag concealing the test. She needed to get out quickly and hide her disappointment about another pregnancy. Her total was delivered and she produced the cash in haste.

"Thank you." She took the receipt and stood staring at me for a second. "I can't believe I went through your line." Uhm ok? You're welcome? "Thanks, for you know, hiding *it*. Nobody can know." We both knew. My imagination went wild thinking about her peeing on the stick and then vomiting when she saw the double pink line. When you don't want someone to see your purchase, I suggest using self-checkout. Needing the job, I didn't say any of the thoughts that were running through my head. I smiled at her and decided saying nothing at all was worse punishment than responding.

Another way that my position allowed me to find out about pregnancies was by witnessing the vitamins being bought. Countless women would go through my line with baskets full of prenatals. There would be five or six different brands. Which one would the doctor approve of? Which one was able to be swallowed? They would have additional supplements packed away. And the same slew of crackers, ginger, tea, and lemons filled their purchases.

Their eyes would always avoid mine. Their small talk would be weak- probably because they felt just as fragile. I'd ask how they are doing and they would smile meekly. If it's such a miracle, why is pregnancy so miserable? It is what each of them wanted to say but never would. They didn't have the guts because they just finished emptying them in the post-apocalyptic inspired bathroom my store offered.

What really would excite me was knowing much sooner than their spouses. Sometimes women wait until a major holiday. We have all seen the pregnancy announcements on Christmas, Father's Day, and even Valentine's Day. It would be such a thrill when the couple would go through my line and I could tell that the husband or boyfriend was completely oblivious. I was always met with the "don't you dare say anything about it" look emanating from the new mother. Sometimes, I liked to start a conversation that could lead to spilling the beans but then steer it off course just to keep them on their toes. It all depended on the relationship I had with the woman.

After the cat leaped out of the bag, women would come in asking how I missed the pills, the tests, the remedies. They would act as if they didn't threaten my life if I spoke about their situation. Suddenly, the cashier that was a threat for knowing confidential information was an idiot that couldn't add one plus one.

Every time this happened my reply would be "your secret is safe with me." It was none of my business to talk about their business- even if they wanted me to. Plus, it became a game trying to figure out how long they would wait to announce. It was obvious when the partner would know. Typically, they would become immediate doters. Arms would be wrapped around their child-bearing partners' necks offering a walking headrest for their weakened state. Suddenly, they would be the only ones paying. Questions would tumble out of their mouths about "honey, didn't you say this morning you wanted...". I would hear about the weird cravings, and lots of flowers would come through the line when she wasn't there. Other times, the real dicks would just disappear and I would never see them again.

Each and every time, their secret was always safe with me.

FOUR

Reasonable Accommodations

A s the months crept closer to my due date my body
began giving warning signs of complications.
Among other scenarios that began playing out at the
store, it was becoming clear to me that this journey of
hope was simply a band aid on my problems.

The turnover was high; they just needed bodies at
registers. They ignored the warning signs of defective
employment and I returned the favor by discarding the
signs of poor management. I was six months pregnant
and only 17 when I was accepted into the company. The
rules and regulations of the major retailer didn't allow
minors to work more than five hour shifts at a time and I
could only work between 4 pm and 10 pm. Oftentimes,
the Leaders would "forget" we were there and more
shifts than not, they would hold us hostage at our registers until 11 pm.

When I was about to pop, I began to receive th
external word lashing from customers about
protruding body. One man in particular decided
perfectly acceptable to call me "a disgusting '

front of his three young blonde boys. Fresh from high school, the words hurt but not as much as it hurt watching the young boys sit placidly by his side. There was no doubt that the flurry of insults emanating from his mouth were the norm in their home. These boys ultimately had two trajectories for their lives- either they will disown their father for his toxic traits or they will make their daddy proud by following in his footsteps.

After the shame of my life's choices was lathered thick onto my skin, the man walked away with his head held high. He was proud of himself as I began to publicly weep at my register. Of course, my Leader came over well after it was done and between sobs I tried relaying the conversation so I could explain I needed to get off the sales floor for a little bit.

Thankfully, a customer who was waiting a substantial amount of time to purchase her items witnessed the man's wrath and was able to translate for me and insisted my manager bend to my wishes. She was my angel I will never be able to thank. My eyes were as swollen as my feet by the time she spoke up and my body desperately needed a rest. Marvin graced me with acknowledgement and was the only good that came out of that place.

As I sat in the break room trying to calm the storm that had risen up inside of me, Marvin brought me cold water and a small snack. He reminded me that yes, this world is a cruel place but there will always be someone in my corner. As quickly as he came, he left so that I could consolidate my emotions and consume my fears in the form of Oreos before stepping back onto the floor. My five minute break turned into an hour. My nerves were calmed as I walked back to my assigned register.

Just moments later, another customer decided to berate me for choosing to carry to term. She told me my legs should have stayed closed clearly I had no self respect. I begged Marvin to let me go home after this but he said my hour-long break was the only grace he could grant me for that day.

My body was heavy with grief. Watching my childhood go while watching the world turn into a place filled with the difficult and horrid villains Disney promised were lurking under the surface terrified me.

When my feet began to swell to the point of concern and the pressure of standing began to be too much, they would not allow me a stool. It was against company policy to provide a stool so a cashier could perform their job. They called me spoiled and entitled when I asked for this accommodation. There wasn't a mother on the management team. I didn't expect them to understand, I just needed compassion.

When it came time, I began taking birthing classes on Wednesdays and almost lost my job over it. The major retailer had strict guidelines for time-off requests and the scheduling Leader, Erik, loved scheduling us minors (who weren't allowed to take time off) when we needed to be home. On my way to my third class, I received a phone call from Erik. His role creating the store schedule was a huge task and it meant he would be stuck staring at screens all day long trying to navigate the schedules of over seventy five people. He was constantly playing the biggest game of Sudoku and it was obvious why he was constantly cranky. Nevertheless, it was still hurtful and frustrating when he would play games with our schedules just to rile us up.

"Hello." It was more of a statement than a greeting as I answered the phone.

"Where are you?" The ruffle of papers in the bacl ground told me he was not on the sales floor. Erik n' was but when he was on the phone, he liked to pretend he was in the trenches with the rest of the team.

"On my way to class. I told you I wasn't available Wednesday evenings due to a birthing class. When are you going to start scheduling me days while I have you? I haven't been a minor for three weeks." It was important to stand my ground and not show my cards. This man lived off siphoning joy from our souls. He would have the upper hand if my emotions bled through.

"That isn't a real class. It'd be a shame to lose you over some silly 'birthing' class. Find a better excuse. I expect you to be here in 15 minutes. Also, nice try. Minors can't work during the day." The pen twirled around in his mouth distorting his syllables.

"I turned 18 three weeks ago. A better excuse will come when you update my employment to the right status- I am not a minor anymore. See you tomorrow." His bluff was called. He loved to intimidate the employees, especially women. It was what he was known for and I'd be lying if a smile didn't creep up on my face when I hung up.

A month later, the grocery retailer denied me any sort of leave when I was about to give birth to my son. I didn't qualify for FMLA because my employment was just shy of a year. The three months of unpaid leave didn't pertain to me and there were no laws protecting me because I lacked tenure. They also never changed my status from minor to adult so no time off was allowed under any circumstances.

Enough was enough and I had to make a choice. Was it to be a present mother and rely on the savings I've been building from saving every penny I earned since I was thirteen? Or, would I give birth and immediately return back to work for a company that refused to protect and accommodate me?

The choice was easy. I waddled into the office that Erik was sitting in and made sure that the papers announcing my intentions of leaving the company touched his slimy fingers. The fear that welled into his eyes could have drowned a whale. There was begging, compromising, and groveling. Suddenly, I was the prized possession of corporate America. Suddenly, he wanted to try to work with me about my upcoming leave. They couldn't lose me.

I turned in the resignation anyway. My intentions were to leave on good terms but I didn't get to finish out my two weeks. Due to complications, my child was born early.

It was the start of a new beginning and I was on the hunt for another job again. After some time and several interviews, I was once again a cashier at another major grocery retailer. Just like last time, I was filled with hope. Maybe this could be my refuge- that I would be able to turn the opportunity into a bountiful career path. They claimed to care about their employees- except here they call them team members and I was to never use the word "employee" again. This company also promised much better pay, there wasn't even talk about how to apply for welfare in their orientation! It was a brand new adventure.

FIVE

Anonymous (Like Me)

The second grocery retail I found myself at was big about making us employees (shit, sorry, team members) feel like our voices were heard and our opinions would be taken seriously. During the probationary period of employment, I warned newbies to study the verbal conventions of each person they interacted with. They never understood until it came time for their 90-day review.

As D-Day crept up, Team Leaders would sneak around asking for everyone to write out answers to a three-question response. We were to discuss what we thought of the new person. Could they be part of our family? Or would we sweep them to the side and sing a parody suggesting "We don't talk about ---"? Did they represent the company well enough to be welcomed into it and buy into the once-killer benefits? Were they the strongest doormat we could find? And for the friendly customers... has the newbie made connections with them yet?

When I started, benefits were calculated based on

tenure. It was possible to have decent health coverage for you and your family for as low as $40/month! Not only did they boast a killer premium, but they had a discount system based on your biometrics. The healthier you were, the higher employee discount you received. On top of all of this, you also had a HSA (Health Savings Account) the company would put about a grand into to help cover any medical expenses you may need to pay out of pocket. This grocery store even paid a few dollars over minimum wage when I was hired. Obviously, none of this lasted. Slowly but surely these incredible offerings were stripped like the lining of a smoker's esophagus.

Because of the jaw dropping benefits, people would flock to work for the major retailer. It took me multiple interviews to even be considered for the once pretentious role. My knowledge in PLU's (the numbers fruits and veggies are assigned so that cashiers can properly charge for the produce) helped me. The banana PLU still haunts me to this day because of the popularity of the fruit (4011 for anyone wondering).

Part of the gambit was making the Team Members feel blindly empowered in our role with the business. Each member of the team would need to respond to questions about the new hire and collectively, they would decide if the newbie would stay employed for the long run. We would create our carefully crafted answers about our new "fam" by hand or type out our responses. Each response would then be typed into the "legal" document for job reviews facilitated by the Leader- I mean Team Lead. There was no discretion. If you pissed off Catty Kathy... that shit would live in your permanent record for the entirety of your career there.

Pretend you are the newbie waiting to find out if they are straight up firing you for showing up with a tank top on and unshaven pits. Or maybe they would offer you some grace and simply extend the probation period instead of canning you for accidentally giving a customer a five-dollar bill instead of a one-dollar bill as change. Maybe you struggle with anxiety and even though you have done nothing wrong, you are terrified that the two guys wearing Oakley sunglasses and Dickies shorts were about to tell you that you are a failure and will not be with the company after today. Sweat beads into your palms as you try to stay calm. Nobody takes a job in retail unless they absolutely need it. Bills need to be paid, mouths need to be fed, and you may or may not be facing eviction from your father's home. Or was that just me?

As my first review approached, I boasted a calm composure though as if I knew the review would go well. Never mind the time when I accidentally told the store Leader the store smelled like old people and dead fish. The Bald Bro's smile faded as the words poured out of my mouth while handing over his newly purchased lunch. His Hawaiian style shirt flopped in the wind that was produced by our sliding glass doors and his flip flops began to look uncomfortable.

"What did you say?" His words twisted around my ears.

"Uhm, this store smells weird. I-I am sensitive to smell I guess. Sorry." My embarrassment was greater than Theo's upset. Even the best of us vomit our thoughts from time to time.

Trying to push the memory from my mind, I sat at the bagel shop across the parking lot with a pair of way too laid back Team Leaders who were to decide if I was to stay or go because of my actions during my 90 day probation. After the self induced angst, the review ended up going well. I began to take a breath as I waited to hear if I would earn a raise. But there was a hitch, and my breath was cut short.

They brought out the team member's comments. They typed them out to hide the handwriting. This is when it came in handy to understand how people spoke. If you could differentiate between their own dialects, slang, and the nuances of their word choice, you were able to pick through the verbiage and see who wrote it. Many times, true colors were revealed and you would be hurled into the world of drama. If Betty didn't like you, her comment would glare at you from the white page daring you to confront her. When David had a crush on you, you would probably feel like you were being felt up on a bad date reading his responses to the questions about you. There was no vetting of comments.

When they were done doling out the petty comments, the pair of Oakley's discussed the differences between the scores they gave me, what the team scored me as, and the scores I gave myself on the job review. It was a three-way nobody truly wanted to partake in no matter how many quaaludes were doled out. The men in Oakley glasses began asking me to defend myself and respond to the middle school-worthy remarks. They glossed over the positive ones because those were just the suck-ups. Or maybe they had a thing with those team members and thought they were like Jimmy Fallon and just loved everyone and everything. Positivity wasn't what they wanted to focus on anyways. It was the improvement they would be after. Positive remarks were rarely made unless you had a stellar Leader (and there were some).

Karl, my hiring Team Lead, made sure to engrain in us that nobody was a "5". If you put on your piece of fate that you were doing the very best you could, he would return it to you requesting that you answer honestly and realistically. This resulted in notoriously low scores and low raises. The President of the Region often praised Karl for his strictness because he felt that it resulted in harder workers. What ended up happening was morale would crash and burn like a car blowing up on a Nascar track. What's the point of doing your best when your best wasn't good enough?

Looking at the average scores, it was imperative that I began to claw my way out of a self-built cave for answers. Emotions would need to be defended when a customer called me a "fucking idiot" and my response was tears. When you cried, you would need to find your own shoulder for comfort. If you laughed too much, you would need to tone it down. There was no winning and your fate was constantly in the hands of Oakley's and jaded adults in nonfunctional aprons. Every step, every breath you took was scrutinized and it was heavily frowned upon to speak up for yourself. And if someone didn't like you, you prayed to God that they also didn't like the management. Shit, did it again, Leadership.

Learning the way everyone speaks was the very first skill you gained in this company. This was a survival tactic that everyone learned the hard way- unless you listened to me.

SIX

Fame

_____

Nestling yourself in grocery retail, no matter where you live, you are bound to run into a famous person. When it comes to me though, I have a hard time understanding who is who in the world. Tig Nataro, we would have one hell of a show together (just sayin'). Over the years, there were many celebrity encounters. While I missed John Lithgow and numerous sightings of bands such as the Wu-Tang Clan, I did get to experience my share of household names.

For instance, my first experience with seeing a celebrity in the store was when Mel Gibson showed up for a quick trip. My little, tiny store here in my sort-of little town was graced with his presence. Everyone was in a flurry trying to sneak a peek at the actor. He was not Tom Hanks (who was rumored to own a home about 20 minutes north of the store) but his aura certainly knew how to throw bystanders into a tizzy.

Unfortunately for him, I was dealing with a rough patch in my life and while I was able to enjoy privacy during that time, he was not allotted the same courtesy during his. Just before he decided to jaunt his way to my town, he was caught in a drunken incident slurring himself into a ditch I don't think he will ever climb out of. Gibson was caught on camera drunkenly mulling over obscenities and antisemitic rhetoric. All of this was caught on camera during a police stop where Gibson was charged with drunk driving.

And hell hath no fury like a scorned woman. That's how the saying goes right?

Anyways, I had a plan. I sent my coworker on her break, and I waited. Like a fisherman waiting to see the Loch Ness Monster, I waited for him to approach my register- the only register opened. He would have no choice but to see me- his favorite type of person, a now scorned Jewish woman. Numerous customers were gathering around him as if they had never seen a celebrity before. His frustration was plastered all over his perfectly chiseled face. I get it, sometimes a guy just wants to get an apple and a kombucha (before all the hipsters discovered it).

As he approached my register, I turned my light off. He walked towards me and continued putting his things down.

"Oh, I'm closed". My smirk gave away my intentions. His scowl grew and spoke for him. Gibsons' eyes rolled and he huffed a little bit. My coworker Autumn, the one who was always trying to outshine me, saw this opportunity and wanted the bragging rights of meeting him. She promptly stopped her break and jumped onto a register.

Before her register was fully signed in and her light on, she excitedly proclaimed "Hi, I am open over here!" Autumn stood at her station twirling her hair and smiled her biggest dopiest smile I had ever seen. He scoffed as he picked up his apple and kombucha. Did he know that it technically had alcohol in it? It made me giggle as I realized he was unknowingly (or maybe knowingly) breaking his sobriety pledge right here in my store in front of everyone. It would take another 5 months for the kombucha Gods to release this information creating a snafu for their sales, customers' lives, and us cashiers who had to be on the front lines of raging former alcoholics assuming we poisoned them on purpose. But, Mr. Gibson was desperate to purchase his fermented tea and apple. Calmly, he proceeded to her register. Autumn began her round of small talk that always came much more naturally to her than to me. Today, I was grateful for it because I didn't know what I would say if I had to continue my conversation with the antisemite.

Customers were showing their protests and interests by which lane they chose. A woman even began crying out of sheer excitement to see him. She was babbling like a loon and between her and my coworker with her hair twirling and obnoxiously fake smile I wasn't sure who the real freak show was. Others came into my line as we loudly snickered about what a disgrace he was to our nation. We enjoyed our time pretending to be Mean Girls in those few minutes as he attempted to leave. It was clear by the way he scurried away that he regretted ever wanting that apple.

Yes, Fabio was an incredible human being and was gracious when I told him I just didn't get the appeal but appreciated how he leaned into the role and allowed women to swoon all over him on Valentine's Day. It might have been a sponsored excursion to my store to help boost sales for his newest product, but he held his head high and smiled wide for each swooning woman who snagged a picture with him. He was a docile giant and while I do not in any way understand the sex appeal, I did understand the attraction to his tame demeanor.

One of my favorite encounters was with Kevin Smith. It was a pretty lax day and there was a man looking at the cheese. In all honesty, the only reason why I struck up a conversation was out of pure boredom. Every centimeter of the area I was stationed in that day was polished to perfection and standing still is torture for me. So, when I noticed a guy who looked relatively harmless and not a total dick, I decided why not? We ended up talking about all the best cheeses. We shared a few chuckles- whether or not his amusement was sincere I will never know.

As the conversation grew, my coworker Danny stormed behind me and gasped "Oh my God! You... You are my hero!".

I immediately became wide-eyed- and so did Smith. I shook my head and admitted my apparent ignorance. In fact, I was convinced that Danny had run into an old friend. Danny informed me this nice, harmless, down-to-earth dude was really a celebrity that is well-known and loved. Before I knew it, Smith was being swarmed by my very bored and overly excited coworkers. To add to his awesomeness, he was equally as enthusiastic for his fans as they were for him. He posed for pictures, allowed them to ramble on, and was amused when I explained that I live under a rock called "drowning in motherhood".

SEVEN

Valentine's Day

The cold nipped at our fingers as we hurriedly rang up each desperate customer. The air was filled with half-dead flowers and still drying chocolate strawberries. We were serenaded with the beeps and murmurs of the registers as products were siphoned from the shelves. It wasn't love encompassing my shoppers- it was the capitalistic incentive of buying love that enraptured them. Each item fell victim to the idea that money would purchase admiration. The store was so packed our check out lines reached half-way through the tiny store. By the time our desperate customers reached our registers, they lost their false lust for the holiday.

It was the same conversation over and over again. Familiar faces would disinterestedly ask what my love was doing for me. "Nothing" was always the response. Some knew I was in a touch-and-go relationship, some just assumed the "pretty face" they saw ringing up their precious items couldn't possibly be in a tumultuous affair. Regardless, he never did anything for me anyways so why would today be different? Insecure men would hear my negligence of the holiday and assume I was open to seduction. They would quickly jump on the false opportunity and I would receive desperate attempts at courting.

Simply put, this girl couldn't have been more disinterested. Dinner in an overcrowded restaurant with no reservation and a movie after a long day sounded closer to torture than romance. Going home and snuggling with my young son sounded better than spending time with a stranger with too much Axe. That stuff will never cover up the rank stench of desperation.

Still, it would've been nice for a half-assed bouquet to land in my lap. It wouldn't kill him to acknowledge me. But, he was busy leaving our son at home with his mom so he could hang out with his "friend" who happened to come through my line that day. Her fiery red hair peaked my attention and my heart sank the moment I saw her. She plastered on a grin that promised to betray me. Scarlette knew it was my line she was in and she constantly was trying to become my bestie. This overgrown child in her cute short skirt and low cut top had the audacity to purchase a teddy bear and my boyfriend's favorite snacks at my register.

It's cute how they thought I didn't know. Everybody knew. But when they were confronted, they acted like we were saying the sky is orange. Before I could muster a witty remark as I scanned my boyfriend's favorite treats, her transaction was over and it was too late. She walked away thinking she was sly.

As the day went on, my mind wandered beyond the register about what could be happening behind my back. Mindlessly, I smiled and shuffled one customer after another through my line. My stomach was queasy but nobody could see that, I was supposed to look happy at all times!

An hour before my shift was up, I was exhausted by the monotonous conversations I kept having with guests. It was excruciating keeping a straight face while my world was crumbling just beyond the automatic doors. Hearing about couples forced plans was mind-numbing at best. Each one came up with the original idea of dinner, a movie, then a bed riddled with roses to set the tone for the evening. And then an older gentleman came in.

His bowler hat concealed his balding head. The veins wrapping around his fingers and neck were distorted maps of his past. They traced the trails of his personal stories throughout his fragile skin. The oversized coat he was wearing gave him a bravado of confidence. It was too much confidence for a man that was hunched with age and old bones. He was holding two bouquets. One was opulent and bulging larger than a stripper with a hard-on. The other was much smaller, meek. Women would desperately call it dainty trying to make up for its size. They are also the same women who claim size doesn't matter. Here's a hint: it always matters.

"Oh how nice! They look beautiful" the mockery in my thoughts were thankfully concealed in my comment as I grabbed the first bouquet from his hands.

"Thanks, they are for my sweethearts" his smile perked up in a crooked way. It reminded me of Oogie Boogie's smile when he caught Santa Clause. This customer was planning something, and I had a feeling neither bouquet was for a daughter. "This one is for my wife." He pointed to the modest bundle of flowers. "And this one? This is for her friend." He began to blush, and a spark ignited in his eyes. Something told me he wasn't joking. It was either intuition or a trigger from the events earlier that day but either way, it didn't sit well with me.

"Uhm, shouldn't you switch it? Maybe your wife should get the bigger one." My personal insecurities bit at his ignorance. Are men this dense?

"Hmm, you're sweet and beautiful honey, but women don't get to decide these things." Ring ring, the 1940s called and would like their idealism back. I grew silent because there was no use engaging with him anymore. Does his mistress have red hair too? His wife must know if they are friends, like how my fiery fiend insisted on befriending me.

His total was paid in cash- he explained that a card would leave a trail. Wow, really? I had no clue, thank you kind sir for explaining how money works. He took his bouquets and started to leave. Just before he walked out the door into the frigid air he turned around, winked, and said "Happy Valentine's Day doll face". The remnants of my peanut butter sandwich began to creep up into my throat as he walked away. I guess men never "grow out of it". Or better yet, you really can't teach an old dog new tricks.

EIGHT

People Watching

I magine the amount of people who dance through the doors of a grocery store. Everyone has to eat and there aren't that many stores to choose from. With the grocery monopoly encroaching, it became a more laissez-faire decision as to who to spill your hard earned cash on. It all went to almost the same company anyways so why not pick the store en route to your destination?

With the plethora of people I encountered, it became clear that my people watching skills needed some major improvement. If my analysis couldn't improve, I was doomed for failure in this industry. If I couldn't mold myself into a likable character in their shopping experience, they would be more likely to not feel satisfied shopping in the store.

To tackle this, I started studying the way men and women would style (or not style) their hair. Hair was the easiest for me because it took the most effort to control. Nobody wakes up naturally with a beautiful wisp of a hairdo on their head. That takes patience and diligence. My predictions for who these people with perfect do's would land them into two categories- either they were pretentious pricks who needed their way or no way at all or were people who took pride in themselves and were trying to convince themselves that they were worthy of nice things. The customers who wouldn't even bother with their hair would fall under either the ideals of being too busy to care or fighting whatever system they felt controlled their hair. Usually, they found a way to blame capitalism for their endless bad hair days.

My simplistic categories left too much room to meander in. I began noticing their clothing. This quickly separated the princesses from the professional good doers. If their clothes weren't clean, it told me that they were either dirt broke and shouldn't be shopping at a store that was overzealous when assigning prices, or they were overly aware of their dirt and they wanted to "show the man" that basic hygiene was also part of the capitalist regime. Regardless, I also knew they wouldn't be able to hold productive conversations and oftentimes I would let them lead the way. There was no use asking them about the newest health food trend I saw them purchasing. No doubt they read about it on some popular "underground" website or even a zine they found at the bus stop.

When customers would tell me they were off for the day but still in a suit, I would question their motives. Why would they sit there in a suit when they could lounge and day drink? Not my type of people and that's all I needed to know.

Customers with normal clothing were always breaths of fresh air. When I say normal clothing, I mean their clothing fits their roles or days. Moms would be wearing clothes that they would be comfortable catching vomit in while still looking cute. Professionals would be wearing whatever outfit best suited their jobs. If they were a lawyer, a suit would make sense. Waitresses and bartenders always were dressed in their required color; and I sought them out. Speaking with other service industry workers was always a wonderful opportunity to poke fun at the public.

Even then, there was too much wiggle room. I began to study mannerisms and while I could tell you by the tilt of someone's head if they were a bitch, I couldn't begin to properly describe it to you. It's almost as if their head was a straight angle yet titled to the side at the slightest degree. You knew you were in for it. If they hung their head like Eeyore, it was obvious to not make eye contact but maybe tell them they looked nice that day.

The way customers' hips shifted to create a gait as unique as a fingerprint began to become second hand for me to notice and analyze. Their self-confidence spoke through the way they held their body. This became the most useful tool to have because it was easier to deal with whatever situation or oversharing you may be in for. Every now and then I would be sidelined with a surprise characteristic trait but eventually, reading customers was like reading a children's book.

Naturally, this evolved into creating full on stories about these people. There were these two guests who would come in and they looked like they were in their 50's or 60's with major plastic work done. I assembled an intricate story about how they were millionaires but clearly had to earn every penny. Their child ran away and slandered them in a lawsuit and they lost every ounce of their trust fund and had to start anew. But, they still had each other and that was enough for them. Eventually, my coworkers assigned the couple the nickname "The Lovebirds" because every time they came into the store they were all over each other. It was a love that could endure hardship and in itself was something to admire.

Another person who would come into my store was the opposite. He was clearly a lost and angry soul. His steps were incredibly precise and he carried himself taller than he really was. To keep in control, he boasted a buzz cut even though he was an aged twenty-something. His frown was plastered to his face and anytime he came through my line he would chastise me and the other girls suggesting we were all doomed for "ass cancer" (his exact words) because we carried our phones in our back pockets. This guy obviously had a basement and it was filled to the brim of conspiracy theories.

Nobody needed to study body language to know that. Just a two-minute conversation would tell you the truth about his inner workings. He probably even had conspiracy theories about me and the little lies I would tell him for fun. Every now and again I would suggest stories such as tin foil doesn't deter aliens. I would explain that it actually attracts them and their spies have infiltrated the US entertainment industry to trick us. He bought it every time. It was easy to get a rise out of him and on particularly boring days, I just couldn't help myself.

The hooker or presumed hooker was by far the most fun story to web together. Being the spider lacing each string of her life was captivating for me on rainy days. She would come into the store with her tits hanging out waking up every man she passed. Dollars would sometimes protrude between her areola and her spaghetti strapped shirt. Her knock off Coach bag would host not only whatever money she made that night but a chihuahua that would stick its head out and nip at our salad bar and go after her breaking bleached hair for dessert.

The dog would then sneeze all over our hot bar leaving the food questionable at best. Her wide frame would falter back with insults every time she was asked to leave her dog outside or to at least refrain from allowing it to hover over the uncovered food. Her lips were contorted not just from the messed up lipstick but from pure offense that her pookie bear was not welcome anymore.

Her escort, pimp, or whatever was always by her side. He would often speak for her but it was hard to take him seriously. While he was tall and his features were grown, his face and clothing choice hadn't left high school. Pimples overtook his face like ants on a cockroach and his clothes were praising a death metal band nobody in our store had ever heard of. Still, he would claim they wouldn't patronize anymore if we continued the discrimination. We always replied that his rebellion would be welcomed because we were tired of sanitizing after them. Who knew what diseases they were carrying and what nonsense they were breathing into the store with their avant-garde lifestyle. Even if she was a hooker, she wasn't well paid nor clean. We were tired of constantly touching the cash she would hand us.

The personalities of each customer perpetuated through whatever disguise they wanted to hide behind and were exposed for who they could be. They were walking stories just waiting to be told and this retail worker was up for the challenge.

NINE

Secret Shoppers

If you are a secret shopper, I have major beef with you. There is a very specialized place in hell for people who get paid to purposely trip up and "secretly assess" service workers. Secret Shoppers are reimbursed the amount of money they spend in the store to assess and report the service they receive during a visit to an assigned department. They are retail versions of undercover spies. Usually, they acted as if they were just as important as a spy for the country when in reality they were more like Melissa McCarthy's character in Spy.

Nevertheless, they would slink into our stores and report back to retail's version of Syndrome. This could be anything from how long it took for their order to be rung up, how long it took before they were greeted, and if they were asked every question the retail worker was supposed to. They also would subjectively decide whether or not we answered their questions according to company policy. On these reports, they were to also walk around the store and report about the cleanliness and overall atmosphere of the building. Oftentimes, they were to report their observations about our appearances as well.

It was well known that their assessments were laced with bias. There was no way to differentiate company standards and their own opinions. The rating scales on the pamphlets they filled out ranged from 1-10 much like the pain rating scale the opioid industry convinced hospitals to use. These undercover appraisals also allowed for comments. The secret shopper was always instructed to describe the person they were assessing and was given little to no prompts on how to do this. Our shoppers were not creative writers and certainly had an odd perspective of the world. I was once described as a short squat girl that looked angry. A few weeks later, I was described as a slight girl with bags under her eyes. My perceived anger docked my score. The bags under my eyes for working while also nursing a baby that never slept also docked my overall rating. I had made Karen uncomfortable by existing. There was no pleasing them and it would have been nice for them to describe my... better qualities.

It was our responsibility to give the exact same over-the-top service to every Susan and Richard that came into our store. Everything was to be squeaky clean, stocked properly, and every item they could ever wish for was supposed to be available to them at any given moment. We were to be experts on everything that was sold within the walls and if we weren't, we had to promise to find out the answer. My favorite line was "Hey, that's a great question! Let's find out together." People thought I was the utmost amazing retail worker ever but in reality, I just didn't want to get into trouble again.

Positive secret shops were a rarity. If the shopper was

in a bad mood, took their job too seriously, or just didn't gel with you, tough luck buttercup... your job security was in their hands. If you got a poor evaluation (anything less than a 100%) you would be immediately whisked into the office to be reprimanded. Leadership would demand to know why I didn't offer Susan a reusable bag for purchase. When I responded that she didn't look like she could afford one, I was immediately met with a speech about how I shouldn't judge a book by its cover. The woman was paying her $35 total in quarters. Quarters. So no, I did not think asking her to buy a $3 bag would be a good idea. I was trying to avoid embarrassing her further. In retrospect, I would have asked simply to upset her if I had realized she was a secret shopper.

It was commonplace to be out of touch or out of tune with the world as a secret shopper. They would also like to make the job into a game and purposely hurl "real life situations" at you such as what the woman did when she chose to pay in quarters. Sometimes, the customer would be on their phone and then claim I never greeted them even though they couldn't hear me over their yakking. I threatened to bring a megaphone with me to work when Leadership chastised me after that incident.

The questions we were instructed to ask each guest are nothing you have never heard before. *Did they find everything okay?* If they didn't, it was your job to find it for them. *How was their day?* This always led to some interesting situations. I got answers that were one-word to full-on verbal novels about their day. *Is this organic?* We were supposed to ask this to save our butts on our purchase budgets because organic produce costs substantially more than conventional. But it all looked the same unless the PLU sticker was magically still on the produce they were purchasing. It seemed pretentious and almost belittling asking someone if their produce was organic or conventional. Oh, Susan, you aren't buying organic apples for your baby? Shame!

We were also supposed to make small talk about the food they were purchasing. Maybe hype them up about a new product or just make it sound like you are two B.F.Fs who happen to love the same food. I can't tell you how many times I scrambled trying to find something to talk about. At one point I accidentally told a man his banana looked especially large and firm. Thankfully, he was not a secret shopper and allowed me to wither away into the abyss of embarrassment.

Lastly, if it was fundraising season, we were tasked with asking each customer if they would be willing to donate to the charitable cause. Watching my customers squirm in front of me and in front of the line behind them contemplating if they would be willing to donate brought more joy than it should have to my day. My coworkers could tell I got a kick out of it and would just watch my register often for the show. Out of sheer spite for the public, I ended up raising the most percentage of money per store sales in the company. I did this three years in a row. Because of this, I was sent on a few trips internationally to experience the amazing things I was supporting. The biggest donation I had ever received was the day after St. Patrick's Day.

My new bae and I had gone out for the American day of drinking. We went out a little too hard and the next morning I had to make extra stops just to puke my alcohol-poisoned guts out onto the side of the road. Still, I showed up to work and through excruciating discomfort, I asked every single person if they wanted to donate. I must have looked awful because the guy who donated a large sum of money asked if his donation would help me leave early. When I told him it wouldn't, he still donated and told me that my night was probably worth it.

Thankfully, there were no secret shoppers that day but it wouldn't surprise me if there had been. They loved coming at inconvenient times, like when the store was closing for remodeling or when we were in the height of a lunch rush. My favorite was when they would bring their friends, grill me as if I was a child in detention, then complain that I didn't sit there and braid their hair and have small talk with them. Yet, if we asked all the questions we were seen as pushy and too "salesy" as one woman put in her comments after evaluating me. It was always never enough and too much all at the same time and we were always left groveling to our Leaders hoping to not be written up.

TEN

Is This What You Call Team Work?

There was some unresolved Bermuda Triangle of interest happening on my team. There were flashy smiles cast from my Leader- excuse me- Team Leader that would land towards me and Autumn. Karl would cast compliments towards like he was fly fishing. We both were hired within 6 months of each other, and Karl was on the prowl. Later, I would be told by Leadership and Human Resources I should have been flattered not disgusted.

He talked of us so highly and so frequently that my supervisors began mocking him. They would joyfully announce that he clearly had a crush on me because my name would rest on his lips during every conversation. The thought of me lounged in his mind longer than I was interested. It made my skin crawl with disgust just thinking about it. While there was reason to talk about my accomplishments in the company, it became annoying and oftentimes I wanted to blend into the crowd.

I grew irritable and restless. When I didn't bite on his

advances, he began to pick on my new boyfriend who would come in during his lunch breaks from the retail shop down the way. When my "Leader" realized I wasn't biting, he then began flirting with Autumn. He would jaunt around the tiny front area of the store trying to flash a smile at both of us, waiting for one of us to reciprocate. His spiky red hair and Chinese character tattoos gave away his age- he was clearly near his thirties but was trying so hard to hold onto his reckless twenties.

As the months eased forward, we were told by our corporate Leadership that it was time for our annual Team Build. Team Builds were a way for the company to rally up team comradery by doing something fun outside of the store while being compensated as if we were working a full day. At the beginning of my time there, we were allowed to choose any activity that supported a healthy relationship between us team members. It was a great way for us to remind ourselves that we were still human and at a cellular level, if we could acknowledge our coworkers as humans, we were bound to gain a level of respect for one another that may not have been there before. Plus, if we seemed happy at work, our customers were more likely to shop there.

My first year there we went to a festival filled with food and historical folklore. We pranced around the festival grounds cockily consuming turkey legs and those of us of drinking age drank beer openly. Laughter and banter filled our day and it was fun to play with my team members instead of bickering with them. It really did stir up a pot of dignity we all desperately needed to drink from.

This year was no different, we were able to choose an activity of choice once more and didn't have to correlate the outing with our company's precious Core Values which was basically the Ten Commandments of grocery retail. We still didn't have to align the gathering with a product we sold or a local producer we purchased items from. I think it is important to point out that this was the last year we were allowed such freedoms and over time, the yearly outing slowly diminished into something that happened only once every few years before disappearing completely.

Our team had grown substantially over the last year and our interests were expansive and impossible to satiate. To quell any arguments before they started, Karl decided to make a choice for us as to what we would be doing for our Team Build. This task also incorporated a new hitch- we had to perform the outing when every shift could be covered. Being the Cashiering Team meant that nobody else in the store was trained to do what we do and we were forbidden to borrow anyone from our sister store. This was his opportunity to bend the rules of what is and isn't appropriate to do as a team. Karl had decided that we would see a newly released movie- it was a jump scare film filled to the brim of guts and blood.

As soon as I saw the flier he made on the small office door I panicked. Horror movies aren't my thing and there was no way this girl was going to willingly subject herself to such a thing.

"I won't be there." My arms crossed over my chest as I informed Karl of my decision.

"Lennox, this is considered a meeting." He replied calmly. Something was brewing behind his eyes.

"Did I stutter? I don't watch that shit." I repeated myself hoping that the message came across.

"Well, if you don't, you don't. But, it would be considered a missed mandatory meeting and you know missing the movie would mean a final write up." He smirked as he said this and my heart sunk. With the way secret shoppers were shopping me it was almost impossible to pass them. My job was always on the line. Begrudgingly, I walked away from the conversation knowing I would be showing up to the movie.

The time had come for us to watch the film of his choice. I seemed to be the odd man out and everyone else feigned excitement. We began to huddle in front of the theater to take attendance. There, Karl went into a spiel about team appreciation and how he was so touched we all showed up. It was a jab at me- the defector for not wanting to partake in this type of outing. Once his mini meeting was over it was time to make our way to the midnight showing of the film.

"Lennox, Autumn, come sit by me." Karl began to grab for our shoulders to showcase that he had saved the two seats on either side of him just for us- his star cashiers.

"No thanks. I don't want to." I explained while Autumn went around me to take him up on his offer.

"I insist. I know you didn't want to be here anyways-I'll keep you safe and make sure you are comfortable." This is when it became clear he was not going to budge. If I denied him, there would be consequences. Everybody was claiming their seats and pretended to not notice me trying to pry away from Karl's grasp.

As the movie began I found myself sitting curled in my chair. Within five minutes my head was buried in my own crevices trying to protect myself from the contents of the movie. Karl found my body language as his opportunity to put his hand on my leg.

"You're okay, I got you." He whispered to me.

I responded by curling further into the fetal position.

Taking the hint his arm was not welcome on my thigh he moved it to my back. The chill of the theater began to crawl up my spine as my dignity slipped out of my body. If it was possible, I would have hurled myself at him and scared him just as much as his actions scared me. But my body was frozen, unable to process the events of the night. When leaving the theater, my soul felt as sticky as the cinema floor- covered in spilled soda and over buttered popcorn. The feeling of his hands on me couldn't be simply shaken off and that entire night I paced my living room floor trying to shake his intentions off of me.

For weeks I sat with an uneasy feeling thinking about the incident and how he had crossed a line. There were no words to describe exactly what had happened yet because the vocabulary didn't exist in my psyche to protect myself. But something was wrong and I decided to confront the current Store Leadership. This is when I had found out they had been childhood friends and were as thick as thieves.

"I don't think that's what happened, Lennox. You know better. Plus, you have a raise coming don't you?" was Theo's reply when I explained the situation. He thought I was blowing the incident out of proportion.

My job review was the next day. Due to my "performance", I was given the lowest raise they could give me. My pay went up ten cents an hour and would stay the same for another year. When I protested the review, Karl explained that I was too emotional and needed to learn how to manage and mask my sensitivity.

ELEVEN

Shots Fired

Time was anything but on my side that day. The clock was mocking me, acting as if I would never make it in time to work. On top of this, my teeth were begging me to go to the grocery store across the street. The household toothpaste ran out the night before and I desperately wanted to brush my teeth using Colgate instead of whatever o-natural toothpaste my work was selling.

An internal debate broke out in my head as my speedometer crept higher. Even it knew it was breaking the law at this point. Ultimately, I knew my job was more important than brushing my teeth that morning. Quickly, my car swerved into the parking lot where my apron and body busted out of the vehicle as if they just committed grand theft. After clocking in, it was clear my boss was preoccupied so I decided it was a good time to speak up about the incident at the theater and the obvious retaliation.

It was always uncomfortable to go into the back office. Not because of the titles and jobs the room held, but the pathway to it was always a disaster. The back half of the store seemed like it was thrown together by a toddler in the midst of a temper tantrum. Maybe the architect decided to play pick up sticks instead of taking a moment to think *should an oven really go in a hallway?* Maybe he had better things to do.

I played The Floor is Lava with the slippery non-slip mats behind the deli as I made my way to the back room. Then, it was time to play Make it Through the Hallway Without Getting Burned. I have so much respect for the kitchen employees who managed to leave work mostly unscathed each day. My clumsy ass would have never made it. The oven was spurting its fuming fury and a pot was bubbling over it. With only inches to spare between the industrial oven and the window on the other side of the narrow hallway, I barely made it past. Only a few drops of boiling water hit me and it hit my apron- success! The office door was wide open and Mary was back there- our Human Resources person. It was time to face the boss level.

"Hey, I need to tell you something. Can we close the door?" I asked as I stepped into the room.

"Sure, to be honest, I think I know why you're here. I already voiced my concerns." A loud popping noise could be heard in the distance as she said this. It sounded like a bad accident- maybe tires popping? We both looked at each other and decided to continue our conversation. The store was near a major intersection and accidents weren't uncommon.

"Well, it's.. it's that I think I am being retaliated against for not flirting back. You know how Karl is with me." My fingers fidgeted with my box cutter deep in my apron pocket to ease my nerves.

"Yeah, I know. You absolutely are. I have talked with

the people above me and nobody is doing anything about it." She swiveled in her chair and we shifted the conversation to our personal lives and how she put in her two weeks because of the clear harassment situation.

Sirens began to wail, cutting our conversation short. One ambulance after another started speeding across the major road next to us. Police cars began filling up our parking lot. We were stunned and didn't know what to do. Were we safe? What had happened?

As the thoughts came pouring into our heads, our janitor came into the room. He didn't knock. He never did and was usually busy being the only living poltergeist the store willingly housed.

"Dude, a bunch of people were shot across the street! Didn't you hear the gunshots?" He was out of breath and had a crazed look. Even he didn't know how to respond to this. "The grocery store was just shot up. That could have been us man." I knew there was a reason why I didn't want to go get toothpaste- but I didn't know it was because a shooting was about to take place.

I ran to the front of the store- we all did. Nothing we could do would stop the onslaught of questions from customers. Suddenly, I was a trauma responder trying to console adults who were twice my age. I needed to process the fact it could have been me but I was told to put on a happy face- be their point person. This wasn't what I was trained for and didn't they know I only took one Psychology class before flunking out of college? The streets were shut down and nobody knew what to do. It was apparently up to me to decide how to handle the customers. Police suggested we clear the building of anyone who was not required to be there. Together, my team managed to convince the customers to abandon their goods and got them out of the store quickly so they could get home. Everyone was in shock.

For four hours our store stood empty. I was demanded to keep busy- and if a customer came I was to greet them. Yet, a two block radius had been shut down and secured. How could anyone come if nobody could get there?

Word got out that the streets wouldn't be open until the next day- police were ordering us to go home. Our store Leader was new to the role since Theo moved and was afraid of getting into trouble for shutting down early. Can you imagine? A reprimand for keeping a store open in hopes to make a dollar while people were laying in body bags across the street?

TWELVE

Are We Friends?

B y simply being kind, you gain a front-row seat to strangers' lives. Growing up, my mom would always tell me to approach people with kindness and curiosity- you never know what someone is going through and it wasn't your job to judge them. Being a retail worker, you get an intimate glimpse into customers' lives. I knew the food they ate, I knew when they were sick, I knew when they were going through a break up, I knew when they were dealing with a death or separation. I knew when they hadn't slept or were dealing with a bout of depression. I was acutely aware of the inner workings of their lives. As a retail worker, I was also there to celebrate their accomplishments such as new jobs, new babies, new chapters in their lives and their birthdays.

How do we know these personal inner workings of our customers' lives? By the way customers communi- cated with us. I have watched women's bodies swell with life and have watched their children grow up. I have watched couples go through terrible divorces and have been there to console them throughout the process without fully remembering their names. You become friends with your customers without even planning to.

It all starts with a grocery list. You find their long lost lists scattered across the sales floor, you scan out their items, you see their grocery carts piled with goods. After a while, you can easily assess what is happening in their lives simply by the food they eat and how they hold themselves.

I personally have found abandoned grocery lists especially fascinating. I love musing about who it came from and oftentimes found myself creating mock stories about the list's mysterious owner. Large parties would erupt in my mind just as often as imagining a quiet night of solitude for my nameless guests. It all depended on what they were planning on purchasing.

But there were times where I didn't really know what to do when talking with my shoppers. I realized pretty quickly in my journey through various stores that we were a free and very untrained therapist for many people. Customers would open up about things that I just wasn't prepared for.

A woman once opened up about how she suspected her husband was cheating on her. Despite the line forming behind her, I walked around the register and held her for a moment as she sobbed into my shoulder. It was me who promised everything would be okay. It was me who told her she deserved better. It was also me who helped her pinpoint if he was or was not cheating on her. When it was discovered that he indeed did the dirty with another woman, it was me who talked her through the process and reminded her his behavior was a reflection of him not her. This was all through our weekly 5 minute meetings while I scanned out her groceries.

Once, a man explained to me he was feeling extremely depressed and didn't know how to move forward. Reaching for a proper response, I asked him who his support system was. He said he had none. I became his support system and found therapists who could help him. After six months, he thanked me telling me that his intentions were not to open up to me like that but he appreciated how I went the extra mile. His smile lit up the entire store and it filled me with so much joy to know I was able to help.

I talked to many women through pregnancy loss. I have talked to men and women through their nervousness in regards to new adventures whether it was moving to a new city or taking on a new job. It is us retail workers that are always here to lap up whatever is resting on your shoulders despite the fact that many of our college degrees or lack thereof have nothing to do with psychology.

Conversations always became personal after one or two visits and it was hard to steer customers away from asking for very personal advice. It was always hard to shun someone away who was clearly needing to open up. So, like most retail workers, I would just sit and listen.

We would cry together and laugh together and I would often pull from my life experiences to guide them through theirs. If I didn't have an experience from my personal life to guide them, I would use experience from a book I had read or from someone else's. Word spread about how I was the one to go to when it came to life advice. Customers would pick my line because they felt like I was the one that would be able to answer their souls's burning questions and guide them to redemption.

Customers felt safe with me because I was an objective force in their life while still being a familiar face. It wasn't anything I wanted to do. I prefer keeping people at arm's length and the last thing I want to truly do is get into the psyche of a complete stranger. Yet, the unsolicited requests would come daily. There was always someone who needed an extra boost, someone who needed a pick me up. And us retail workers would always try to pick up the pieces no matter how shattered the mirror was.

Sometimes though, the tables would turn and it would be customers who would comfort me. When I was pregnant I received a blanket for my unborn child from a woman who came in every few months. Somehow, I captured her heart and she gifted me a blanket she knit herself. I will keep the fluffy pastel rainbow blankie forever. When a woman found out that I was working on the day my son was sick, she went home, and came back two hours later with multiple boxes of legos for my son to keep. She explained that her kids were too old for Legos and she just wanted my son to feel better and become excited about something. Customers would go to bat for me and say the things I wanted to to my Leaders about the injustices they witnessed in the store. They would also cheer me on with my accomplishments when I shared them.

When you work in these environments, you form relationships and alliances you would never imagine. It is something I am grateful for. It was an odd community but a community nonetheless.

THIRTEEN

Unenthusiastic

For over a month we knew our Assistant Team Leader Stacy was leaving the company. She had publicly announced her concerns through mockery and professional communication that our store was a "Boy's Club" and all of the Leaders were showing predatory behavior. The Store Leader protected his buddies as he turned his cheek on their actions and Stacy's concerns. When his Assistant Store Leader pressured his subordinate (my coworker) into sex, it was her that was cast out of the store through threats of no raises and losing her status as a full time employee. They suggested that if she was really that disgusted by Phil's behavior she should leave and stop telling stories about his unwanted approaches.

Appalled by this suggestion, Stacy decided it was time to leave. She was tired of watching helplessly as her team was harassed and assaulted by Leadership. Stacy was also not quiet about her earning her degree by the end of the semester. This was her get out of jail free card.

Her intentions of grooming me to take over her role were not unnoticed. In fact, until I rejected Karl in the tiny cash office, the grooming was celebrated. Karl and Sandy would show me all the ways information was stored throughout the company. They showed me how to count the drawers. They even showed me how to write people up. The duo went so far as to teach me how to email corporate and earn a response as well as how to effectively communicate with the team. Each responsibility Karl showed me was laced with intentions beyond work. I knew that he was doing the same to Autumn.

Then one day, us three were crammed into the tiny cash office. It comfortably fits one and we were clearly well over the occupancy limit. Autumn, Karl, and I were crammed so tight our elbows were unintentionally rubbing together in this god-forsaken cash office. There was banter, there was joking, and there was instruction on certain functions of the Cashier Department. I have no recollection of what led up to his comment. I don't know if it was provoked by the close quarters of the room but my dear Leader decided to discuss his intentions openly.

"Wow, I'm in a tiny office with two hot chicks. Dreams really do come true. I don't even know what to do with myself!" He turned to see our responses. Autumn began to twirl her hair. I almost puked.

"Fucking perv" I spewed. It was impossible to hold it back anymore.

"Excuse me? What did you just call me?"

"I didn't stutter, you're perverted." My arms were crossed. If I could have pushed the two aside and lunged for the door I would have but the truth was there was no room, not even an inch to move them. Baby was in the corner stuck in a tiny room with two idiots.

"Uhm, your boyfriend is older than me." He scoffed.

"So? He's not my fucking boss." My mouth spurted at him. Autumn's hair twirling stopped. Her eyes shot down. She knew. She knew what he was doing was wrong. He knew what he was doing was wrong- he just didn't care.

After that, I spoke of his indiscretions. I went to the store Leadership who brushed me off. Phone calls and face-to-face conversations with Human Resources got me nowhere. They all said the same thing, there was no proof and he claimed he did nothing wrong. Instead of quitting, I pretended the incident didn't happen. It was easy to turn a blind eye on the allegations and personal experiences I went through when it was the hands that fed me.

The rest of the company loved the way I held my head up high- how I showed my dedication for the store by pulling all-nighters for them. When this was going on, my son was a baby and ended up with croup during every season change. I would spend endless hours in the E.R. with him- often not leaving until 4 a.m. Then, the next morning I would show up to work at 6:30 am on the dot. Why? Because I had mouths to feed. Thankfully, I had a support system to help with my sick child.

Oftentimes, I would stay late to cover shifts my coworkers couldn't finish. I worked through migraines and was harassed by Karl suggesting I didn't know what a migraine really felt like. I explained that the room was literally spinning and almost vomited a few times from them. I felt like I had to defend my body's natural response to stress. I had to defend how my body func-tioned. Those were the days they thought I was hungover. When you are a single mom that is working and trying to earn the right to go back to school, there is no time to frivolously party.

However, no matter my convictions, nobody believed me. Doctors would also just assume I had a drug and alcohol problem due to my early onset motherhood. So if a doctor wouldn't believe me, why would my boss?

Regardless, I would train my colleagues, count the register drawers, I would even lock up if it was requested. When it was time to clean the bathrooms, it was always me. Once I protested suggesting it was the other girls' turn to clean them.

Karl smirked and rubbed my shoulder. "But, Lennox, you do it so well. You don't want us to think you don't care about your role here at this store do you?" He wouldn't hesitate to put me in check mate. On the day of my mini protest, I had a family function to go to directly after my shift and it was ghastly to think that I would reek of the knock-off cleaner and piss. My grandmother didn't need to smell that- especially on her birthday. Afraid of being written up for insubordination I obliged and scrubbed the bathroom multiple times until Karl was satisfied.

Ultimately, my grandmother did sniff out the bathroom cleaner after I was directed to clean the bathroom three times that day. By the third check, Karl finally agreed the bathroom was clean enough. My grandmother thought I was demoted when I showed up at her home later that evening.

Eventually, the time came. Stacy went on to do bigger and better things and left. She gave me all of her codes. She put in a good word. She even trained me on all of the behind the scenes jobs I would need to perform that Karl refused to train me on. She even told me the interview questions ahead of time and how to properly answer them.

There I sat, in front of five men watching me intently. I answered every question exactly the way they wanted. They grilled me for over an hour- much longer than the others. It was a warm day and the sun shone directly into their eyes until they were satisfied with the interview. Later that day, I found out I didn't get the role because I "didn't understand the requirements".

For six months I worked hard as a cashier as well as fulfilling responsibilities beyond my job description. While my supervisor was too busy policing me around my new boyfriend who would pop in just to say hello, I would make sure everyone received their breaks and helped count drawers. She was still upset with me for breaking up with her cousin and was convinced I was up to something like sweet-hearting (where you give someone a non-approved discount). Our janitor was often too strung out to perform his duties so they would be slathered onto our daily tasks. Safety walks (making sure the store was tidy) and cleaning the bathroom became the team's responsibility.

The intensity of my job took everything out of me. I was put on academic probation because I flunked college algebra for the fourth time. My dreams of breaking out into a dream career slipped between my fingers while I pursued the promotion. My focus was on my job, not my academics, and it even took a toll on my motherhood. Working different hours every day with split days off was doing a number on me but my dedication ran thick. Anytime I was called into work I showed up. Every time the phone rang or a text message came through on my time off, it was answered. There were no questions about whether or not I would be able to handle a more superior role.

Karl was incredibly aware of my over the top achievements. He would tell me how impressed he was of me. But the compliments began coming in a little too hot again. Two days after Christmas I had finally purchased a jacket. The double doors on both sides of the cash registers allowed the brisk winter air to nip you to the bone- the store's HVAC was placed in the building when the Egyptians were building pyramids and could barely keep up, leaving us at the mercy of the outside weather. For two months, my bones would shiver in the cold because there was no jacket to keep me warm. My money went to my son and nothing else. Not to mention, I was now paying a substantial rent to my father during a recession for a single room. This jacket meant I was finally taking care of myself.

As I was cleaning my register, Karl came over. He grabbed onto my jacket and rubbed his hand down the full length of my arm. "Wow, this jacket is nice." He contemplated the feel of my new clothing. "It helps that a beautiful girl is wearing it."

My eyes rolled. He didn't deserve a response.

"What? It's nice. It's called a compliment" He tsked and walked away.

"What a creep!" A young woman said as she approached, acknowledging she witnessed the whole thing. I stayed silent. She knew the compliments if one could call them that were not new nor would they be stopping soon.

After several weeks of ignoring these grand gestures, it was brought to the store's attention that the staff needed to be expanded. They were to bring on two new cashiers and create a second supervisor position. I jumped on the opportunity right away but so did my counterpart-Autumn who loved every compliment Karl flung at her. It was beginning to become clear she was actually enjoying them.

We both studied for hours, constantly quizzing each other and promised to respect whoever was granted the role. We did our due diligence. She was able to convince Karls friends, sorry, Leaders, to sit down with her, tell her what they are looking for. When I asked, they were too busy. They wouldn't give me the time of day. I outsourced to our sister store and allowed those conversations to be enough.

It was beginning to be clear that the interview date was nowhere in sight. Regardless, we studied hard. Karl let us have our own supervisor codes and let us "practice" being supervisors. We were granted permission to make big decisions and were both tasked with counting drawers and ordering the grocery bags. None of this was done with a raise. We were hungry for the position and too young to understand we were working harder for free.

Eventually, I began to become frustrated. I wanted to know when the interview would be. Karl had begun to become cold and his compliments were fading. His sights were focused on the other girl who was more…receptive of the unwanted advances. They even showed up at the Christmas party together. That should have been a clue. While I was relieved that the unsolicited attention was finally fading, I began to get a sinking feeling in my stomach.

On one particular week day, I had requested the day off to move. My friend and I were moving in together and I needed to be present to receive the keys. My phone began ringing at about 10:15 AM.

"Hey, it's Karl. Call me back." My voicemail played back at me. This was 25 minutes after the missed phone call. My heart raced with each ring as I frantically called back. Was I getting fired? Did I count a drawer wrong? Did I not press "send" on the order guide? The possibilities were endless and it was an eminent doom I was looking at.

"Hello?" His voice was calm.

"Hi, you said I needed to call you?" My phone sat between my ear and my shoulder as I lugged a box into my first apartment.

"Yeah, so uhm, Jack and I just realized we never told you when the interview was. It's today. Can you get here in an hour?" My heart dropped and so did the box my tired arms were carrying. Before my answer came, my mind began to calculate exactly how quickly my son could be dropped off at daycare, change my clothes, and get to the store.

"Yes. See you then." My roommate said she would take over the rest so that I could go to the interview. Thankfully, the daycare agreed to take my son even though the day was not paid for.

After rushing to the store, it was clear the Leadership team was waiting for me. One of them had the audacity to exclaim something about being late for an interview wasn't creating the best start. I held my tongue; they didn't take kindly to back talk and this promotion meant everything to me. We sat down in the hard metal chairs-cold this time due to the time of year. They bit through my thin dress and it was imperative I didn't reveal my discomfort. Discomfort is part of the job after all.

The boys began hurling questions at me- questions that were much harder and more intense than the questions they asked during my interview for the assistant

Leader position- one of higher standing. Exhausted and frustrated, my replies began to shorten because there was no right answer.

"If a customer was in the store and wanted to do a fraudulent return, how would you tell them no?" Jack's smirk crept across his face. This incident just happened and he felt that during my training I had made the wrong choice. While he gave no redirection, nor a solution, he had just explained that the wrong choice was made and the company now suffered immensely because of it. Apparently a multimillion dollar company couldn't afford a $45 scam.

"Well, if the customer is not one who shops here often, then the return would not be accepted. If the customer is a frequent shopper, it is important to keep them happy. Keep them coming back for more and the money lost over a single item would not be worth the lost revenue of the total customer." My legs shifted trying to keep the cold from numbing them.

"So how would you know?" He sat up straighter.

"Excuse me? How would I know what?" My head cocked uncontrollably.

"If the customer was a frequent shopper. Do you understand now?" He was frustrated but I held my guard.

"Well, working full time and honestly over full time, I have been able to make connections and relationships with all of our frequent customers. It is obvious who is a frequent shopper and who is not." What kind of question is that anyways? Was he really asking if I could recognize a face?!

"Ok, well, thanks for your time. It's too bad you didn't do any due diligence and ask us what we wanted in the role but you did well." Karl stretched his hand for a shake when he said this. Were we just meeting? It was as if we hadn't worked together for a year.

Two weeks went by and I heard nothing.

Then, I noticed my shift changed. I had three "clopens" (for those not in the service industry, it means you work the closing shift then turn around and work the opening shift). When I protested, explaining how nobody in the store was asked to work such a turbulent schedule, I was directed to Autumn. Apparently, she received the role and everyone tried to keep it hush-hush. They knew it was wrong. They were afraid of my reaction.

Later that day, I asked what I had done wrong in the interview. What did I need to work on to get a promotion? Karl explained I was "unenthusiastic" about the role and lacked energy during the interview.

FOURTEEN

I Ruined Her Christmas

The company decided to finally remodel one of the stores and purchase a third location in town. Instead of announcing this amazing new addition, us cashiers were tasked to blindly ask people for their zip code so the company could analyze where the best location would be for their third store. The data was used to figure out where they could open a store without hurting the business of their existing ones. No matter how many times I explained the situation and the reason for asking for their zip codes, customers were convinced their information would be sold on the black market to track their mundane lives. Never mind the fact that there are thousands of people who reside in one code, customers were livid. We were their punching bags.

When they refused to give up their vague personal info, it was me who put in my zip code to avoid the meltdown. I was accused of being a stalker, a fascist, and a sociopath when prompted for their residency's postal code. The same mindset was used when people complained about the prices as if we had any control over them. We had no say in the prices and honestly couldn't afford the food ourselves. It would always blow my mind watching people come in and out of the store with just a few items and spending hundreds of dollars. I knew better than to suggest they shop elsewhere. Secret shoppers would always rat us out if we defected.

Soon, it was time for the big store closure. Holding true to their standards, the company decided to not waste money on marketing and had the store print a couple of signs on regular printer paper explaining that the store was closing soon and to expect a full liquidation. My store Leadership didn't understand how little the public pays attention and inferences weren't really their "thing".The store would not be ordering more products and as items diminished, it would create a void on the sales shelf in lieu of the items. But, because the company decided to be cheap, we were left with many unhappy and disturbed guests due to the lack of communication.

"Wow, you would think you are going out of business!" Some would say.

"Better start looking for a job, I heard that McDonald's is hiring" Customers would tout.

"What is this? The apocalypse?" Not having gluten free bread was apparently a sign of Doom's Day approaching.

"It would've been nice to tell me that you decided to close shop." Nope, not my fault. I verbally told every Dick and Jane that went through my line the past few months the store was closing temporarily to be rebuilt. It wasn't my fault they didn't listen.

What didn't help matters was that this amazing and clearly intelligently superior company chose to close down right after New Years. We were specifically instructed to not purchase anything for the store after December 1st. Any idiot can do the math. How would suburbia entertain their one percenter guests if their favorite gluttony was closed and didn't have the vegan chicken they needed? By December 20th, our shelves were as barren as the trees back East.

Customers became more disgruntled by the minute and a fit of hysteria hit the store. No matter how many times we explained to them the store was closing and was being rebuilt, they didn't seem to get it. It was the end of the world and I was to blame for it.

On December 23rd a scraggly old woman waited impatiently in my line. The other two registers were broken at the time and I was the chosen cashier to ring in the groceries. Autumn was bagging the groceries I scanned trying to make herself look useful and Jerry was busy herding the carts in the parking lot. The line was at least 35 people long and almost touched the small liquor section in the very back of the store. Before I could even get a word out the woman began pointing her finger. It reminded me of the witch in Hansel and Gretel.

"You!" She accused.

"Hi, how are you?" I gave up asking if people found everything okay. It was obvious with how bare our shelving was that they didn't. If a secret shopper came through my line, I was prepared to tell the company to suck a dick over it. Avoiding trouble with the customers was my only concern at this point unless provoked.

"You, you should be sorry for this!" Her anger bubbled through her frothing lips.

"Is this an organic apple?" This woman was not my vibe. It pissed her off when I refused to acknowledge her situation.

"You're out of everything I need! Now, I need to

drive to yet another store and hope they have my things! I'm an old lady, I can't be driving around town like this!" Her finger was still wagging at me. First of all, these weren't her things yet, she hadn't purchased them. Secondly, if she is this old and couldn't read a sign, she had bigger problems to grapple with.

"Well ma'am, the company has been advertising they are closing this store to remodel it to better suit the modern times." It was hard not to smile. "We also have signs on all of our shelves and our front doors explaining the closure and the liquidation process. Plus, everything that is left is on a 30% clearance!" This was turning into a game. My slippery sweet reactions were infuriating her more. Pretty soon, steam was going to pop from her ears like a cartoon character.

"Well, I hope you're proud of yourself because you ruined my Christmas. I don't know what I'll do. Maybe I will serve my guests peanut butter and jelly sandwiches. I'll be the mockery of the family thanks to you." Her order was almost fully rung up. Getting this woman out of here was fully dependent on how fast Autumn could bag up the groceries.

"We're out of peanut butter and regular bread but I heard the jelly we have left is quite tasty!" Almost accidentally, the sarcasm slipped out. Can we just blame word vomit for a second?

"You ruined my Christmas, and I am going to make sure nobody supports this store again." She huffed and handed over the $200 she spent on three bags of groceries.

Thankfully, when the store closed down I would no longer be a cashier. The constant verbal assaults were supposed to die down once I was in a new team. Originally, I didn't get the role in the Cheese and Spirits department but someone dropped out. Besides being insulted that I was lapping up the role sloppy seconds style, I was beyond relieved to be moving away from Karl's team and customers who thought I was responsible for their first world problems.

FIFTEEN

Bone Dry

The store opening was a smashing success. We were pumping customers in and out like...well... I don't really know what because I had never seen anything like it before or after. It was as if we were the new circus in town. Maybe that metaphor will work?

Friday's were the busiest days and this Friday was no different. My role that day (it changed frequently due to the team I was now in) was to be in the bar- slinging beers for day drinkers who get their kicks from drinking in a bar in a grocery store before the weekend began. It was even too early to be Happy Hour so these schmucks were paying full price for their craft beers.

As I was gearing up to rinse the glassware, I noticed the water was not turning on in my bar sink. What the fuck? My main concern was keeping calm and not alerting the customers. My only choice was to find Leadership, this store was honestly just a polished pig. It was important to walk away calmly and act like nothing was wrong. Before pretending to rinse anything, I placed the glasses down slowly and calmly as my eyes began to scan the store to see where Leadership might be. This was not something I wanted to radio over. Yet, a coworker of mine beat me to it.

"Leadership, do you copy." A Panicked voice crackled through.

"Copy. We know. Talk to us in the back, not over the walkie." Janet's voice was stern. This wasn't like her. She was the bubbly blonde who was surprisingly likable. Sometimes, we would forget she was in Leadership simply because she was fun to be around. Janet was one of the many new hires for the store- our employment numbers almost doubled by the time the new store opened.

"Yeah. Okay." The voice replied. Many of us decided to invite ourselves to the mini meeting to find out what was happening. I went to wash my hands in the bathroom because the gloves that are provided for us made my hands stinky and itch. My hands begged for relief before I addressed the situation in the bar.

Motion sensors rarely sense me so the faucet not dispensing immediately wasn't anything new. I tried a few more times to no avail. Then I heard a giant "What!?" and decided that something really was up. Something was not right.

"Yeah." We could only hear her side of the conversation.

"Ok." Silence.

"Shit. Shit- sorry, ok." She listened closely.

"Yeah. Ok. Thank you." Janet hung up and slipped her phone back into her pocket.

After taking a huge breath, she almost calmly explained why the water for the entire building was turned off. There was a blinding error on the Leadership's part and they thought the water bill was a janky phishing scheme. But nope, the bill was as real as these pages. So, just like any other user, the water company shut that shit down and they shut it down quickly because of how much the store owed. She also explained she had no true access to the information to pay the bill because she was too new. We would need to wait until our Regional Headquarters could contact the company and pay the bill as a third party. Until then, the water would be shut off. There was no telling how long it would take to restore it.

In the meantime, she instructed Autumn the new Sign Maker (she was placed in this role when someone spilled the tea about Karl promoting her while dating her) to create signs that stated the bathrooms were down for maintenance. The lack of transparency bothered many of us. Our customers deserved to know there was no running water and honestly the health department should have been informed. Instead of closing the store or even just the venues that needed hot water to function, Janet told us to perform as if nothing was wrong. This meant dishes piling up in the dish area because our dishwasher needed to wash everything by hand using the water in the three compartment sink. I was expected to serve beer using glassware that was washed in 5-hour-old dishwater.

The water was so cold after an hour that the soapy mess couldn't even take lip gloss off the rims of the glasses. Wine was being thrown out left and right due to customers refusing to sip anything from a cup that had grease streaks all over their freshly poured beverage. Men began complaining the lipstick marks on their glasses were not "their shade" and would ask for their drinks to be repoured. But the truth was, every single glass in the bar was dirty at that point. No amount of scrubbing could clean off these mugs because of how cold and old the water was.

My final straw was when a woman called us out. She simply went to use the restroom to wash her hands. She noticed the sign suggesting the bathroom was closed and she began asking questions about how long the closure would last. When I couldn't give an answer she became suspicious about the store's integrity. This woman then realized I hadn't washed my hands between handling cash and handling her glass of cider. For some people, this may not be anything to worry about but she was a regular and knew my habitual hand washing between each customer and especially between cash and food. Yes, it left my hands raw and bleeding by the end of the night but it was worth knowing I was keeping my customers as safe as possible.

Putting the pieces together, she walked over to the juice bar area and asked for a latte. They denied her and claimed the machine was broken and was not dispensing hot water. By the time she got back to me her script was set.

"Hey, so uhm, let me understand this correctly. You didn't wash your hands between handling cash and pouring my cider. Then, I went to wash my hands and the bathroom was closed. And now I can't get a latte? Is the water in the store down?" Her mouth twisted in a curious and accusatory way. We were not allowed to tell the customers the truth- the water was down and we were doing everything we could to get it back.

"Let me grab Janet for you, I really am not sure what is going on." I obviously did but this conversation was well over my paygrade.

When Janet came over, she explained it was just a coincidence everything was down. I don't think it fooled this customer, but it fooled the others. We were told that if we called the health department we would get a final write-up because Leadership was figuring out how to get the water back. No laws were broken if they were trying to make the store safe again. But didn't Yoda say "do or do not, there is no try"? I was too afraid to call and lose my job over basic hygiene and I think the woman was afraid her favorite place to get drunk would close down if she called too.

SIXTEEN

Not a Drug Dealer

In any service industry role, it's our job to accommodate the needs and demands of each customer that waltzes through the front doors. It's our job to understand quickly how to serve them and to customize each experience. Being in an area that is heavily infiltrated with worldly tourists, you would think we would have conversions near each scale. Not only for us to understand the needs of our foreign guests but also for them to understand the lbs to grams ratio. This is America after all and our forefathers just had to stick it to the king and break from taxation without representation. To throw salt in the King's wound, they just had to change the numerical system in which we measure length and temperature. While I always wanted to understand the metric system, it was still too mushy in my mind to flip a conversion quickly in my head.

A man wearing a beret and a puffy jacket came up to the deli counter I was stationed at one day. I greeted him with my smile and asked him how I could help him.

"Mortadella." he scoffed, staring blankly at me.

"Okay, uhm, yeah I can do that but how much do you want?" I started grabbing for the deli meat because it was going to take a moment to peel the casing off the fancy bologna.

"How do people usually order it?" His cologne was beginning to smother me as he spoke. There was also a hint of moth balls lingering in his aura.

"Well for this, people usually order it by the slice. Is that what you would like to do?" My voice was still clinging onto a forced style of sweetness.

"Hmm, ok. Can I have 45 grams?" His face was straight as if I should be able to do the conversion easily.

"I'm sorry, this is embarrassing but how many grams are in an ounce?" I asked. It wasn't like me to ask for help on these kinds of things but it was busy and I needed him to get what he needed and leave. My humility would need to be put on hold so nobody thought I was being lazy by not having a quick turn-around time for this gentleman.

"What are you? An idiot?" He scoffed again and folded his arms. He wasn't about to tell me and I genuinely wanted to know. It's not like I could have whipped out my phone and done the conversion myself in the moment. Having a phone on the sales floor was an instant write up. Plus, think about all of the health code violations that would pop if I touched my phone with my gloves.

"No, I am an American that was raised in the American Public Education System. I didn't do so well in science so... here we are. I genuinely am trying to be helpful" The mortadella was getting heavy in my hand and it began threatening to plummet towards the ground.

"You Americans, I'm from Canada where we do

things right." I wasn't contesting which system was better. "I just need 45 grams. Why is that so hard?" He began playing with his mustache from irritation. The conversion was still alluding me and it was difficult to maneuver through this interaction.

"Ok, but, how much is that? Do you want me to give you a certain amount of slices?" My frustration was growing stronger. Wasn't the saying when in Rome worth anything here?

"Just give me 45 grams." His mustache twirling stopped and the straight face returned. Maybe he didn't know how many slices that was? Was he being purposely difficult to prove his point? Either way it was taking up too much of my time.

"Sorry, not sure what that means, I'm not a drug dealer. I'll just give you what I think that is." I began to guess how many slices 45 grams could be as I turned toward the slicer.

"What did you say?" Concern and disgust washed over his face.

"I'm going to guess because the only people who can do that conversion here are drug dealers." I replied between the clink of the slicer setting and the hum of the now spinning blade.

He received what I thought was enough and instead of thanking me for trying he walked away. His silence worried me that there was a write-up coming. Customers loved to complain and Leadership rarely took our side. They were concerned more about the customer feeling right and praised than our dignity. If this guy did complain and they did write me up, I almost deserved it- I guess comparing a pretentious Canadian's measuring system to drug dealing isn't the best idea. At least I was honest.

The suspense was killing me about potential trouble and I eventually spilled the beans to my new Team Leader Jeff about what had happened. I asked him if we could print the metric system conversions by the scale. I asked him for help converting the measurements into how the scale would read it. After chastising me for being disrespectful to a customer, he declined my request. He suggested I brush up on the metric system. Jeff reminded me it was my job to memorize the conversions and be aware of our global clientele.

SEVENTEEN

Here's Your Sign

Alcoholism has been clinging on for dear life here in America. With cannabis crawling to legality, alcoholics are beginning to become outed and outnumbered. And if you are wondering if you have a problem with liquor, you might want to think about where you partake. Is it at home only? Or maybe you liked going out on the town. If you do, where do you frequent? If it is a grocery store... well... that's your first clue.

Back in my day, my employer would ask about our ideas to better the company and turn them into something (obviously, the company enjoyed the profits and credit for a team member's innovation don't get silly now). A southern employee came up with the brilliant idea to create a bar in a grocery store.

It was no secret booze racked up a profit like no other. It was cheap to make, and consumers rarely bat an eye at the exaggerated sales price. This Florida Man dared to ask the question... how much more money would the company make if they actually let customers consume the alcohol on the premises? Not only would they purchase a glass (or five), but they would also then want to keep the buzz going and buy a bottle (or three) to take home. It was a two birds with one stone situation our money-hungry CEO couldn't pass up.

Quickly, bars were resurrected inside the nationwide chain. And just as quickly, customers began flocking to my store specifically to get a buzz on. I witnessed first dates, anniversary dinners, break-ups, flings, affairs, and everything in between in that bar. Tears were shed, laughs were shared, and life stories were frequently told. My ears and shoulders were always ready for whatever decided to come my way. While there was a lot of fun to be had, there were many questions I had about the people who frequented the venue.

Understanding how each person handles booze is a soft science at best and it was a craft I had learned on the fly. Simple body movements and the slightest flicker in their eye could give away their buzz. A month into the gig I was the person people would entrust to evaluate someone's intoxication- everyone except Riley my fellow bartender. He didn't understand this because he was usually too busy talking and flirting with anyone who owned a vagina. My opinion meant nothing to him unless I wanted to suck his dick.

One gentleman was a day drinker. He would sit at the bar and schmooze with anyone willing to listen. After a few months, he realized that he knew my mom and was a client of hers- she was designing his house! But as the project went on, his visits to the bar became longer too. He would relish in life's big questions and gulp down one beer after another. While he was a kind man, he would often ask personal questions I would never answer in a work setting. He would pry for information about my political beliefs, my finances, and my life story. I would give him little bites of my story, but they were always heavily guarded and reserved. Conversing with drunks in a grocery store was always a delicate balance. Spill too much, they think you are their B.F.F., be too guarded and well... you just lost a customer. Nobody likes a closed door.

After a while, I asked my mom who he was. She explained that he was telling his wife he was going to the grocery store for lunch and he shouldn't be drinking. Obviously, I wasn't supposed to know this. He was having lunch, but nobody knew these meals were liquid and fermented- maybe he was telling a little white lie? Maybe in his mind, this was lunch?

Regardless, it was obvious my assumptions of him were correct- he was hiding more than he was sharing too. A little secret shared between friends was good enough to keep the tips coming. Apparently, we both could tango across bartop conversations.

Another example of my bar being the precipice for a new Alcoholics Anonymous member was when a woman had come in with a "friend". This was particularly awkward for me because she went to the temple I did growing up. They purchased two bottles of wine (one for the bar and one for home). As their luncheon went on, I noticed they were pouring their own bottle which was legal according to my store because there were two people. If the bar wasn't full and I wasn't the only bartender on duty, maybe then I would have noticed her sly indiscretions.

But the truth is, I didn't. I didn't notice that she poured the entire bottle and had opened up the second. I didn't notice that her "friend" hadn't touched his wine- or barely did. I didn't notice this frail toothpick of a woman polishing off two bottles on her own accord. She had swapped the screw-top bottles slyly so the bag still looked like it held the second bottle untouched. With 50-plus people who needed to be served, my observations of her were lacking. She knew what she was doing though. She was sneaky and her tactics were effortless.

That was when it all went south. Soon, she was excusing herself to the restroom. Ten minutes went by and she wasn't back. I called for my store Leadership to check on her because her date realized she had swapped the bottles. It made me feel better knowing that he didn't even know. Was she really that deep into alcoholism that she swindled the person right in front of her?

When Janet went to check on her after me vocalizing my concern, she found the woman's small frame laying on the bathroom floor. She was defeated from her own game and was miserably helpless. Janet held her hair while she heaved into the bleached toilet and immediately used her walkie talkie to inform me her date needed to come get her. They both were to leave immediately.

At least she wasn't the heavy-set guy that had to literally be carried out by my other Team Lead. Thankfully, it wasn't me who over-served him. Three beers before he was too drunk to stand, I warned my fellow bartender, Riley, the customer had a few strong drinks and should be cut off.

Unfortunately, Riley was more concerned about what a woman's place was uninterested in my observations and opinions. He also always wanted to one-up me as if life was a huge dick swinging contest. It was a game for him to see how many belittling comments it took before I broke down and snapped. There were no hiding spots in the bar and customers would watch him lash me with one degrading comment after another. When my fiance would come to visit me at work, Riley would flirt relentlessly with me as if I was even into him.

Sometimes I wonder if he began serving the already impaired man more beer just to prove I had no place in a bar. Regardless, his recklessness ended up with him and our Team Leader holding the 400 pound man up as best they could and plopping him on the cold metal chairs out front. It was our Team Lead who sat with the man and listened to him babble about how the world had gone to total shit until the taxi came. My Team Lead was the one who helped the taxi driver load him into the doomed cabbie.

When it came time for the reckoning from severely over serving a customer, Riley blamed me. When I touted I had cut the man off previously and Riley refused to comply, it was a "he said she said" moment and we ended up both in trouble. Never mind the camera that captured the entire situation. Store Leadership watched the video of me refusing to serve the drunk guest. The camera also caught me giving the man his first check and Riley starting another tab for him. They chose to ignore the footage. We were both verbally reprimanded for overserving because they "couldn't prove" who it was. Leadership just didn't want to admit Riley was truly at fault and deserved the true consequence.

The real punishment would have resulted in Riley getting fired and the bar couldn't afford to dispose of such a "charming" and "wonderful" bartender. They didn't like to discuss it was him who personally almost killed several bar goers by overserving them. Eventually, he did get canned, but it was for time and attendance and nothing more.

EIGHTEEN

If You Build it... They Will Come

That was the motto. Build the displays big, build them high, and then watch them fly. We would be tasked with piecing together ridiculous pairings of products with each season or holiday change. Beer, cheese, and olives would be expected to be perfectly aligned into a pyramid of goodness and jaw-dropping beauty. Parmesan and fig bars cut into triangles would need to look like a well-rounded and irresistible glob of glory. At the registers, whatever various departments were trying to sell would be shoved into little baskets as impulse buys for customers. Daffodils and protein bars would fight over the small confines of the plastic boxes placed before each guest as they purchased their goods. To accomplish these tasks, we would pretend the items were puzzle pieces and lean on our knowledge of psychology and color theory to organize the products into an aesthetically pleasing display.

Anything our corporate masters would throw at us, we would figure out how to sell it. They would never give us ideas or examples of how they would display things like Red Witch Cheese and lumpy pieces of honey-infused chocolate bark. But we would always find a way to create a jaw dropping display of the items being pushed for the season.

We would create handwritten signs that were filled with wit to entice our customers towards our products. We would match yellow or red into every display because it is the easiest color for the human eye to see. Using these colors would guarantee to catch the eye of every passerby. Each display would play on the culture of the customers the store serviced. These displays were mini-research projects and constant practice in advertising.

And each time we created our masterpiece, the products really would fly off the displays. The quick sales caused us to have to reorganize and rethink how to make our dwindling products look just as enticing as they did the day before. Think Burning Man grocery style. At one point, I had beer, Parmesan, bags of tortilla chips, and chardonnay all in one display due to quick thinking and product availability. It was a constant game of Tetris with different products depending on availability. The result was always a pyramid of gluttony.

This skill didn't come easy for me. To start, my hand-writing was atrocious and after placing my carefully thought-out wit onto the cooler doors of the beer aisle, I was verbally fired from ever touching a marker again. They said it looked worse than a middle schooler's hand-writing and it was an embarrassment to the store. To be fair, my handwriting isn't the best but beggars can't be choosers with this. The result was me feeding my wit to coworkers who would scribble my banter onto each display.

After being barred from writing anything, I was desperate to feel useful. My attention swerved to our ever increasing spoilage. Each day, we found ourselves scanning out loads of cheese customers were too nervous to touch. They didn't want to take a chance on something they had never tried and we couldn't demo out everything we had to offer. Instead of accepting defeat, I created a "Petite Fromage" display in our cheese case. It was a great way to get new cheeses into the hands of customers and it helped us save money on spoilage because the tiny bits of cheese were more palatable for explorative foodies. I created a mini waterfall of cheeses that were not selling well and wrapped them in almost bite-sized pieces. They careened down the middle of the cheese case as if they were a river of novelty full of daring new flavors. My river of opportunity was a wild success. My Leader Philip will forever claim it was his idea, but it wasn't. He actually fought me on it until a Corporate Champion came in and praised the innovative and well thought out program.

But, I got cocky after my accomplishment and began tinkering with building displays on the sales floor. After carefully placing items on top of one another, I ended up with a retail version of Frankenstein's Monster. Philip didn't have great bedside manners and he quickly remarked that this was also an embarrassment to the store. He offered no advice on how to correct my janky pyramid of beer and cheese dip (sans the bread or pretzels because Leadership wanted customers to have to walk around the store). Instead, he insisted I stopped trying to build floor displays and questioned my ability and competency as a retail worker. He was disturbed I had worked for the company for a few years yet couldn't build a proper display. Each role I played before this one left no room for me to build a display so the skills to build one were never learned.

Then fall came around. We weren't prepared for the holiday crusades and none of us were in the jolly high season spirit. Yet, the Corporate Champions rolled out another program. It was something about Stuffed Brie. We were to follow the recipes or create our own and place a beautifully stuffed brie into a plastic box. The idea was to make a yummy appetizer for our frazzled guests to serve.

With the company recipes, what ended up happening was finding a giant slop of mess threatening to vacate the plastic box the day after it was made. Customers would pass the appetizer by without a second thought. Nothing enticing was going on in those plastic boxes. The shelf life was short at only three days, yet, they wouldn't even last that long. The drippy drooly brie was not selling and it was important to figure out a way to boost sales while avoiding the mass amounts of spoilage we were scanning out each night. Creating our own recipe took time we didn't have because we had to list out each ingredient, weigh it out, and then type it into the not-so-user-friendly system so other stores could have access to it. It simply wasn't an option but something had to be done to save the program.

Without permission, I set up a station where I would facilitate customers creating their own version of the cheesy treat. This was the first time I truly went into the mindset of asking for forgiveness and not permission. That very statement held me back from a few raises and promotions- besides being overly emotional and unen-thusiastic, Karl explained to me in my last attempt to earn a supervisory position I wasn't gutsy enough to take on a Leadership role. It was time to prove my commit-ment to the store and my career.

I stacked a rolling cart with brie and every ingredient

needed to fulfill the recipes corporate gave plus a few rogue ingredients to fulfill my own ideas of what a yummy version of the dish while avoiding a totally sloppy and sloshy mess. Next, I grabbed a sample display dome and carefully placed my new creation into it so guests could try it for themselves. It was a concoction of brie, chocolate, and nuts. I layered my two favorite types of crackers next to it and before my station was fully set up... I had customers wanting to know more about this B.Y.O.B (Build Your Own Brie) program.

By the end of my shift, we had sold out of the cheese of honor and three of the main ingredients to create the new appetizer. When Leadership came in the next day, their jaws dropped. Customers were upset they couldn't get the specific accommodation their friends boasted about because we had sold out. I couldn't technically sell them a Stuffed Brie under a different barcode because the specific cheese brand didn't exist in the system, and it would throw off our number tremendously. Despite the prices being the same, there was a huge difference between a "Stuffed Brie" and "La Fromagerie". No matter how I explained how easy it was to make at home, customers wanted me to create the appetizer for them. They had to wait two days for our next shipment to come.

Despite Anna ordering double the amount of the cheese than the last order, we sold out before our Monday delivery. When the brie flew off the shelves on a Tuesday, it was a shock and my team finally admitted I was onto something. We had to triple our purchase and hope to make it through the weekend. Suddenly, even the crackers were flying off the shelves for one charcuterie board after another and before I knew it, the Cheese Department finally was the cool place to be.

On the weekends in November, I turned my interactive display into a Teppan-Yaki table. I wowed guests and threw little snacks at them while throwing watered-down jokes at someone else. The display turned into a crowd-pleasing show and customers who normally did not shop at the store came to see me perform because it wasn't being done anywhere else.

That year, my store crushed every store in the state in sales for the partially thought-out brie promotion. The other stores were too afraid to bend the rules slightly and create a performance out of the stuffed goodness. But I wasn't and it paid off.

Pompous emails began flying talking about how Leadership led us to this incredible innovation. Pictures of my superiors floated around the company and it began to catch the eye of stores across the country so they could put on the same performance. I was never mentioned despite my role in birthing the program.

NINETEEN

I'm Barely Okay (I Promise)

In my Psychology 101 course during high school, our teacher went into grave detail about how depression works. She went straight up to us and gave us the biggest Cheshire Grin she could and explained how simply forcing her face into a smile, dopamine would protrude from its hiding spaces and be released inside her brain. If you did it enough, you would be able to trick yourself into being happy. There were never promises about how much happiness you could feel, but the promise was there that you would be able to begin to feel at least some happiness.

No matter how hard I tried, after a few years, the trick didn't work. I could no longer pretend I was okay with the situation at hand. To think someone should be able to put on a bubbling face right after their boss chewed them out in the cheese cooler is asinine at best. It didn't matter if granny died- you were to show up and be grateful for your job. Leadership would remind us weekly how they could replace us in a second. They would hiss and gripe about our lackluster demeanor. We were always to act as if we were on display.

"Smile, you'd be prettier" men would say to me. My resting bitch face was apparently offensive to the guests who frequented the store.

"I'm not a model so beauty isn't really part of the job description." My tone would stab them in an imaginary wound.

"Well, shouldn't you be happy? At least smile for me, you would be so pretty." Their arms would begin to rest on whatever display was dividing us. It probably hurt when they got hit in the head a million times as a baby, but I don't think that was the pickup line any of those men had in mind.

"Am I making you uncomfortable?" I would stare them down and not look away. The entire store could be on fire and my gaze would remain fixed on their fragile masculinity.

"Just smile, what's your problem anyways?" If the conversation would get this far, I knew how to win the joust.

"Oh, making men feel comfortable wasn't written in the job description. In fact, it never stated anything about women either. I guess my job is just to serve." My stare would remain on my jousting partner. My smiles weren't gifts on Oprah's twelve days of Christmas episodes. I owed nobody a smile and I wasn't about to just frantically pass one out even if that meant a poor review from a secret shopper.

While customers thought our job was to act as if we were working in Disneyland, Team Members would often try to throw on the facade for one another as well. My coworkers were dealing with severe health issues, familial struggles such as children in prison, and we were grappling with inflation. Between customers, we would try to prop each other up to help support one another. We were exhausted from rickety schedules; we were stressed out about daycare and how to explain to our kids that we wouldn't be able to take their birthdays off. We missed one milestone after another that our babies hit. Banter between us moms would help control the chaos in our minds about the constant struggle.

Daycares actually have a rule to not mention if the baby is talking or walking until the parent does. Most of the time, it is the daycare workers who witness these miraculous moments and us parents are just riding on the lie suggesting we magically saw the event first. We do this despite the fact that deep down in our souls, we know we weren't the first to listen to the little babbles forming into words in our babies mouths. We tell ourselves our babies are just natural walkers when they confidently take their steps for the first time in front of us.

We weren't okay because we were living paycheck to paycheck. This feat was even with inflated wages. The minimum wage my state offered was a joke and it kept encroaching on the company's lowest wage. Slowly, the bare minimum crept into the shadows of the company's policy. When the minimum wage went up, our wages weren't inflated to compensate. Pretty soon, people who had worked for the retail chain for just a few years were earning close to what I was making as a tenured employee. My eight years of experience and our new coworker Iris's six months were separated by 50 cents. Still, it was the most money any of us would be able to earn with our perceived experience so we stayed.

Iris truly believed the amount of dopamine being released through forced grins would be enough to get her through her day. She would always smile and ask how I was. I would always reply that I was okay and try to move on. We all knew I wasn't okay. Most of the people I worked with weren't okay. Iris wasn't even okay. Her boyfriend was a terrible human and made her life hell. Between her shitty homelife and the demands of the job, she really bought into the dopamine effect.

According to everyone around me, I brought the team down with my second pregnancy due to my physical limitations. It didn't help that I had slipped into an undiagnosed depression. Quietly, I became swallowed by a hungry and fierce bout of despondency. Anxiety was pulsating throughout my entire body. My movements and thoughts became jagged with no way to fully vocalize what was happening inside my brain.

Yet, I showed up for my shifts ready to work. But because I didn't burst out into a song fit for a sing-a-long every time someone asked me how I was, it was depressing the team. What was worse was Secret Shoppers revealed I wasn't throwing smiles at every customer and one shopper even noted I looked as if I was on the verge of tears. The experience was off putting to them, and they wrote down that because I looked as if I was in emotional distress they would not be returning. They mentioned how I was extremely knowledgeable and helpful but looked sad and despite my efforts, they scored me as failing.

One day, Iris confronted me and said I was too much of a downer. She explained I should be grateful for my life. She told me she stopped asking how I was doing because she got sick of my negativity. When she said this I also realized it was she who sold me out and it was her words that knocked me to a whopping 10-cent raise. I sat there in the hot sun groveling with Jeff to give me a raise during my annual review. We bantered back and forth sitting on the oversized brick planters in front of the store as he publicly reviewed my yearly performance. My Team Leader decided with my Store Leader I didn't deserve a raise at all that year. I begged to differ. They decided to meet me in the middle with an insulting raise and made sure to tell me it was because they couldn't risk a scene in front of the store. I had caused enough grief and I was certainly going to pay for it. They said I was bringing my personal life into work too much.

And instead of anyone asking if I was okay, or what I needed, they crucified me behind my back which resulted in the lowest raise possible. By doing this, the team had made it clear I was no longer a welcomed member.

TWENTY

Reasonable Accommodations (The Reprise)

S oon enough, my second pregnancy started to take a major toll on my health, it was obvious and couldn't be ignored anymore. They were beginning to grapple with the idea of me being permanently stuck in a depressive state. It didn't help that my husband had been laid off. A month later our young dog was diagnosed with terminal cancer. Our cars kept breaking down and each repair was equivalent to multiple months of rent. To top it off, when our dog eventually passed, our cat ran away and our tortoise ultimately succumbed to old age. All of this happened within a few weeks of each other. This was not normal and the stress being pressed upon us was immense. To further the situation, our 4 yr old son and his nanny were hit by a police car while crossing a marked crosswalk. They thankfully were ultimately okay but the nanny quit quickly after to tend to her wounds. Adding legal battles to heartbreak, to fear, and less than half our household income… well… the physical and mental health issues mounted.

Noticing the severe changes in me, my doctor began

limiting the hours I was allowed to work. She wanted me on a fixed schedule- trying to keep the stress low. Her explanation was that unpredictability can lead to physical stress within the body and to help stave off my pregnancy becoming a high risk, she needed to see some normalcy in my life. She stated working 30 hours a week would be okay for me because otherwise, we wouldn't financially survive. The only condition was that I was restricted from working extreme hours. No more early 5am shifts and no shifts after dark. The lovely clopen was no longer an option despite how much management loved to schedule it. The predictability would counter the amount of hours I was to be on my feet lifting large items. Monday through Friday 8 am-6 pm was her preferred hours of operation for my gestating body. In a normal job, this would've been fine.

But this wasn't a normal job. This was retail.

When my shaking hand turned in the paper stating I could no longer work whenever they felt like scheduling me, I knew things were going to get hairy. Memories of when I tried to adjust my schedule due to my first pregnancy at my previous job began radiating throughout my brain. While everything inside of me wanted to believe this time things would be different with this company, my gut knew it would be a battle I wouldn't win. Why? Retail will not accommodate.

All of my previous baggage began flooding back to me as I handed in my doctor's note stating my new restrictions. Retail is not for families. They are not for mothers. And they certainly will not accommodate. I immediately thought about my previous Leaders at the other store and how they retaliated against my doctor's orders and refused to even give me time off to give birth to my first child. Thankfully, FMLA couldn't be denied this time because I had been with the company for several years.

My new handicap was met with rolled eyes, huffing, puffing, and the silent treatment from Store Leadership. My coworkers side-eyed me and began making comments like "must be nice" and "spoiled". None of them had experienced pregnancy, and none of them were even in a serious relationship. Most still lived with their parents and had no actual bills. They didn't understand my world. Their comments slid off my shoulders. The pain from my sciatic nerve being pinched didn't allow me to mull over their ignorance.

Over the next three weeks, nothing really changed. My schedule was still wonky, my blood pressure kept rising. I would leave work at 10:30 at night and clock back in at 6 am. When my doctor found out, she called my store. That is when things changed. They accommodated me for exactly 2.3 weeks after the phone call with my physician. Then, the dreaded page to the office came through the walkies each department had.

Two store Leaders met me in the tiny office. They had a manilla folder on the desk and asked me to sit down on the old and dingy couch. They must have found it from a Craigslist ad suggesting it was free. No doubt the gray fabric was used in several homes before landing itself in a grocery store office. The smell alone reminded me of a dorm room. Hints of salt emanating from the fabric told me it was on the boy's side of the living quarters.

As I sat on the couch they both looked at me. One looked like he was annoyed about wasting his time on this conversation. It was easy to see that he wanted to find a reason to fire me but couldn't. The other had the eyes of a puppy that just got into trouble for pissing on grandma's shoes.

"Do you know why you are here?" The annoyance leaked through Jeremy's stature.

"Should I?" Tears began welling up. I knew why they called me in, but they would need to be the ones to say it. His chair swiveled and handed me the manila folder. The sad puppy (Mark) lowered his head. He had a good heart. The folder flopped open.

The words "Job Description Change" were printed in bold mocking me. Mocking my status and mocking my disposition. Nope, there was no way my pen would hit this paper.

"If you choose not to sign this then we will be terminating you right now. You are no longer able to perform your job duties within reasonable accommodation. We are doing you a favor." Jeremy explained the situation as if this was perfectly legal. Unfortunately for me, he could read my mind. "My wife is pregnant right now and she isn't using it as an excuse to get a better schedule." First of all, no pregnancy should ever be compared to another. Secondly, his wife worked three four-hour shifts a week at a dive bar. That was less than half of my scheduled hours. This is also her first child. The second pregnancy is always much different. Kudos to the happy couple who seem to live the perfect life.

"I deserve reasonable accommodation." There was no use pretending to be strong. The hormones had me almost wailing at this point. I saw the bills not being paid, the already empty cupboards bearer, the broken-down cars decaying in my dirt driveway.

"Unfortunately, it has been determined your schedule restrictions are not actually reasonable." Mark sighed as the words left his mouth. His remark was met with a smirk from his partner. After the meeting I found out Mark vocalized his concerns about what was happening to my status to corporate before the meeting took place. A year later, he was demoted.

Tears began to stream like a wash flooding during monsoon season. "Explain." The word left my mouth in a deep and heavy gasp.

"You need to be available more. There is nothing left to explain." Jeremy replied.

"I need time." To think, to breathe, to figure out yet another plan B.

"I'll clock you out so you can use your lunch break to think." Mark began to get up and was clearly as uncomfortable as I was. It was suspected that he was grabbing our Human Resources who was not present in the room. Or, he was really going to clock me out illegally as per the company policy (nobody was allowed to use the time clock on behalf of another team member no matter the status) to let me think. If Charlie came in, the fight would be over. Charlie was incredible at finding the rules and regulations to support the actions of Jeremy. She would have found a way to dismiss me on the spot. If Mark clocked me out, I would lose time to find daycares for my son and figure out how much it would cost to get the transmission fixed in my car. Both circumstances couldn't be risked.

After a few minutes, my pen met paper. My status went from full-time to part-time. I was no longer promised anything more than 4 hours a week. My health insurance was immediately terminated. My tenure of 6 years was gone with a stroke of a pen.

TWENTY-ONE

When Do I Work Again?

No promises have ever been made about consistent schedules. One week you may have Thursday and Sunday off. The next week you may work until the Tuesday after and just get one day off. With the way the weeks were operated, it would make sense to have a Tuesday off and then wait until Saturday to have another day to yourself. After that, you might wait until next Saturday and Sunday to be relieved of your duties. On top of this, you wouldn't find out until a week in advance when you would work. During that week, you may close at 10:30pm and then be expected to clock back in by 7am. If reading this paragraph didn't give you whiplash maybe you would have handled the situation better than I did. But, I liked to be able to plan things like appointments and family gatherings.

This expectation was after the company outlawed the famous clopen (when you would close the night before and open the next morning). The retail giant bent after dubious amounts of complaints that management was using clopens as punishment as well as a way to force us to quit. When we quit, there was less paperwork for them to fill out than if we were fired. Before this rule was enacted, you could have worked until 11pm and be scheduled at 5am the next morning.

For the early birds out there who love shopping the second the store opens, please bring the workers a coffee or just plan on being a decent human being to them. Chances are, the people dumping olives into the olive bar are sleep deprived and have zero patience. Cashiers are probably dealing with massive headaches as their registers chirp each organic vegetable you just had to purchase at 7 am. And the grocery stockers are probably reeling because the departments weren't faced (when you bring forward the products so that everything looks full to the brim).

For a year or so, anytime I requested time off for a big event or simply requested a day off after the event, I would mysteriously be scheduled at 6 a.m. the next day. Request denied. It never stopped me nor anyone I worked with. Would we come in still fucked up from the night before? Absolutely. Were we able to complete our tasks? Sometimes. Did we complain? Hell yes. There was always a reason for adding me to the morning schedule on a day I rarely worked. Retaliation was never listed but it was clear it was at the top of the list.

The struggle was real. I was walking a tightrope like so many others between hosting a real life and working in the world of customer service. And when we did need to make requests, it was difficult to accommodate them. Team Leaders would adjust the schedule so that the numbers made sense- not the schedule of our lives. In short, it was difficult to function beyond the walls of work.

When placing my time off requests I had to be

careful about my word choice when writing down the reason as to why I needed the personal day. My Leader during my time in the cheese department was frustrated with me and acted like I was asking for special favors to… you know… have a life and be an active parent. He didn't have kids and didn't quite understand the semantics that go into parenting. He also made it very clear it wasn't his responsibility to make me available for my children and would often deny requests for me to go on class field trips, take my kids to shows, and holidays. John loved to deny holidays- it was probably a special hobby of his. He told me I knew the job I signed up for. To be able to participate in my children's lives I had to feign illness. Magically, my colds that year would appear on the same day as recitals. They would brilliantly go away the next day and I was able to walk back into work and complete two days worth of work in a single shift. Sometimes, requests turned into our own game and us team members would swap shifts to help accommodate each other's lives.

One example of this was when I requested the Friday evening and the following Saturday off for my dad's wedding. Suddenly, those were the only two days I was scheduled that week because of the slashed hours. They weren't abiding by my doctors orders yet, they did decide to slash my hours "to help my disability". My shift was 10-6pm on Friday. The next day I was set to work from 6am- 1pm. The wedding was going to be a rager starting at 3pm that Friday and my relationship with my father was rocky. If it wasn't for me having two referrals under my belt, I would have called out. Thankfully, one of my coworkers was desperate to have that Friday morning off and swapped shifts with me. I worked the early morning shift, showed up at the wedding, and then stayed until

9:30 pm. This didn't bode well with my father and my job was one of the reasons my relationship with him fell apart.

If I hadn't shown up the next day to work I probably would have been fired. Staying any later would have nearly killed me due to my 6 am shift the next day. I was on the precipice of preeclampsia during this time and the long two days only made my symptoms worse. Being in retail meant being tugged in all directions and I began balancing the will to live, and the will to afford to live. It was a choice I had to make and I decided to earn my wages at the cost of my health.

TWENTY-TWO

You Can Go Home

W hen I came back from maternity leave I was given two options: work in the kitchen doing whatever work was needed or be let go. They really enjoyed waving the possibility of canning me in my face. It was always a checkmate situation and the store knew that. We still hadn't overcome our financial woes at home and there was no other choice but to be thrown into the kitchen. I was scheduled to train the next week during my singular four hour shift. There was little to no time to become reacquainted with my team or the updates for everything as well as learn a new trade.

After my first shift back went by, I was stationed in the bar. This was welcomed because it was a department I had previously worked in and enjoyed greatly. The nuances of the different types of beer were fascinating to me and I enjoyed the long conversations with customers. An hour into my shift, I was told I would need to cover for someone's vacation in another venue. No biggie, this kind of stuff happens frequently and I enjoyed having more skills under my belt. I was told I was going to have a few days of oversight to make sure I was comfortable in the area. The training went as follows:

My Leader, Stewart, walked me to the Taco Shack. He told me this was the station I would be working in. Out of the venues in the kitchen, this was the second most terrifying role for me. The first would be the bar chef. I wasn't a strong cook and knew nothing about cooking meat as I was a vegetarian. It was implied I would need to learn how to cook for the masses very quickly.

He guided me toward the kitchen nestled behind my new station and vaguely pointed at a wall in the walk-in (a giant refrigerator) where I could find my ingredients. Stewart quickly moved to the oven and thought I needed to be told how to turn on the burners right next to it- I think he thought "I don't cook meat" meant "I don't know how to use kitchen equipment". This isn't entirely false, an industrial kitchen is much different from a household one but the basics were well, basically the same. After the 20 minute Kitchen 101, he brought me back to the Taco Shack and told me to "feel for the levers underneath the counter" that is apparently where I would find the plugs for the hot wells I was to keep full of water. Steam from the hot water would rise up keeping the displayed food hot.

I was then informed my first day manning the station was today and he had an appointment to go to- I was to work alone and lunch was starting in thirty minutes. If I didn't have everything ready by then it would be another "talk" on whether or not I could handle retail. I told Stewart I would do what was possible but it was going to be his problem not mine if the task couldn't be finished in time.

Sweat began to bead under my apron. Thankfully,

everything that needed to be served hot was magically placed in the alto-shaam (a giant steamer where you can heat up food). My trusty friend Pam noticed Stewart was throwing me into a situation where I would not succeed. She took her smoke break then between sips of her Cola, she made sure each bean and meat made it to the warmer in time for me to pull off the impossible. By 11:05 am, the station was set up- minus the levers on the bottom being propped up. Little did I know the hot water keeping the food warm was draining quicker than the wells could fill. It only took 45 minutes before this was caught and one of my other coworkers quickly realized what was going on and saved the day from another potential catastrophe. Burnt water really reeks. The water in the wells only burnt a handful of times after this before I was in the habit of closing the drains appropriately for good.

As much as I hated being at the station, I have to give credit where credit is due. This is where I learned to cook. Every time I would come back from my weekend the meat and salsa would be depleted. My task was to cook vats of chicken, beef, and pork within a two-hour window. I would be expected to prepare and fill two cambros filled with three different types of salsas, grate cheddar cheese, and crumble pounds of queso fresco. During the window of time when my shift started and the lunch rush began, I was also expected to take the temperatures of each station, ensure my coworkers had their breaks, and deep clean the coolers.

Oh, did I mention the rotisserie was also my responsibility? There I was, a stark vegetarian, ramming about 30 chickens onto giant skewers at 10:30 in the morning and man-handling them into a rotisserie oven that was taller than me. Sometimes, I would sing songs from

Sweeney Todd because of the size of the oven. Other times, I would walk around the kitchen asking if people liked my chicken centipede (it was the Disney version of the Human Centipede). It was not a small task to be in charge of this station, and while I grumbled through the entire process, I am pretty confident in my cooking to this day because of it.

When my coworker got back from vacation, he was stationed at the bar and I was told to stay where I was. It was explained to me that the corporate wanted his personality type in the bar area and mine right where it was. The sales have skyrocketed for the Taco Shack since they scheduled me there. Why mess up a good system? This broke me. I wasn't meant to be in the kitchen in this capacity. Baking was more my style but actual chef work was a whole other world I didn't want to live in.

If I told you a year later there was a position open in the bar I would be lying. I have no clue how much time passed between the initial job switch and the opportunity but does it really matter? There was a bartending position available and they wanted someone to work mainly days and just one close. It was my time to shine! My application was filled out, I did my due diligence, and I was ready to rock the interview.

A few days later, I was told I didn't get the position. There was no true explanation. I knew it was my availability. I tried hard to work daycare hours because it was nearly impossible to find a sitter outside of those times. The sitters who were available to watch two kids during odd hours were incredibly expensive leaving me in a pickle. Stewart didn't say much about denying me the permanent position- he didn't need to. He was promoted and began working in the corporate offices within a week of the bartending interviews.

Stewart had promised me at least a shift at the bar every other week to keep me happy. He alluded he would discuss the arrangement with Dwayne, his replacement. This wasn't much but if it meant I wasn't going to come home with raw chicken juice from ramming extra rare rotisserie chickens onto a giant skewer once a week I was going to take it.

When my next bar shift came around, I showed up ready to work and noticed a girl I didn't know standing in my spot. I asked who she was. She replied with her name- Danny. Danny explained that it was her first day and she was told I would be training her.

"Well, glad someone decided to tell me that." I didn't mean for the spark in her eyes to burn out so quickly by saying this but it was the truth. I had no idea I was to be training her. The role of Team Trainer was stripped from me when I was stripped of full-time status during my pregnancy. According to company policy, I wasn't allowed to train her. Yet, here I was and there she stood doe-eyed and eager for her brand new role in this pretentious grocery store. Rage sifted inside me and before my soul could sedate it, it took the reins. Yes, I showed her where everything was. Yes, I showed her how to use the cash register, change a keg, and set the bar up to perfection. I wasn't a monster, just a pissed-off exhausted human. She was the innocent bystander caught up in a theoretical gang fight.

It was time to do roll-ups (where servers prepare the silverware by literally rolling it up into the napkin) and there was no silverware to be found. During my time racing around the store trying to figure out where hundreds of sets of silverware ran off to, I ran into Dwayne. Now, before I continue, Dwayne is a great guy and is a very wonderful human. We had a good rapport except on this day.

"Hey Lennox! Did you meet Danny?" He asked cheerfully.

"Fuck off." I stomped into the walk-in. The silverware definitely wasn't there but my anger needed to go somewhere.

"Excuse me?" He retorted.

"You heard me. Fuck. You." I stormed out and slammed the giant door so hard it bounced back open. I was startled by my own strength but wanted it to be clear this tantrum was far from over. The silverware wasn't found but it was time to return to the bar.

After showing Danny the rest of the ropes, I took a ten-minute break and cried in the bathroom as all the girls do in romcoms. It's true, we really do cry like that and yes it is embarrassing. On my way back to my doomed colleague, Dwayne stopped me and told me to go to his office immediately. It was a tone I had never heard from him before and could tell he meant business.

"What's your problem today?" He may have been nice but he needed a bit of coaching when it came to addressing people. I slunk into the office chair and began twirling in circles. I ignored his statement- it was obvious what my problem was. "I'm going to ask you again, what is going on with you today?" He looked genuinely confused.

"Uhm, you're having me train the person who got the job I wanted. Don't you think that's a little fucked?" I spat at him.

"Wait, what?" It was beginning to be clear he wasn't the one who wrote the schedule.

"Danny? The newbie that is now working in the bar? Yeah, it's my job to train her. I thought I wasn't a team trainer anymore. I also thought that I wasn't fit to work in the bar. How dare you have me train someone for the job I wanted? You know this isn't the first time? Remember my stories about Karl? Having me, the cashier, train the supervisors after I was denied the positions? You're no different than them." It was either stop there or go further and continue to dig my own grave. I had already dug out the first full shovels of dirt.

"Okay, first, yes, that is fucked. I'm sorry. I thought she was starting tomorrow, and I would never have done that. I did not make this schedule. Secondly, you didn't get the job because you are unwilling to work weekend nights. This has nothing to do with your skill. And thirdly, I would recommend you go home before you say anything else. If you continue this crap, I'm firing you." He has never sounded sterner before.

So, without saying another word, I collected my things and went home.

TWENTY-THREE

This is Halloween

The first several years of my time in retail, if we worked on Halloween we were allowed to dress up in costume. Obviously, the dress code had to be followed so we had to get a bit more…creative and innovative with our costumes. Goodbye tropes of sexy nurses and Chucky masks spurting fake blood.

Halloween was the day where instead of seeing us workers, you would come in and see girls in poodle skirts and men in baseball jerseys. As eager as we were to dress up, we were pretty lazy with our creativity. Nobody wanted to offend anyone and certainly "risqué costume" would be a pretty frustrating thing to be fired for. My couple's costume the year prior of a priest and Catholic school girl would have meant immediate termination. There were also no pregnant nuns running around the meat department for the same reason.

"And you left your job because?" Says the ominous hiring person.

"Oh, I dressed up as a pregnant nun and walked around the store with a bottle of water in a paper bag wanting to really dig into the character" would be the reply…if you answered honestly. If the interview lasted any longer, I think it's safe to say it would be your day to purchase a lotto ticket.

On a hot July afternoon, I was strolling through a competitor's aisles. My kids went gaga for the frozen orange chicken they sell and momma needed an easy dinner. Since I was there, I might as well make a trip out of it! My cart was filled with all the goodies: spinach dip, pizza, orange chicken, and lots of snacks. But, this story is less about my ability to eat like a college student (or five-year-old that can turn on an oven) and more about what happens next.

As I was saying, I was waltzing through the aisles with my kids and suddenly it hit me. I knew what my Halloween costume should be for work. Yes, it was several months early but come on… when an idea slaps it slaps.

I texted my grandpa: *Hey, can I borrow one of your Hawaiian shirts?*

He texted back within seconds: *Ok?*

With his blessing half the costume was completed. I hunted for the nearest employee to begin the process of completing the outfit. As I asked for an old name badge, the employee looked at me like I was crazy. He even asked me to prove I worked at their competitor by pulling out my nametag, apron, and discount card from my ever-so-distraught baby bag/purse. He was still super suspicious. Thankfully, I was extremely persuasive. When my new friend realized there was a brilliant plan at hand, he excitedly looked for the Leader on duty. My creativity and persistence left the MOD with more questions.

We went through the same gambit. I explained where I worked and how I was going to dress up in the competitor's uniform as my costume. My creativity and persistence left the MOD with more questions. Despite his suspicions, he eventually gave the final okay to my plan. He went to look for a name badge of someone who was no longer with the store. Thankfully, it took him no more than a few minutes to find one because my daughter was pretty much over the situation. In one moment I was both wrangling a 2 year old out of hell and accepting an old name badge from another grocery store with a very simple and totally dress code appropriate costume in mind. Thinking back on this, it would have been a very easy way for me to infiltrate a store and maybe even perform a heist. Maybe that's why the Leader was so hesitant to give me a two year old nametag.

The waiting game began.

One month passed.

Two months passed.

Three months, and here I went straight into October. Nobody had any clue what I was planning. Halloween was the best time to work because it was so fun to play dress-up at my job. Usually, my creative ideas would be boasted throughout the months of September and October. But this year, I was radio silent. Being so quiet about my upcoming costume had my entire store concerned.

Like clockwork, ol' Hallows Eve sprang up and opened her arms to creativity and mischief. That day, I put on my grandfather's Hawaiian shirt, clipped on the name tag from the competitor, and waltzed right into work. I was officially "Kathryn" from "L.B'S". Where everyone looked much happier.

A few people got the joke immediately. More people gave confused looks. One woman even asked me what store she was in. I guess in a sea of 50's poodle skirts,

sports jerseys, and the occasional stereotypical representation of a decade passed walking around I looked the
most normal. I told her she was at L.B's. Just kidding, I
wanted to though because the joke was clearly lost
on her.

As the day progressed, the laughter, confusion, and
complete misunderstanding of my joke only continued.
"Kathryn" was working in the Taco Shack. I was
building one burrito after another, plopping cabbage
onto burrito bowls, and sandwiching overly juicy tacos
into cardboard boats just like any other day. Displays of
the meals I offered at my station continued to get built
and the dress code was never broken. Everything was
going smoothly, most of my coworkers and team Leaders
who got the joke thought it was hilarious. They would
walk by me just to double over in laughter. My humor
was celebrated until my Store Leader decided to get
lunch from my Taco Shack.

"Burrito, tacos, or a bowl?" I said as he approached
me. My face was straight, not to try to act cool but
because my outfit no longer tickled me enough to give
my customers flair. It was lost on me that my next guest
was the one who ruled us all.

"Uhm, where's your name tag?" He asked. Theo was
regaining his composure in the store since moving back.
Because of this, the joke was not funny to him and his
smile faded. Theo's lunch break just turned into a
lecture.

"Right here! I'm Kathryn, how may I help you?"
Spunk and energy re-entered my body and I began to
stand a little taller as my pointer finger touched the
competitor's name tag.

"Oh. Very funny." He did not find it funny. Arms
began to fold over themselves and his head looked me up

and down carefully trying to find the flaw- find the reason to force me out of my costume.

"Burrito? Tacos? Bowl?" I asked again.

"Oh, nothing, I don't support my competitors." He said as he walked away.

The rest of the day and actually, the rest of the week he didn't even look me in the eye. There was no solid reason to have me change my costume and nothing ever was stated in the store or our retail bible book suggesting we can't dress up as our competitor's employees. I never thought to check on it but I have a sneaking suspicion that if your retail bible suggests "thou shall not cloth thyself in the robes of the competitor" you can probably thank yours truly for the rule. And if it isn't written in there, you now have an idea for your next costume.

TWENTY-FOUR

It's a Burrito Not a Life Lesson

W orking in grocery retail showed me why the obesity situation is so dire in America. Please don't get this confused with me suggesting I am healthy. I just understand the predicament. It was my job to cater to the quick demands of guests, prep the food, and ensure that the display food was constantly looking its best. It was a juggling act at best but it was my juggling act and I enjoyed having multiple things to do at any given time of the day. It was fascinating seeing how much people- especially teenagers could eat.

Tuesdays were always a doozy. Like clockwork, the parking lot would fill up with Mercedes Benz, Range Rovers, and BMWs while pretentious high school children would crowd our store. We were situated across the street from a very prestigious school that bred incels and entitled assholes. They loved the Taco Shacks Tuesday special and would flock to my station every week.

There have been incidents of children telling me how dumb I was to not cash in on whatever the cryptocurrency was before BitCoin. One kid told me if I didn't sell her MLM makeup I would be "saying no to a lifetime of opportunity". They would try to make a buck off me by framing their Ponzi Scheme as a way to help me climb out of my dire situation of working in the service industry. Sometimes, the children would explain to me I worked in retail because I didn't graduate from their pretentious charter school. It was fun watching their faces contort in confusion when it was explained to them their school didn't exist when I went to high school. Even if it had been built, I would have scoffed all the same and refused to go.

Tuesday once again reared its monstrous head, I was stationed at my usual place in the Taco Shack. Scooping copious amounts of beans and rice into cardboard bowls and nestling in too many ingredients into the itty bitty corn taco shells was the task at hand. I passed my time by imagining the overstuffed tacos falling into the laps of the prissy teens messing up their newly dry cleaned clothes.

At approximately 3:30 pm, a woman and her teenage dream daughter walked into the queue for their midafternoon lunch. It was obvious they were arguing. Little moments like this always gave me a slight rush- it was a personal soap opera waiting for me to witness. I had the opportunity to see people at their best just as often as I saw them at their worst due to my job. This mother-daughter duo was somewhere in between. Their argument was not about to stop on my behalf and the snickers flew between one another as they approached me.

"See?" The woman pointed heinously toward me after asking her if she wanted a burrito, burrito bowl, or taco.

" Hi, what can I get for you?" I ignored her

comment, it was my way of expressing she was as worthless as I seemed to appear. I just simplified my original question because she might not have understood it.

"See this? You could be scooping shit into containers and relying on people like us- taxpayers to pay for your bills." She clearly was never told to not disrespect anyone who handled her food.

"C'mon, mom! I just need a year break before going to college!" The daughter whined. Her Kate Spade backpack began to slip off her shoulders as she rolled her entire body in frustration.

"A year turns into two, which turns into three, and before you know it, you turn into her." The woman pointed directly at me again. I had gone from human to subject in a matter of seconds. It didn't matter my life story- apparently, I was the example of a failure.

"Mom, I won't turn into her! I have a backup plan." Her blonde hair started falling out of her ponytail and she started to whisk it away from her face. Apparently, besides my body standing in front of them, I did not exist.

"You better. And I am done having this conversation with you." Her mother then looked me dead in the eye. "Burrito. Make sure the beans are strained correctly. I need steak, cheese, and pico. And make sure to wrap it correctly." Her arms crossed over her body as if my servitude was a nuisance.

Retaliation had to be subtle. Nobody talks to me like that. Her burrito was soggy, poorly wrapped, and I definitely "forgot" the cheese, but I added two helpings of sour cream. Oops, sounds like this girl was too stupid to follow orders being barked at her. She on the other hand was too busy scoffing at her daughter to notice I made her meal completely wrong. She would find out in due time.

As I handed her burrito over, I told her "You know, my friend is teaching right now with a master's degree and making less than me. She has debt, I don't. This job pays enough for me to take college a course at a time so I never have to deal with debt. Do I still look stupid to you?"

The Mother of the Year didn't know how to respond but her daughter looked at me and mouthed "I'm sorry". A lesson was probably learned that day but it wasn't the one Mother Dearest intended.

TWENTY-FIVE

Team Member Appreciation Week

I f you are underpaid, overworked, or both, you know what this week is all about. It is casual freebies, pranks, games, and maybe a tote bag filled with cheap items from Oriental Trading Company. Every single item in the obligatory tote bag gift is "fun-sized" and almost useless. Nevertheless, my kids certainly enjoyed it when I came home with fun new toys and single serving treats for them.

One year, during our yearly reminder of lackluster wages, our corporate Leader wanted to come by and do a little "checkup" on the store. When the big bosses rolled into town, the bells and whistles flew out. All of a sudden, purchase order budgets were able to be magically blown. The sales floor would be stocked to the brim almost threatening to spill over with fancy new products nobody wanted and would ultimately go to waste from spoiling. We were to be cheery with all customers to a fault. And we should never ever skip a beat in service.

When it was announced Robert was going to pay us a visit during this time we had mixed feelings. How would we keep up the demeanor of a well-functioning store while still participating in the mandated activities of the week? Should we nix the coveted pie-eating contest? Maybe the corn hole was too distracting and needed to be nixed. I personally wasn't willing to give up ping-pong (hi, store champion over here). And none of the women were willing to give up the 10-minute massages being offered. So, how would we incorporate this outlandish week with a store visit from a bigwig?

I suggested we have a Robert Day and dress like him as a joke. For the first time since the Halloween incident, my sarcasm caught the attention of my store Leader in a positive way. Theo thought it was hilarious and felt it was easy to pull off while keeping up the tempo for the week. He quickly implemented the plan into the daily themes.

The one condition was that nobody was to spill the beans and tell Robert we would be dressing up like him. We had it labeled as "Dress Up Like Your Hero Day" on the required calendar to send out to the region for bragging rights.

Flaunting your ideas through email was part of the ultra hip club the company tried to portray. Store Leadership was to constantly send emails to the region about the happenings in their store. Cool cheese display? They wanted to show off your work and put their name on it. Amazing sales because a team member created an interactive display that caught customers attention? Cool, let's shoot off an email and act like it was the Leadership's idea.

If a store did something that was a big hit, an email went out. It was a big dick-swinging contest of which store made their team members seem the most productive and happy. It was also a way to make a week that was supposed to be relaxing and fun into a competition.

That's how these companies do it, they pin us against each other and then try to call us family. They want us to believe our jabs at one another are friendly fire. To some degree, it was. We aren't paid more based on large sales. We would still come home with meager checks no matter what the store made. Yet, we all cared. We all wanted to do well and make Daddy Warbucks proud.

Word spread quickly throughout the store about the plan. We just had to all show up in a purple polo and khaki pants. I would love to bet my right foot that the consignment shops were very confused as to why so many people suddenly wanted purple polos and khaki knickers. It wasn't really anybody in the store's style, but we wanted to poke some fun and felt that dropping a few bucks on shitty clothes was worth it.

It took this man, this man with a vision a whole two hours before he realized we had all dressed like him. None of us said a thing and just tried to speak to him as normally as we could. His first clue was Theo encouraging Robert to make conversation with us. That never happened. Usually, the two co-conspirators with a vision leading us into victory found themselves holed up in private quarters of the Leadership offices. So, when the algorithm was thrown, we thought it would be obvious.

Theo and Robert walked around and talked to us as if we were important that day. But if we talked to them for more than two minutes and especially if we were complaining, their eyes would glaze over. Theo in particular had such an uncanny ability to look right through you. It took Robert almost ten years for him to remember my name. Ten years of monthly pop-ins, greetings, and how do you do's before he began to recognize me.

Sometimes, I enjoyed the anonymity. But it also

made me worried he was the man we were all relying on to steer this ship home. If he couldn't connect with his crew, how would he connect with our vision?

In the middle of him speaking with someone in our sandwich area, he broke out in a huge grin. My laughter broke the moment of silence as the realization took over him. I loved a good prank but damn it was hard to not just burst into laughter when he walked into the store. When the beans were finally spilled everything I had been holding in spewed out.

"Uhm, wait.. what's going on here?" He spoke softly and was clearly amused.

"Dress Like Your Hero Day!" I shouted out of turn, I wanted to take credit for this one.

"But… who are you all dressed as?" He had to have been kidding…right?

"You!" three of us shouted and doubled over in laughter.

"Come on, wait, did you all plan this?" The man was blushing. Either from the embarrassment from us calling him out on his singular outfit or the fact that it took him so long to figure out the joke.

"You're just our hero." I replied and made sure to lace my words with heavy sarcasm and minimal giggles.

TWENTY-SIX

I Wouldn't Google That

The Special Order Table was the focal point of the holiday season. For some time, the "grand opening" of the table would be celebrated by creating a giant feast for customers to sample every item in the catalog. This display was so large it would give Costco wet dreams each year in anticipation.

Mountains of sweet and fluffy mashed potatoes, rivers of stuffing, and a downpour of gravy would entice guests to come inside. They would be greeted with Heirloom Turkeys displayed as if Martha Stewart was coming for dinner. Perfect hues of orange, brown, and white were delicately placed across the table. At the end of the buffet, mini dessert samples were propped for onlookers and kids in need of their next sugar fix.

Everything was free to taste. Every team member ate lunch on the house that day. We stuffed ourselves silly and pretended we were truly contemplating purchasing a meal for our families. The meals themselves cost more than what we made in a week. Our joke was lost on many but we still enjoyed the private sarcasm between ourselves.

A few years in a row, I was pulled to work the Special Order Table to greet customers and gather their orders. This was deemed as a role of honor because customers would come into the store who normally didn't shop there. It was my duty to persuade them to do all their shopping at the store year round. Suddenly, I was the one with all of the answers and my job was to oversee hundreds of extremely special Thanksgiving Dinners. If the count was off, it was my fault. If a turkey didn't show, I was the reason. In a short span of about three weeks, I spoke with hundreds of people and my job often emulated that of a secretary at a high end call center. I was simultaneously answering phone calls and helping guests who were standing in front of me clueless as to how to handle a party. In a world of instant gratification and a mass amount of aging Boomers, asking anyone to wait on hold was a sin punishable by spit flying at you while slurs of disappointment piercing through your ear drums. The huffs and puffs of impatient guests would send me into an internal flurry. It was imperative I never showed the effect they had on me.

My coworker Danny would always remind me that soon those same people telling me my generation is the cause for the world's demise would be on life support. We would joke around about what we would tell the Susans and Barbaras as we theoretically pulled the plugs and watched their terror as they realized we had the final laugh.

When I was able to focus on the customers, they rattled off their anxiety ridden orders. Most of the time they were giving standard requests such as wanting a turkey a certain size and needing to purchase the right amount of sides for their families. But there was one specification that kept coming up I just didn't understand. Guests wanted their turkeys spatchcocked. This word confounded my vegetarian soul. Cooking meat was only something I did at work and the word itself just wasn't appetizing. It left me with insatiable curiosity.

When I was growing up, the internet was a budding rose that people flocked to. Teachers didn't fully understand it so they didn't teach us great online researching skills. I could skim the fuck out of an encyclopedia but when it came to Google, I thought all you had to do was type in the word and the correct answer would magically appear.

Rule of thumb, be more cautious about what terms you type into Google. My naïve fingers delicately typed the word "spatchcock" into the search bar of my company laptop.

It wasn't poultry that popped up but there was definitely meat on full display. My shock and horror paralyzed me and I couldn't close the window fast enough. Suddenly, there were a slew of naked men with dicks bigger than the average porn star right in front of me. If the computer was facing the wrong direction, my newfound kink would have been on display for every customer in the store to witness.

As soon as I regained consciousness, I clicked repetitively to close out the window. Obviously, the computer wasn't the newest model, and the lag time was making me feel as if my secret humiliation would be let out. Sweat began to bead on my forehead attempting to showcase my embarrassment. This Millennial didn't know how to Google basic chef terminology.

Fear began to sink into my soul as I realized my Google history was still sitting there waiting to be discovered. I quickly began to clear the cache. Wracking my brain, I tried to think of any other way my search history would need to be wiped to avoid being reprimanded for searching a rather lackluster fetish on company time. But my answer was still left elsewhere and the question burned into my thoughts. What was a spatchcock turkey and why were people so interested in it? Did they even know it was a sex term? At least it was fun to listen to grannies tell me how they loved it when it was spatch-cocked now.

Tepidly, I typed in *what is a spatchcock turkey?* I held my breath and clicked "go". Thankfully, turkeys popped up cut in half and splayed open. This intrigued me and I began to go further into my wormhole of questions. Obviously, it made sense to do this if you were wanting to cut down on cooking time, but what didn't make sense was how to keep the bird juicy. Knowing now how to search on the platform, I began typing in things like *benefits of a spatchcock turkey* and *recipes for a spatchcock turkey*. Suddenly, I was an expert at cooking a turkey sliced down the middle. It was just another tool under my culinary belt I wouldn't use. No amount of knowledge could turn this vegetarian into someone who cooked meat willingly.

There was something I would take with me for the rest of my life though. I now knew to never Google just a term. I knew to also never Google something with the images as the first page to pop up. So, I may have gained useless culinary knowledge but at least I walked away possessing some research skills under my belt. Those would not be wasted and helped me create incredible lessons for my department that were used for a few years after I left (I loved creating them so much that when I was dismissed from my duties as the trainer I still curated them) .

Nobody would think research would be a large part of retail but it was. While spatchcock was my first experience in using said skills, once I had them down there was no stopping me nor my team. We utilized this newfound talent to keep up with the fads drifting in and out of the foodie world so we could stay one step ahead of our gastronomist guests.

Left to our own devices, we would research ways to make our displays more enticing- what colors were popular for that season? What ethnicity was the newest food trend? How modern or postmodern should we go with our lettering? Each display boasted a large amount of research backed decisions to make each shoppers experience enjoyable and trendy. My mishap at the Special Order Table was just the beginning of a vast set of skills I would need in the future.

TWENTY-SEVEN

Storewide Meetings That Should Have Been Emails

B oosting morale was always the backhanded reason for holding store meetings. Being crowded into a store with people you were sick of seeing was the perfect solution to our woes according to the corporate Leaders. It was no secret the morale between employees, management, and their superiors was becoming extinct faster than the existence of dinosaurs. The meteor named "The Customer is Always Right" was what killed the hope we clung onto. It was imperative to keep us thinking we were more than just robots plugged into the system.

In addition to boosting morale, it was apparently unacceptable to pass on certain information in a small group setting. Our twice weekly mandated team huddles (mini meetings that consisted of 3-5 people on the same team) were not sufficient enough to spread company wide news. Nor could we take any more of our precious time during operating hours to discuss a simple procedure change, publicly shame someone (anonymously of course) or simply praise someone for their lackluster effort but beaming smile. Awards would be passed out, accomplishments would be shared, and there were always snacks. Though, the snacks would've needed to be laced with gold before they were worth the amount of grievances I heard from the back seat on the way there. No daycare in their right mind was open during our scheduled store meetings and most of us had spouses who worked odd hours. Those that didn't were straight up single and solo parents. Our kids were in the same mess of frustration we were in as we entered the mandated meetings.

At first, the store meetings happened once a quarter. When that didn't pep us up to the corporate standard, they bumped it down to twice a year. They thought by having us gather before the twilight of the morning we would be thrilled to drown in each other's misery. Pastries and burnt coffee would be laid out due to the bakers coming in at 3 am to provide for us. I always felt bad for them. Despite their attempts, it was too early to eat. Delicious delicacies such as croissants and muffins grew cold and hard like our jaded personalities. The bakers would forever be marked as martyrs but their food was rarely eaten.

Concert-worthy speakers would be planted in the middle of the store where we gathered to hear our brave Leaders speak. A microphone would be passed from each speaker's grabby hands giving them their minute of lime light. Their voices would scratch our eardrums with their over amplified enthusiasm. With a store of fewer than 80 people, there was no reason for the microphone except to invoke a false sense of excitement- a false sense of security. It was their job to masquerade as if the company wasn't floundering.

Teams would discuss their incredible innovations.

Team Leaders would boast about profits as if they were single handedly responsible for them. But honestly, it was the embellished pricing system that helped show an increase of sales. The free publicity didn't hurt either. With the rise of social media, the one-percenters were all over our luxury branding. They willingly spoke about how it was the only place to purchase groceries. Funny videos began popping up on different media platforms. Videos from shenanigans happening in the parking lots to videos about how our groceries were the only way to feed our nutrient vacant bodies were launching our brand through the vines of global awareness. Any press was good press and our growing sales proved it.

Our groceries were pure like the video creators claimed and this confused customers. They thought the slogan our company boasted meant our cake wouldn't make you fat. My vindictiveness would sprout the moment someone suggested the contradiction. I would explain the cakes were made with real butter and while they wouldn't increase your risk of cancer, they would make your ass bigger. We would sometimes discuss the confusion in our meetings and address the proper way to inform our guests of the discrepancy. This was Leadership's way to calm down my pep and make sure everyone knew I was not the role model for this conversation.

When the chastising and slight blame would finish, specialized teams such as the trainers, would distribute store-wide knowledge and we would all pretend to care. At first, I did care about this portion of the meeting. This was until I lost the role of Team Trainer due to my scheduling needs. When I was labeled as a trainer I loved it. Together, we would build lessons out of sticks and straw pasting them together with catch phrases we birthed ourselves. We would construct interactive exercises and lectures about recycling and the importance of following store protocol. Once, we even created a parody of Vanilla Ice's "Ice Ice Baby (Too Cold)" and used it to discuss how to properly recycle and why we should participate in the Earth-saving practice. We were the underpaid cheerLeaders always ready to pep up the crowd.

Near Halloween, the entire store would be encouraged to wear our costumes to the mandated gatherings. It was their way to vet out any unwanted representation as well as make sure nobody showed up dressed like the competitor again. Jokes would be thrown about what Wes Anderson character was portrayed the best. Being in retail left us with an odd sense of humor and it was always fun to lean into the characters we portrayed.

As time wore on, the meetings held at the first flush of morning were occupied by morning breath and grumbling hung over bellies. Everyone began to self medicate through their employment and it would show during the early mini conventions. The sound of defeat and frustration being passed around in whispers would fill the voids between our peppy speakers. Rolled eyes and sighs from overtired team members would infiltrate the phony vibe and once they started they didn't stop. It was the most depressing audience wave ever.

The only things that woke us up were the raffles. IPods, Fit Bits, and gift cards would fling through the air if your name was called. We would pay attention to this bit but quickly would lose patience when the same five people kept winning. These raffles lasted the first several years of my employment. Without warning, the major retailer took those away to save themselves the Benjamins.

The company began opening stores like they were a

Mattress Firm and forgot to look at the actual financial gains. As a corporation, they touted how they never had to pay for advertising. The grocery vendor was so busy gloating about how amazing they were they didn't notice the crash in their financial stability. To address this, an emergency meeting was scheduled in the twilight hours of a Wednesday.

When we all began piling into the store, the sun wasn't even daring to wake up yet. It was the beginning of Spring and our company was clearly getting ready to be part of a new adventure.We didn't expect a giant screen to be nestled in between the two speakers. We didn't expect them to begin the meeting with a movie. But the movie was short. It was a total of one minute in length and we suddenly knew- our employer was going under. This was no ordinary video, it wasn't a competitor's, it was ours. It was the first commercial this company ever funded.

Suddenly, even the "parent on duty" who was designated to watch all of our kids and pretend to listen to whatever droning conversation was blasted at us started to pay attention. Each meeting we would trade kids to help alleviate the agony of dragging our precious angels to work. Jodi's arms were filled to the brim with her own babies as well as my toddler, my seven-year-old, and three other batches of offspring. Her eyes sprung up the second our logo popped up.

"We're going under." I whispered to her. The wiggling minors couldn't even distract her from what was happening. This was bigger than what it was portrayed to be. The retailer tried to play it off as a step in the right direction.

If the advertisement wasn't a huge announcement like they claimed, they could have summed everything up in an email. The Corporation was still tight-lipped about any financial issues they may have been having and I naïvely thought they would be able to save face with their bougie ads. They were to be showcased during the Super Bowl where they would instantly gain millions of viewers. Despite their free publicity from various social media outlets, they still decided that a commercial was the best course of action. Buckets of money were being poured over the financial wildfire they sparked and it was us who were supposed to feign enthusiasm.

It didn't take long. Other retailers and one greedy billionaire began sending offers to the company as if we were on display at a Puppy Mill. Our CEO held onto his ignorance but we knew better. The advertisement was a warning of the future. Before we knew it, our company was haggled over like a cheap prostitute and landed in the arms of a new pimp.

TWENTY-EIGHT

Caught Me Red-Handed (Wasn't Me)

F or starters, it was me.

It was a slow summer day. School wasn't quite back in session and the seasonal residents hadn't flocked south yet. So, it was just us stuck with the summer heat and not much to do. These were the months I would whip out paper clips and clean out the itty bitty areas a regular clean would never touch. Whatever station I worked at always was the cleanest because I would clean down to the screw rivets. Sales were that low.

To pass the time between customers, we were discussing the most amount of money we have cost the company by breaking things (accidentally of course). Stories of shattered rotisserie oven doors, chemical spills, accidentally snipping fridge lines, and the occasional rogue cart hitting a fancy car were flying in through air. Was it bragging? Not quite. But it certainly was fun to think about the money we siphoned from the CEO's pockets through our own clumsiness. We fit the role we were given- a burden to society. Except me.

On my very first day of working with the retailer, my

assigned register was broken. It was a double drawer register but the bottom drawer was permanently stuck shut. There would be no second till in there. It was the first thing they told me- never slip money into the bottom drawer because it would never be rescued. We also were not allowed to open our register till completely if we were accepting a twenty-dollar bill or higher. When customers would hand over a Jackson, we were to slip him through the outside of the register into the under belly of our till so he could rest safely under the smaller bills.

The protocol was set into stone because the store wasn't in the best area. It could've been worse, but it absolutely could've been better. Anyways, the inevitable twenty came through my line and I was so nervous of fucking up, I fucked up. The bill found itself on the wrong side of the cash box and was lying helplessly trapped in the second drawer's belly.

By the time I confessed my mistake to Karl, I had two options. We break the register to get the twenty dollars, or I take the written warning. The last thing I wanted to do was to be known as the girl who broke a register on her first day. The written warning was received by rolled eyes and an annoyed signature acknowledging the situation. The bill was there permanently and listlessly waited for the jaws of life to free it from its hell. When the store was later bulldozed, I can almost guarantee you Mr. Jackson went down with it.

After taking my coworkers down memory lane, I proudly exclaimed my choice to not break the register. Without skipping a beat my boasting continued. They listened to me explain that I still had not broken anything expensive. There was no need to mention my habits of taking home thousands of sharpies and box cutters. They weren't broken, just unaccounted for.

But sure as shit, within five minutes of our wretched conversation, I began to serve a customer. She was a docile and kind older woman. All this sweet soul wanted was a quarter-pound of tuna salad. It was people like her that made this job tolerable. We looked forward to serving the kind ones. Sometimes we would even fight over who got to serve them because it was always such a breath of fresh air when customers would treat us like humans.

What she got was a lot more than store bought tuna salad. She didn't deserve the show she was about to witness.

Being short meant struggling to reach things in the big display cases. The deli case was so wide I simply couldn't reach over and scoop anything from the bottom platters. Your girl had to walk all the way around and open the case from the front. Lifting the giant glass dome was part of the gig and thankfully, the hydraulics always surprised the guests. If I didn't take the extra steps to scoop the various salads from the front of the case my boobs would have been smothered in whatever was towards the top of the deli display. Not only was the idea not enjoyable, I couldn't help but to think about the food safety concerns of my dirty apron raw doggin' various salads that were to be sold and eaten right away.

I went quickly into my spiel about how my mom told me the best things come in small packages as I waltzed around the counter to lift the large glass door open for my new favorite customer. Charming guests into not noticing the extra it took me to scoop their lunch into a plastic container was part of my mini standup gig. The woman politely went along with the conversation. She let me flash my words at her and even bought into my spiel.

And then it happened.

As I lifted the convex glass case, I felt a moment of resistance and then a giant crash. All eyes were on me. Fear flew across my face. The woman immediately began telling me it was okay, if I needed to pay for the broken item she would help me pay for it. It was still unclear to me exactly what had happened. The moment was stretched out so long that it snapped back quicker than a rubber band. As I regained an understanding of my surroundings, I realized the brand-new food scale we used to weigh and tag our deli items was off the counter and smashed into about 20 pieces. My teammates that were just ogling at me about my accomplishment of not breaking anything in almost a decade were in hysterics. The sentiment was lost on the angelic woman- she had no idea what conversation preceded this incident.

Dwayne came out immediately from the depths of the kitchen and was initially infuriated. He couldn't hold the anger for even a moment and burst into laughter when he realized what just happened. My sweet savior of a customer began to grovel with him, explaining I had done nothing wrong, and it was clearly someone else's fault. Bless her heart for immediately coming to my defense.

To ease her soul, I explained between giggles I had just boasted about never breaking anything important and then here I go breaking one of the most expensive items in the deli area. When the real story broke, she too burst into a smile and laughed with us as we figured out how to literally pick up the pieces.

TWENTY-NINE

Is This How You do it?

L ong after I was denied the bartending position, one of the bakery cake decorators left. She wasn't the lead decorator but there were only two of them so she was still incredibly important. For someone who loves baking, decorating was a whole other beast I had yet to tame. It at least was less gross than spilling beef blood on me and definitely smelled better than the raw chicken juice that would always drip into my shoes. Plus, Dwayne understood I was just about done with my role in the kitchen and was very aware my patience wouldn't last forever.

Dwayne shared the happy news of the open position and recommended I apply for it. He made it clear this position would not be simply handed to me- I needed to prove myself worthy of the role. He explained there were many talented people out there who would love the position. Dwayne also reminded me the lead decorator, Sarah, was a finicky human who wanted to work with someone with a solid skill set under their belt.

Sarah pulled me aside the day word broke out about

my submitting my application. She explained she needed to work with "a real artist, not some housewife that can smear frosting onto a cake-mix cake." Her bright green hair huffed in annoyance as she rolled her beautiful blue eyes at me.

"Great! I am not a wife yet and definitely have never baked anything from a box. Looks like I'm in!" I replied with a smirk. Little did I know, this was a great foreshadowing of our relationship to come. Sarah couldn't take me seriously and was insisting to Dwayne I didn't get the role due to inexperience.

As the interview approached, Dwayne asked me to create some examples of my work. He told me that while he wanted to see me smile again, he couldn't detriment the team with my not quite novice skill set. So, each night when I got home, I made a box mix cake (sorry Sarah) and tried my hand at frosting cakes into a beautiful masterpiece.

Every day I would become defeated and my fiancé worried I was wasting my time, money, food, and hopes. My cakes were so bad my biggest cheerLeader asked me if this was something I wanted to pursue. He witnessed the endless heartbreak and let downs from the last several years, he was trying to spare me another disappointment. The frosting was coming out uneven and filled with crumbs. Sarah began feeding me tips and tricks that were unhelpful- such as a real decorator doesn't rely on a crumb coat. She would taunt me and ask how the decorating was going and even asked to see pictures. As someone who loves a good self-deprecating joke, I showed her a few pics from my first catastrophe of a cake. I laughed to ease my pain. She jeered at my cake, satisfied thinking I couldn't land the role.

The day of the interview finally came. My stomach

was upset and my head felt heavy. I wasn't ready but I couldn't show those cards. I wanted to be given the chance to do something I felt was an art- something I enjoyed. Maybe I wouldn't hate going to work as much? As I sat down in the conference room, I felt like I was breaking out into a cold sweat. Dwayne and his replacement, Olivia sat me down and asked the very standard questions.

"How long have you been decorating for?" He asked me as stoically as he could.

"A total of two weeks and a day." I replied. They loved my sense of humor and how it sliced through my apparent nerves. Smiles broke out for a millisecond across the oversized table.

"And what makes you believe that you will be an asset and not a burden for the team?" Ouch, that's not like Dwayne to talk like this.

"Well, my determination, my lack of ability to understand the word no, oh, and my charming personality." My hope was that the last question was just to poke at me. Thankfully, I was right because they both started laughing. We all knew I was not known for my charm.

"Okay, okay, all kidding aside, you need to show us your work. What do you have for us before we consider you?" Olivia straightened her back and flashed a Cheshire Cat Smile. I wanted to trust her but for the first time in a while I couldn't read her intentions. Her beauty mesmerized us all but today was not the day to get lost in her aura. My portfolio was nothing impressive but I needed to act with confidence and keep a straight face- Sarah would surely shoot down my candidacy if she saw what I had accomplished. Luckily, she was not invited to the interview.

Confidently, I pulled out my phone where my portfolio was created. I handed it to them and stayed silent, sat up straight, and pretended I had an air of dignity. Slinking back into my chair would have been preferred but a tough backbone is a core prerequisite for retail.

I don't think they were ready for what they were about to flip through. They found themselves looking at the first cake I attempted. It was covered in crumbs and globs of frosting were dripping from the sides. I attempted to write the words "Happy Birthday" in bubble gum pink frosting but it looked more like a ransom note from someone who just stole your cat.

The next cake was no better. There lay a cake with blue frosting, gobs of crumbs, and drawings all over it. Some may say it was a disaster, I would like to say it was reminiscent of Picasso and an interpretation of what I envisioned the world to look like. It was abstract and perfect for the head of an art department; if that person was being fired. And then the giggles and red cheeks began spewing from my Leaders. They had finally swiped to my final creation.

"What, the fuck is this?" Olivia and Dwayne could barely get the words out. Tears were almost rolling down their faces in laughter.

"Oh, this is my interpretation of a rest stop. You see, I made this cake with a retiring sanitation worker in mind." What they were seeing was a cake filled with perfectly written words and phrases such as *fuck off, Mary sucks dicks, cunt ass mother fucker, your mom tastes good.* These phrases were adorned with perfectly drawn dicks and boobies of various sizes. To add a feminine affect, I added in a few butterflies and flowers that looked like they had taken a rather large dose of acid.

The real story behind the decoration was my frustration trying to get this cake-decorating thing down. It was so much harder than I expected and it was unlike me to do something well the first time I tried. I had spent an hour trying to decorate an 8x8 square cake with the tools my fiancé bought for me as encouragement. As it was becoming clear to me I wasn't getting the hang of the craft immediately, I began to become upset. Tears welled in my eyes and I just about gave up. My fiancé suggested I take a break and try again the next day. But the next day was the interview and I couldn't risk not having three cakes with apparent improvement to show.

My anger and ultimate demise of never getting out of chicken duty reeled through my psyche. I couldn't give up just yet. My escape was just around the corner and I couldn't turn away from it. Instead of continuing to torture myself, my kitchen, and ultimately my family, I took my anger out on the cake. I practiced my letters and phrases by just writing and drawing what came to mind. I didn't need to fit into a box, I just needed my anger out. My intentions were not to show my bosses the end result. Yet, they saw it.

Between gasps of laughter and wide eyes, Olivia and Dwayne looked at one another and told me that yes, I had gotten the role. The interview was more of a setup than anything and they couldn't risk losing me. But there was now a condition of me accepting the role.

They were to be there with me as I told Sarah. I was to show her my last cake and explain it was the reason why I landed the role. The look on Sarah's face was priceless. Dwayne and Olivia sedated their laughter and spite as we watched the color fade from Sarah's bright hair as she realized she would be faced with training me.

THIRTY

Caffeine is a Girl's Best Friend

I t was no secret Sarah was livid I had landed the cake
decorating role. She was not the patient type and
even though she swore she would teach me how to decorate a cake properly, she would often leave out important
details during my training period. Details such as how
much butter and sugar needed to be used for the buttercream frosting, or the exact amount of heavy cream
needed for the Signature frosting were always left out of
her mini lectures. Sarah would even go so far as to show
me difficult and overly advanced cake decorating techniques she knew I would not be able to master. Her eyes
would roll and her breath would huff and puff with frustration as she hovered over me struggling through the
not so simple designs. Even though I followed her
instructions well, the concepts were a bit too advanced
for this rookie.

Frequently, I would come into work seeing her
holding a cake I decorated talking to Dwayne, Olivia,
and anyone else who would listen to her. Reading lips is
something I have prided myself in doing and there was

always something being said about how my designs looked as if a child made them and how embarrassed she was seeing them displayed in her cake case. If she noticed me watching her complain to our bosses about my creations she would stop her conversation with them and pick it up with me.

"This cake is shit!"she said once as she threw a Strawberry Shortcake into the nearest garbage can. She would rather waste food than sell decently decorated items. It was a game of hers to see how many of my cakes she could toss in front of the team before I cried. I never cried in front of her but would often slink back to the walk-in to sob my wounded heart out.

Sarah didn't stop her comments. She would go beyond my lackluster cakes and poke me whenever she could. Her behavior turned into a Mean Girls situation and it was clear that her comments weren't about to stop anytime soon. Maybe I didn't work out like she did. She would tell me how it didn't look like I was losing weight and her weight loss was real because she went to a clinic for it. Sarah began to get under my skin and it was showing. I didn't want to let my team down and I began to think Dwayne had made a mistake by taking a chance on me. My nerves forfeited any appetite I could conjure and I was left sipping coffee for many of my meals.

Despite my efforts, the comments kept rolling in. I was too naïve to relate to Sarah. Maybe I wasn't risky enough for her. Whatever the underhanded comment served, I was ready to lap it up and wait until the moment struck that I could serve it all back. Whether or not we ended our time in a B.F.F. status didn't matter to me.

Within two months I began to get the hang of the wrist flicks needed to adorn the overly sweet cakes we sold. Once my wrist began cooperating, it was hard to discern my cakes from hers. When the time came, it was me that was asked by our assigned Corporate Champion to create a picture portfolio on how to create things like fruit tarts and the other desserts our company offered. I wanted the world to know I was a more than capable decorator by now and without her dismissing me, I probably wouldn't have cared as much.

"Whatcha doin'?" She asked as I was taking pictures of my fruit tarts.

"Oh, didn't they tell you? I'm making a picture portfolio for new hires across the company. Didn't Jenny ask you too?" It became a game to wait until she was working to begin taking photos of my tarts.

"No. She didn't." The realization came over her. She was no longer the store's Prima Donna.

"I'm so ready to be done with it, it's taking up too much time. I have cakes to make for the weekend." Brushing off the award was part of the game. Her reaction wasn't enough for me and it was my time to serve her the same dishes she served me. "What are you and Evan doing this weekend? I saw you have the entire three days off you lucky bitch." Butterflies welled into my stomach as the words spewed out.

"Nothing." For the first time she had nothing to say.

"Really? Oh what a bummer, is he just going to come over then? Don't waste the opportunity!" It was all a facade, I knew why she was doing nothing but I wanted to hear it from her mouth.

"We just aren't okay? He broke up with me." She said quietly and slunk away from my station. The two other women we worked with stopped what they were doing and looked at me in shock. Nobody ever served Sarah the dishes she loved cooking before.

As time went on, Sarah began to not show up for work. Whether it was an illness, a family emergency, or just a no-call no-show, she quickly became unreliable at best. But if she didn't show…how would she have the boasting rights that she hooked up with someone in the walk-in cooler? How would she be able to explain to me what a fuck up I am as a decorator? How would she be able to belittle every person around her through exasperating every insecurity we all held about ourselves?

For weeks at a time, she would not attend to her duties and it began to put a huge strain on the team. Suddenly, I was the main decorator, and it was my job to follow the budget for the mini cakes, correctly assess how many we would need to order each week, keep stock of how much cake we had on hand, and to handle all special orders. This goes without saying but it was also my job to decorate enough cakes to keep the case full and ensemble them in an enticing way.

It was also my job to maintain the sales floor and make sure the packaging of those "store-made" goodies were properly taken out of a giant package and placed into a tiny plastic one. Between all of these roles, it was also in the job description to handle the afternoon bake if we ran out of bread, help with the juice bar when they got slammed, and attain a happy and personable attitude at all times. The last one was the most difficult to master and usually, my sarcasm and spite leaked through my fragile will.

Even though I was curating multiple roles at the same time, I was not granted my full-time status back and was consistently scheduled just 30 min under the full-time status bracket. My schedule would be five days a week racking up 35 hours total. This meant no health insurance as the company did not offer part-time insurance policies. The store also denied me a raise regardless of how many hats I wore in a week. According to them, I was lucky to have the job and needed to understand my place.

As word got out I was pulling double duty, my team began to question what was going on. They would try to help by checking for outdated products on the sales floor or even jumping in to replace sold cakes in the case before I got there. They were the real VIPs always silently trying to lift me up. These women were the crux of my survival and I am forever indebted to them.

When my coworkers found out my daughter was still not sleeping through the night, my son had multiple extracurricular activities, and I was trying to study to get back into college. They were astounded that I was standing up straight. With an unreliable schedule, it was difficult to manage a regular life. Between my two kids, the demands of the job, and some sprinkled hopes and dreams for a better future, I began to exhaust myself. But, I persisted and showed up every day at 6:45 a.m. on the dot.

After several months of Sarah calling out, those sweet women started to buy me a coffee each time she didn't show as a token of respect. As I walked towards my station, I knew if there was a piping hot peace treaty waiting for me that the day would be rough at best. As much as I loved the coffee, I would have given anything to see Sarah's snarky mass of green hair at her station. But, the triple shot of espresso and sweet taste of chocolate melting into a hazelnut haze always gave me exactly what I needed to pull double duty on only a few hours of rest.

THIRTY-ONE

Fresh From a Box

If I told you the name of the store you would immediately comment to yourself that everything you have ever purchased was "so fresh". Overpriced? Absolutely. But it's worth it if the food you are getting was grown "local" and as fresh as you can get it. To be fair, it might be as fresh as it comes. Just don't confuse the statement with the product being grown in a backyard down the street.

The scratch kitchens we boasted about went away when grumbles from unhappy customers began to infiltrate our corporate teams. Customers hurled their disdain towards the retailer over the lack of conformity between each store's products. They complained the items they purchased looked and sometimes tasted different depending on which store they visited. The company responded by creating a program that would ensure stability with recipes, flavors, and aesthetics.

To accomplish this, the food became fresh from the freezer. Fresh from a box. Everything would come ready to be prepared with distinct measurements for each item.

It was like HelloFresh but for a major retailer. The prized tuna salad came from a kit in a box thanks to the whiny Karens out there. No longer were meals prepared on site because we couldn't risk the fallout of having offerings different from the store across town.

The only fresh things you would find if you walked back there were a bunch of grumbling cooks and a new relationship falling apart between the team members who decided dating at work was a good idea. Even the food for the Taco Shack and Bar began showing up at the store pre-packed in vacuum sealed containers nestled inside a cardboard box. All of the ingredients were ready to be thrown into a package with a confusing label stating the product was "packed fresh". Customers constantly confused this phrase with the food being prepared anew in the small kitchen the store provided. My once drool-worthy carne asada recipe in the Taco Shack began coming in par-baked and the team member thrust into my old role would simply "finish it off" in the oven.

The same ideology was used in the bakery. We could slap on stickers stating "baked fresh" on almost everything because our ovens would take the partially baked bread and finish the job. As long as the food came up to appropriate and safe temperatures, it was sellable and able to be labeled as freshly baked. This is also why we could sell cold holiday meals but never offered to heat them for you. Our ovens couldn't handle turkeys of that caliber and it would be impossible to cook 200 of them within a few hours harboring only one working oven. Between the verbiage and the approach to our interesting standard of advertising, I felt like I was jerking off the head honcho himself.

And all of those cakes my customers would vie over?

Those come in frozen. All the mini cakes were purchased from a company elsewhere. We would pry the cakes out of their original boxes and tear them apart from their native cake boards. Next, we would plaster the pre-made cakes onto the signature pink and white boards our customers loved so dearly. When guests would ask what the recipe was, I would tell them I was under a strict legal requirement to never give out the secret. That would always give Dwayne a good chuckle because I was never under any such scrutiny. Sometimes, I would give them the website to the bakeries we plagiarized and told customers if they ordered through them it would be far cheaper. If anyone just read the 12 pt fine print on the price labels… they would have realized this themselves. We technically never said we made those cakes in house but it was certainly not advertised well that we didn't.

Our "Signature" aka in-house cakes were no better. The cake blanks (these are the layers of sponge cake held together by frosting) would come in like our personal Hans Solo's and be stuck in a deep freeze. For them to even be manageable, we would need to thaw the sponge cake according to each flavor. Chocolate always took the longest… but vegan chocolate was its own little night-mare. To this day, my heart is convinced the chocolate vegan cake never truly thawed.

I would assemble our Signature Cakes in the store with the in house frosting (there were so many tears over the Signature Frosting). Fusing together the frozen pre-made cakes and our freshly made frosting was enough preparation to slap a "prepared fresh" sticker on my sweet treats.

Eventually, even the frosting was sent in pre-made. What was the point of even having appliances when nothing was actually being made in a kitchen? And if we really had no products baked fresh, these customers would be just as well off going into a college dorm looking for the perfect meal to impress their mother- in- laws.

With everything coming in a box, we were constantly left with surprises. We would play "How Fucked Up Will This One Be" anytime we had to grab more cake. On a good day, the blanks would come in uneven and wonky. Many times, I was tasked with making a three layer cake that contained cake blanks measuring at 2 cm on one side and 3 inches on the other. It was a gentle game of Jenga on those days but after time, I began to get the hang of it.

Regardless of the way the cake came in, the assem- bled delicacy would look even. Sometimes, I felt bad for handing over a cake that I knew would crumble to my unsuspecting customers. Someone would certainly get a surprise with an all-frosting bite. Depending on the person, it would either be the best day ever or biggest disappointment when their mouths were filled to the brim with the titillating frosting. I had always been curious about what happened when people cut into my Jenga cakes. Nobody called to complain, maybe my cake skills held up after all.

No matter what, it was my job to create an even and jaw dropping cake that would make every housewife jeal- ous. Sometimes, I felt like a fraud. I was the enemy making everyday people feel bad about themselves for not knowing how to make a cake "as delicious" as the ones sold in the store. If anyone bothered to make a cake at home, they would have been able to make one much tastier than the machine made sponges we sold. The secret is to use half the sugar, one more egg, and hand beating the shit out of the batter (this gives the cake an incredible texture).

Sometimes, customers would bring in a recipe claiming it was the best one they ever had. My first reaction would be something along the lines of telling them to make it themselves. My next reaction would be to expose the dirty truth about everything simply being assembled in store- nothing was actually baked here. It was fun explaining to my entitled guests I was happily declining their demands.

Customers would always become irritated at the denial of their request. Mainly, it was Boomers who would get riled up and explain to me the customer is always right. Coincidentally, those lovely souls were hardly correct in their accusations. But with no flour, no sugar (except for powdered) and no real ingredients or tools to bake a cake, how could I even dance with the idea of insulting our precious corporate recipe? We did bake the asparagus... maybe I should have offered an asparagus cake?

THIRTY-TWO

First Impressions

I n retail, hiring newbs was like opening a book you're not even sure you want to read. You never know what you're going to get. As hiring professionals reached into the bag of applications, it was hard to tell the difference between the stale chocolates and the ones that were actually sweet.

Retail offers a slew of different roles that attracts a large assortment of humans. Add in a very lax felon hiring rule, you never know what kind of person is walking through those doors.

Before I continue, I feel I need to say this- being a felon and not having a degree does not define who you are. It does not make you a bad person, and it certainly does not mean I look down on you. What I will say though, is that I truly believe your past reflects your behaviors. If you are a felon and you haven't had the opportunity to do some personal work, there's a high chance you're still dealing with whatever trauma you encountered while doing time. If you do not have a college degree, there is a life story back there. It is very rare that someone just decides they don't want to go to college. A choice like this is usually made for you through random circumstances in the cards you were dealt.

As a kind reminder, my journey with the company started when I was on the precipice of 20, a single mom, and college dropout. Just looking at my situation upon hire you would have never known that I was a formally straight A student who found herself in sticky situations.

Still, most of the people I worked with, had a college degree and chose not to work in their studied field for a number of reasons. They usually didn't jive with the professional world of their degree and the amount of debt they were in made them wary to take out more money to earn a second Bachelor's.

Typically, if you are applying for a retail or service industry position you are probably "going through it" as the kids say. Not many people dream of working in this field and after a few years, it shatters your soul like a broken mirror in a domestic dispute.

Because of this, I stopped bothering to remember people's names unless they made it through their 90 day probation. To be even more clear, it wasn't too difficult to make it through. If they didn't make it, it was because they realized this "easy" job wasn't easy at all and they would run back to their corporate careers with their tail under their legs. People tended to be on their best behavior during their probation and Leadership was always desperate to lower the turnover rate. Blindly, our Leaders would turn their cheek to many situations. If you think I am joking about it being easy to pass the probation period, I have a little ditty for you.

The day was a random one. I think it was February because it was cold and dark. The store had hired a new baker despite my words of warning. Something just wasn't sitting well with me about her but the team was desperate for an extra hand. Plus, upper store Leadership made it very clear I needed to keep my mouth shut about my opinions and stay in my lane. My years of experience were not welcomed. Because I had been demoted multiple times, my reasoning meant nothing to my superiors. They were going to hire whomever they pleased.

At 7 am my Team Leader, Liz, came up to me with a smile that said not only was today going to be rough, but I wouldn't believe the reason why. She wasn't the most animated human being so seeing her like this sparked my interest. Still, I had three jobs to do and ended up buzzing around her listening as intently as a kid in a classroom on the last day of school. I knew Sarah was calling out again, it was why I came in early without being prompted to. But our newbie baker was starting today so at least I would have some help.

"You're never going to believe this." Liz leaned onto the cake case so I couldn't ignore her.

"Sarah called out?" I asked haphazardly.

"Well, yes, but we knew that. Thanks for coming in early. It's about the new girl." Girl was a stretch, this woman was older than my mom.

"Spill." My interest was piqued. An expired cake dangled dangerously at the tip of my hand in suspense.

"She isn't coming in today." Whoop-dee fucking doo. This would be the third person they hired and didn't show up for their first day.

"Looks like you're stuck with more interviews. Sucker." I wanted to come up with something clever to say but it was too early and there was clearly juicier gossip to follow.

"Well, I just talked with Theo and he said we can't

fire her. She called an hour before her shift so I guess it counts even on your first day." Liz continued to smirk.

"So, who calls out on the first day? How could we not fire her?" Now I wanted to throw someone in the oven Sweeny Todd style.

"Dude, get this… she called us as her one call. She was arrested on her way to work. Something about an unresolved DUI and a non-existent driver's license." Liz thankfully had the same sense of humor as me and it felt safe to giggle and roll my eyes. "There's more, she said she was going to call her daughter but knew she wouldn't pick up. The new girl told me her daughter wouldn't bail her out anymore." Liz said all of this in one fell swoop blowing through her words to make sure she relayed the story correctly. I think she was trying to believe it herself. Was she thinking we would bail her out so she could work? Liz and I couldn't figure out what the red flags meant.

New Girl lasted just under a year before she was finally canned. There were many safety concerns but Leadership was trying to turn our 80% turnover rate to less than 50% year over year. This woman who I purposely forgot her name would slam speed racks around anytime she would be slightly inconvenienced. Despite the giant metal racks almost hitting us on a daily basis, the store was trying to stick to their year goal. They ignored our grievances when she would yell at us so loud customers could hear. They ignored her lack of concern for basic food safety. Leadership ignored the constant complaints about feeling genuinely unsafe around her.

What did her in was when she served a customer a cake labeled vegan when it wasn't vegan. The customer had massive stomach issues because of it and it was almost me that fell victim to the Blame Game. As soon as they realized I was off the day the cake was purchased, it only left one other culprit. Apparently a customer being slightly poisoned was more important than the obvious safety concerns for the people who were around her every day. Despite my Leadership's efforts to dwindle the turnover rate, they had to let her go before she passed the year threshold. It would have saved us a lot of money and time if we had just taken a phone call from jail as the warning sign.

THIRTY-THREE

Sharpies

S lowly but surely my home was filling up with flair from the company. Aprons with the company logo plastered on it, reusable bags exclaiming how much they love me, pins and hats stained with God knows what plagued every corner of the house. But it was the Sharpies that caused the most grief. It was those writing tools we had to always have on hand. It sounds silly. It sounds whiny even to complain about the trauma sharpies caused but there is so much symbolized by the smelly permanent markers. In grocery retail, it is imperative we keep everything nicely organized. We can't live- I mean work- in a pigsty now can we?

Every Cambro (the thick plastic containers we would store massive amounts of salsa, pasta, icing, etc. in) had to have a food safety label. Each label was required to have the name of the product, the date it was created, and the date it expired. It also needed the time you packed the product and the time of day the food must be thrown out. In addition, you had to always mark your initials to tell the world you are the one responsible for the products safety and cleanliness. It was expected of you to accomplish all of this on a 1x1 inch sticker that disintegrates with any sort of humidity/liquid. Simple enough right?

Every single item needed its own shelf life and it was up to us to memorize them. There were hundreds of different products requiring different lengths of proper storage. Food was to be tossed the day before the expiration date because as the saying goes, "today's date is too late". The trick was that every few months, the shelf-life of products would change. I don't quite understand the difference between March and May but for whatever reason it made the sugar last either more or less time, the butter would suddenly be okay for shelf storage, and the eggs would go from a one-day shelf life to a three-day.

As bottom-feeder employees, we didn't get email notifications of such changes. Shit, we never saw a computer screen unless we were forced to watch the active shooter training where the company suggested we use our keyboards to deflect a bullet. It's hard to decipher where they got their information about possible tools on hand because there has never been a keyboard in an industrial kitchen. I think the rusting pans would have done more good than a keyboard from the 1980's sitting in the next room.

We would be at the mercy of our great and powerful Team Leaders to not only look at the email explaining the shelf life changes but to also print and display the changes for us all to see. Regardless of whether or not they did their job- we were held to the utmost accountability for us to do ours. Ignorance was never an excuse when we were caught off guard by new rules.

This is one of the reasons we were terrified to take

time off. Regardless of our presence in the store, we were held accountable for our previous actions. We never knew what new rules we would be held responsible for when we returned. I took a week off for a small summer vacation with my family one year and when I came back I walked into a written referral. It was supposed to be two write ups but my Team Leader took pity on me and decided one was enough. As I waltzed back into work refreshed with a well-earned vacation, I was abruptly taken into the office to "have a talk".

I will spare you the details of the entire conversation but here is a summary. Apparently, the dates changed for the Signature Frosting. It went from seven days to four while I was on vacation. During my time off, our third-party food safety auditor decided to grace the store with her presence for a surprise check. On the Cambro, I had given the product five days instead of seven because at that point I was checked out and already in vacation mode. Well, my vacation was eight days. She came on day six.

Not only was the Signature Frosting considered expired by my miscount, but it was labeled now with too many days rather than not enough days. While I was gone, nobody was bothering to check the dates or fill in for my job. And even though the frosting was perfectly in code when I was there, I was still held responsible for the frosting going out of date and never being disposed of when I wasn't remotely near the store. The short answer to the dilemma was that I wasn't supposed to set my team up for success by creating frostings for them to use. I was to make sure there were no products in storage.

Which is the second part of this mini sob story. My store Leader wanted me to be written up for having an empty cake case during my absence. Everything I had created to support my team was sold during my absence prematurely. The expectation was for me to take time off and work at the same time. This is when cloning would become handy. I was responsible for tasks completed whether or not I was there.

THIRTY-FOUR

Schedule Me This

After working in the bakery for three years at 35 hours a week, I was getting tired of not having benefits and not being fully represented. These 35 hours still took up five days of my life every week. This meant five days of hustling small children out the door at 5 and 6 am. Five days of scheduling daycare pick ups and rushed meals. Five days of driving across town multiple times to make sure my son got to his after-school activities while juggling a job that didn't give a shit about personal lives.

And then one day the phone rang in the Smoothie Bar. It was Desmond, a Leader I had a while back. One I had trained and helped lift up to Leadership. He was kind, he was a pushover, and I hadn't taught him all the tips and politics of the game. Giving him all the tricks would have meant not being able to finagle my own wants and wishes. I needed him in my back pocket for future use and this was my moment to shine. He informed me he was looking for a cake decorator for his bakery and he desperately wanted me on his team. I was the desired decorator in town by this point. Not only could I decorate, but my work ethic shone through the corporate bull shit. In my short time in the bakery, I had climbed over Sarah's carcass the second I had a chance and relished in becoming the decorator people wanted- to put it politely, her attitude made her cakes taste and look like shit.

Before responding, I took a few breaths and clutched the phone tighter. I knew I wanted full time. I knew I wanted to work closer to home. I also knew I wanted to get the fuck out of the store I was in because it was filled with predators that disguised themselves as management. The store was unsafe and crawling with men waiting to prey on us women. Desmond knew this. Desmond was also trying to play the game- who would fold and would either of us win?

"Ok, I'm interested. But..." I wanted him to guess what my caveat was.

"Yeah? You would be willing to come to this shit hole?" He was relieved due to my interest but didn't get the intense request I was about to lay in his lap.

"Sure, whatever, just get me out of here. But, I no longer have childcare on the weekends and would need full time before I consider leaving this store." My brave face was put on. I kept telling myself not to stutter, to stand strong. This needed to be a moment of strength.

"I'm confused. We really want you here, and I know you hate the Leadership. They're pigs." It appeared some of my cards were already on the table.

"I need full time and weekends off. The store I am at right now does twice the amount of business as yours does and I can make enough cakes on my own to suffice a weekend here. I don't see why I couldn't do that at your dinky store." My voice was firm, collected, and for the first time in a while, possibly intimidating.

"You know we can't do that." He explained with little reasoning.

"Sure you can, you make the schedule. You have the power. Just don't advertise it. Let them figure it out." I held my ground.

"Like I said, you know I can't do that." His voice filled with disappointment.

"Sounds like it won't work. Toodles!" I hung up before he could respond further. The corporate market we worked for had some strict rules about full time employees. We had to be available to work seven days a week and available to work during all operating hours. The second you had a commitment outside of those hours you would become demoted and lose all benefits.

Desmond and I played this game of back and forth for four months. When October rolled around, it was clear they were heading into the holiday season with no decorator. It was such a specialized skill they needed and they couldn't risk hiring someone with their own agenda. I was the perfect fit for a few reasons. There was no training that needed to happen. I also had no clue how to decorate anything besides the way the company wanted me to so there would be no secret motives, no defecting, and absolutely no chastising the company's outdated decorating style. Plus, I worked my ass off. My name was plastered around town as the girl who never stopped. There was no question about my loyalty and they knew I would be around for a while.

In complete desperation, Desmond half excitedly hired me and I began working full time again. After four years, I finally regained my status as a full time employee. Health insurance was restored and a consistent schedule was on the horizon for the first time in my life. The cherry on top of this sundae was the ability to leave my store which was filled to the brim of homeboys abusing their power to get laid.

THIRTY-FIVE

OSHA's Worst Nightmare

OSHA (Occupational Safety and Health Administration) only actually came into one of the stores a few times and offered a warning for the infractions they found. It was the feds way of trying to keep an eye on businesses to ensure safety was the company's number one priority. The agency was spread too thin and underfunded so they rarely showed up. But, when they did, we were ready to show off our duct tape ridden store. They would tell us when we were going to receive a visit and that gave us time to discuss what parts of the store were to be labeled as non functioning. It gave us time to figure out temporary fixes for our dangerous appliances.

When I started my final role with the company, I was placed in the oldest and most ill-kept stores in the city. It was the only store in the town to not be remodeled-instead the corporate machines decided to continue polishing the little turd and kept wondering why it wasn't booming like the other stores. Whispers of the location being the most profitable filtered through the city but anytime I asked to see numbers, my bosses became too busy to stop what they were doing. I can't speak to everything that was wrong within the walls but I can tell you about my first day and what was seen as totally normal to them. It became normal to me too after a few months.

To start, when given the safety tour (this was something every new team member was part of. The store Leadership would walk you around the store to show you where exits and safety equipment were), my new boss... Mary Anne showed me the emergency exits. She walked me to the kitchen where she showed me the emergency exit door that would lead us to a courtyard which was gated. Mary Anne placidly told me the gate in the courtyard was always padlocked so if I didn't know how to jump a fence it would be best to bust through the styrofoam wall in our walk-in cooler and hope the receiving door wasn't blocked, broken, or where the danger began. Then, we waded into the back storage area through stacks and stacks of unshelved products vicariously placed as towers simply to prove to me the other side of the walk-in cooler was indeed styrofoam and easily maneuvered. A year later, those stacks dwindled to nothing as the company shifted its ideology from stocked shelves all the time to a "Truck to Shelf" mentality.

The walk-in freezer was another situation on its own. I was told the door got stuck frequently and if I didn't know how to use the ax then I better wedge the door open with something. Thankfully this was where we stored the Food Bank donation bins and they were always by my side when I would have to venture into the great arctic blast.

Those bins always looked out for me except the one time a volunteer from the local food bank came slightly later than normal. The docent pulled the bin that was wedged between the freezer door and the door frame so he could collect the tax write-offs, excuse me, donations. I was startled by the bin moving and the freezer door closing. Quickly, I ran from the back of the freezer to the door, fearful of it slamming shut and therefore trapping me in the arctic tomb. Unbeknownst to me, the volunteer was right next to the door and as I swung the door open in a frenzy of fear, I almost knocked him to the ground. What was worse, he was disabled and walked with support. It is unclear who was more startled, but the truth was because of that door, I almost took out a disabled volunteer from the Food Bank. I still feel horrible about the incident.

Anyway, as the tour came to an end, Mary Anne took me to the front of the store where the other half of my department resided. On that day the sewer was backing into the store via the Smoothie Bar "Dish Pit" as they called it, leaving the area smelling like a water treatment plant and unusable. According to Mary Anne, this happened frequently and it would be expected we clean up whatever pops out of the drains. Plumbers were constantly perplexed by the grandfathered piping and there was little they could do to prevent the situation from happening again. Their only solution was to completely dig out the pipes and re-do the entire store. This was not a feasible option according to the major retailer so we witnessed backed up drains constantly. I made a mental note to never be the first person to walk into the dish area ever. And if I was, I would turn and walk away silently. Sewage and cakes just don't quite make it onto the Foodie Adventures Bucket List.

Then it was time for my cake case, my new to-me baby. Mary Anne showed me the back area of it first. Besides being totally filthy, I discovered quickly the sliding doors fell off the case with ease and zero warning. It was my very own "pop goes the weasel" toy. She also warned me about the thick glass shelves and how they didn't fit well. It was important to handle placing items there with care. Not from fear of dropping and ruining the items but because the wrong touch could send the glass shelves careening to their death at any given moment. This would ultimately shatter glass everywhere and be yet another safety hazard this store bore.

I think she waited to show me the front of the case on purpose. This was by far the most important part of the tour. The heavy display glass was designed just like all the other display cases. While yes, you could technically load and unload the case from the back (as long as the doors felt like cooperating), you could also lift up the giant sheath of glass to load the case from the front. Every display case was supposed to have a hydraulic system to hold the glass safely in the air. When she held the glass up as if she was holding a first-place trophy, I asked why she didn't let it go.

"Oh, I guess that is important. The hydraulics don't work on this case anymore and you will need to keep this propped up at all times if you are loading/unloading anything from the front. Being short like me, I think you'll be doing this a lot. Always keep a speed rack with you or have someone help you." She said it so plainly. Nothing phased her anymore. Later, I discovered the reason the hydraulics didn't work was because the glass did break before. But, the replacement glass was too heavy for the antiquated system and the company did not want to "waste" money purchasing a whole new case.

"So which speed racks have brakes on the wheels to secure it properly?" I was too naïve to realize the answer.

"Uhm, none? Speed racks don't really come with brakes. At least the ones we buy don't. Just don't nudge it." Mary Anne didn't flinch as she said this.

I can't tell you how many times someone moved a speed rack unknowingly risking my life. Becoming a ninja wasn't really in the job description but you learn quickly how to open a glass case and quickly take the product out of it before the glass hits you. Another skill I acquired was quickly opening the glass guillotine and letting it hit my back to keep it open. There were many days customers would bump my speedrack sending my trap door in a spiral. Sometimes, newbie workers would try to "help" me and begin moving whatever was propping the case up. I would always holler startling anyone around. Watching their faces melt like mine did as I explained the situation was always fun to see. Their reaction would always remind me I wasn't the crazy one.

Despite my valiant attempts, it was hard to keep the peace between me and my glass case. There were so many times I would pray it didn't hit me. But, as time went on, there were many awful days at the store. I would beg the Gods to prove my point that the case was unsafe and needed to be replaced immediately. I would plead with the powers that are much greater than me for the glass door to slip and genuinely crash onto me sending chards of glass in all directions. I envisioned something like the end of Fight Club- maybe I would pull out a cigarette and walk away as I dropped a match and lit the whole place on fire. Fire and glass would consume everything around me in an epic explosion as I walked away with my internal battle wounds. I could have been Jack Moore.

THIRTY-SIX

Rules are Rules

C ompany policy was black and white. If you were not going to make it to your shift, you best inform your Team Leader with at least an hour's notice. This was actually shortened from their original timeline of two hours because people were getting fired left and right over their tardies and absences from last-minute illnesses. While the big wigs claimed there was a before/after hours line to call if you are coming in before the store opens, it was rare that the Team Leaders would actually check it before calling you asking why you didn't show up.

I had two kids in daycare by this point and mornings were always a hectic blur. My daughter, Alice, was scratching her head and behind her ears as I corralled the kids into my car. She was an antsy little thing and I didn't think twice about it. But, sure enough, when I went to drop her off at the daycare things didn't go as planned.

"Oh no you don't. Nobody leaves their kid here until their head has been checked for lice." Tammy called out.

She had a line of kiddos waiting for her and one on her lap. Like a chimpanzee, she began picking through the little girl's hair who was sitting impatiently on Tammy's knees. Tammy was a wizard at styling little girls' hair but today was different. She didn't have bows in her hands and there were no hair ties to be found.

"Excuse me? I am really late for work, I really need to get going." Was she serious right now? Was this really happening? I was caught off guard by her sternness, she wasn't the serious type.

"Dead serious, there is a huge lice outbreak in one of the school districts. They don't have a policy about sending infested kids home so now we have an infestation, and are trying to nip this in the butt." Tammy dismissed the girl who was on her lap and hoisted the boy waiting behind her up onto her knees. She began combing through his hair and sent the little cherub back home with his mom almost immediately. "Alright Alice, you're up. How are you doing today sweetie? Tammy has missed you so much this weekend!" Tammy began combing with a fresh comb and it only took a few moments to find out why Alice was scratching her head.

Suddenly, my entire body began itching just by thinking about it. Lice has struck. Lice was in my daughter's hair and she would need to go home. My first reaction was her. She must have been so uncomfortable and frustrated she couldn't verbalize exactly what was going on. She was only 3.5 for Christ's sake! It's not the bird and bees talk but we certainly never explained lice. It is one of those parasites that are out of sight out of mind.

Work needed to know of the discovery too. It was only 20 minutes before my shift started and my husband was out of town for a business trip with his new job.

Thankfully, the store was already open. Still, it took eons for someone to pick up the phone.

"Thank you for calling America's Favorite Grocery Store!" Jeremy was too cheery. Reading through his syrupy tone, it clearly had already been a stressful day. I was going to be making it even worse.

"Hey, it's me, I know you know who it is." My words dripped out of my mouth.

"Oh hey, you okay? You're supposed to be here in 15 minutes." Jeremy laughed. It was the kind of laugh that was playful yet laced with contempt.

"Uhm, so, about that. I actually can't come in today. Alice has lice. Like a full-blown infestation on my kid's head. The daycare turned her away and I need to get this crap off my daughter as soon as possible." Keeping a firm tone was essential. Jeremy wasn't exactly my supervisor, but he was one of the Leadership minions and saved my ass more times than I will ever be able to count. My nine lives of favors were running thin with him. I needed to at least try.

"You're kidding. Please tell me you're joking." There was no more laughter in his voice.

"Wish I was, are you the MOD right now?" It was 7:30 am on a Monday morning, if Leadership was in, something was up.

"Yeah, it's me. I will mark it down. Are there any special cake orders?" Thankfully, I knew the answer.

"Yeah, there's two for today, both made sitting in the walk-in. Hopefully the cooler didn't drip too much on the boxes but a couple of the girls can fix the cakes if that happens." I lost my trail of thought because Alice began asking why she couldn't go to daycare. "Look, I have bigger problems right now. I gotta go. Please tell them I called out an hour in advance." My plea was to try and save my butt. I already had a write up for writing the date on a vegan frosting wrong on accident, and I felt another one was coming because a customer thought I was making her life difficult because I refused to put the local college logo on the cake despite the company policy forbidding us to use any copyrighted material. Nevertheless, she felt I was rude and purposely trying to upset her. If that write up went through and now this, I would be on a final.

Two days had passed, and the lice situation was resolved. Alice's daycare checked her and offered tea-tree oil to help repel the pesky little parasites. Everything was golden on that side of my world, it was time to find out my fate at work.

My stomach was in knots but calling out again could have been the nail in my frail coffin. So, I walked in and before I could even clock in, Mary Anne and Annie (one of the Store Leaders) told me to meet them in the office. Desmond was enjoying a day off and couldn't save me. As they called for me, I knew Jeremy didn't fudge the call out time. There were papers waiting on Annie's desk and Mary Anne made sure I saw her sign them.

"Hey, where have you been?" Annie said with a huge smile.

"Fighting the good fight against lice. Want any? I probably have some eggs saved for you." Mary Anne laughed, Annie knew me longer and knew it was more of a threat than a joke.

"And you chose not to call out with an hour's notice." Mary Anne piped in, trying to keep business as usual.

"It was more of a finding out within 30 minutes of my shift situation. The daycare was checking kids because there is a huge outbreak. I didn't know. I honestly would have called out earlier if I had known."

Suddenly, my hat and apron became tight and no amount of twiddling with either was fixing it.

"Still, you know the rules. We need you to sign this." Annie shoved the referral towards me.

"You're kidding." There was no way this was a reasonable punishment. Wasn't losing three days of pay to combat bugs in every ounce of hair and linens in my house enough?

"Nope. If you keep pressing this, we can make this a final very easily." Annie had a twinkle in her eye. It was becoming common knowledge I was a thorn in her side.

"Ok, but my daughter was ill. What if we got into a car crash? What if my mom died of a heart attack? What if my house was on fire?" Would they still write me up then?

"Well, your first call should be to us so we don't fire you. Then feel free to call the police or paramedics or whatever. You would still get written up but at least it wouldn't be a final for a no call no show. Rules are rules. I don't make them, but I sure as hell enforce them." Annie sat there staring at me. She was just as curious as I was about my next move.

"So, if I don't sign this..." My sentence was interrupted.

"You can go home and when you return you will be on a final." Mary Anne suggested. Her arms were crossed, she hated wasting her time on other people. Without saying another word, I signed the referral simply because I couldn't afford to lose my job.

THIRTY-SEVEN

Black Out Dates

H olidays do not mean family gatherings when you're working in retail. They mean longer hours and tumultuous schedules. When everyone was busy worrying about weight gain, I was worried about weight loss. Racing back and forth between the kitchen and sales floor left little time for breaks. Add in massive amounts of call outs and there goes lunch!

We would sneak bites whenever we could and receive multiple warnings for not taking our breaks. The empty threats never came to fruition. Sure, Leadership could have taken one for the team and covered our break for us but they were always busy trying to look busy. Holidays meant you would be worked to the bone and left droopy eyed and soulless come Christmas morning.

During the months of November and December it was pure betrayal to the company if you requested even an afternoon off. It didn't matter if your mom flew in from Montana. You would be working when you were told to work or you would be spending your mom's vacation searching for a new job. Birthdays would shimmy to January when you were able to pretend you were human again and request a night off. Family gatherings would happen without you and you would be stuck with the leftovers of funny stories about your grandpa talking about his Nazi friend who was, despite his alliance with a party that relied on mass genocide, a really nice guy. Aunt Bertha would comment about how she never sees you and your grandma may or may not call you to explain she is pretty sure she will die before next Christmas. If you loved her, you would come to her Christmas Eve party at 11am.

This created huge tensions between my family. Not everyone understood the desperate situation I was in when I politely declined one gathering after another due to my schedule. To add insult to injury, it was always paired with me asking if they could babysit my kids because the daycare was closed. Childcare always made things complicated because the daycares ran on holiday hours. It wasn't lost on me that I was asking my loved ones to pull double duty during the holidays because they would find themselves chasing around my crotch goblins while also putting together a giant gathering. A gathering I would never be able to attend.

Because of this, holidays never meant much to us retail folk. We knew this would be the case when we applied for the world of retail. We understood going into the job our lives were not our own during the jolly season.

But blackout dates (times when we couldn't request time off) are perpetuated throughout the year. When someone else needed time off to go to their boyfriend's cottage in France, you were expected to shift your life to accommodate their leisure. If you requested time off to volunteer at your kid's soccer game, your teammates couldn't even contemplate breathing outside of that request. Our lives revolved around each other's worlds to the point where we would discuss and collaborate with coworkers before we even planned our personal lives.

We would often start the conversation with each other by asking what plans each person had in the future. This would evolve to calendars being whipped out and snide remarks about how everyone felt they were being the accommodating one when really you needed the other person to bend just this once. Susie would throw hands because she wanted to go on a hot date and thought it selfish I was requesting time off to watch my son play his saxophone.

And for whatever reason when Leadership requested time off, that meant the entire team was gridlocked. Leadership also could approve their own requests to have a life. With just two clicks, their requested time would always be approved while you were left creating Power-Points about why you deserved to have an extended weekend for your birthday.

During a particularly heated debate in April, my Team Leader announced that she would be gone for all of June because she was backpacking in Spain with her boyfriend. Hearing this, my ears perked up. My birthday was that month and I had already requested five days off to do a staycation with my family. We were going to do the kitschy tourist things around town I loved. I was going to sleep. I was going to day drink and enjoy cute clothes without worrying about grease stains from butter and kitchen grease drippings.

Mary Anne explained she denied the request as soon

as she had the inkling she would be out of the country. If I had bothered to look at the scheduling app, I would have been aware of this weeks ago. Knowing that this was supposed to be a first come first serve situation I argued my case. That week in June is notorious for being the lowest week in sales for the entire year. The two of us could be gone and the team wouldn't know anything different. In other words, the team could pull up their big girl panties and survive.

Mary Anne wanted nothing to do with my rebuttal. She suggested I suck it up and deal with it. My job needed me and I needed to perform my duties with grace and gratitude. She made it clear three people were on the waiting list for my position and she had no issue calling them and letting them know the good news.

She made it clear she was going on a once in a life-time journey and I was being childish for demanding I have my birthday off. All the while she had just finished taking two weeks off for her birthday. It was a case of the birthdays and I informed her she could schedule me but I was pretty certain I was going to have food poisoning that week.

As she scoffed and walked away, the rest of the kitchen looked at me with dropped jaws. Nobody said "No" to Mary Anne. She was the prissy grunge princess everyone adored (and were slightly afraid of) at the store but her tactics didn't work on me. I wasn't afraid of her boots, her stare, or her attitude pretending she didn't care. Yes, she was my superior, but she also didn't know how to handle true conflict.

The debate was not going to be settled until we were both granted our time off. It was a rarity we were heard by our head honchos but that year I was in good standing with Annie. Because of my argument to Annie about the situation, each person on my team was granted a week off of our choice that summer because of the semantics I used in my one person debate. I was everybody's hero because I paved the way for us to have a reprieve before the holiday slaughter happened again.

THIRTY-EIGHT

Pandemic Woes

In the mornings, my store held mini-meetings. We made sure our families had the groceries they needed. Paper towels were carefully awarded to employees as well as mac n cheese, milk, and other kitchen essentials. Toilet paper was locked away and hidden so if our home supply ran out we could buy some. The rolls of toilet paper in the public bathrooms began to be stolen by desperate customers. They would walk out of the glorified outhouses with wads of single-ply paper bundled under their jackets, purses, and diaper bags. It was incredible and terrifying that so many items were suddenly hard to get. Products began to become unavailable. Aisles were emptied faster than we could stock them and it reminded me of a post-apocalyptic world where there are few survivors. You could smell the old wood of the store and the fearful intentions of the shoppers as they scurried throughout the building. Covid-19 was showing us a side of humanity my coworkers and I feared but never wanted to acknowledge.

We slung the products that showed up onto the shelves while we tried our best to take care of one another. Most of the venues were shut down due to potential contamination so we were all part of one team. We snuck extra breaks, snuck each other snacks, and tried our best to laugh. Laughter felt better than the fear lurking under our breath.

As a store, we decided to not allow our families and children to visit us because it had become too eerie. Suddenly, trips to say hi to mommy or daddy were banned. Our kids did not need to know the severity of this situation. It was becoming more "man vs. man" every day and they didn't need to see the side of humanity we were witnessing in the store. Collectively, we wanted our kids to still believe there was good in the world. Let them cling to what was left of their idealism and their childhood. Nobody knew how long this was going to last.

The news ticker came in one morning, Disneyland was officially closed. Hysteria was about to break out again- I braced myself and so did the people I worked with. Schools were closed and us parents were now scrambling with teachers to understand what distance learning would look like. My title shifted from Cake Decorator to Grocery Minion to Makeshift Teacher within a few weeks.

Some of us were wearing masks, others not yet. It wasn't mandated yet. Fear ran through our veins as we questioned each customer that walked through our aisles. Could they infect us and our children? I begged my Store Leader to implement curbside pick-up out of fear for our safety. He claimed the company refused. We had the technology- we were owned by a man worth billions of dollars! It would be the perfect time to roll out the

Pristine Shopping Experience. Yet, despite record-breaking sales, the intention of the CEO was to cram as many bodies as possible into the store. But don't worry, they counted them as clients marched in to make it look like they were controlling capacity.

As we placed items on the shelves, we became almost immune to the physical fights breaking out over the last of our shelf stable kitchen essentials. We were forced to add Grocery Store Bouncer to our job description. I winced at an altercation between two women over a bag of flour because I knew the grounded wheat would go bad before those women used it. Thinking about their faces as one of them opened the flour months later only to find it crawling with weevils brought a blended mix of pure joy and despair. Personally, I could have used that bag. My stress baking was at an all-time high and I was blowing through flour like an addict blows through cocaine. How much food was to be wasted because of ignorance? We didn't need to bunker down for a year, but you wouldn't know that by observing the fights over canned green beans and paper towels. This wasn't us prepping for doomsday- we were just asked to stay distant from loved ones and wear masks. Yet, in the day of clickbait and fake news... our fears were inflamed and nobody could tell the truth from fiction. Not even us.

Due to the lack of protection and the fact that my children were labeled as "high risk", I took a seven week sabbatical. The company offered one for the first bit of the pandemic and while it was unpaid, I felt it was necessary. Everyone working at the store was forced to return- nobody could pay their bills otherwise and millions of people were being laid off from every company imaginable. This made finding another job almost impossible.

When we reported back to work, we had shown up to a store that was still operating under abysmal conditions.

After severe pressure from the corporate community, our company decided we would finally receive hazard pay. A whopping dollar an hour. We were told to be grateful, but it needs to be analyzed. My health was worth about seven dollars a day (if we worked our normal shifts and didn't stay longer). That wouldn't even buy us ibuprofen at the hospital. Our health insurance wouldn't cover anything until we paid over $6k deductible despite our high premiums. I could bring this virus home to my asthmatic children, or my husband and that fear rattled my bones. The daily allotment of hazard pay broke down to $1.75/ day per person for someone like me who has a family of four. Our health was worth less than a drip coffee at a gas station.

We were getting flooded with emails and videos from corporate telling us how much they loved us while they were safely tucked away in their homes. A TV was installed in the breakroom just so they could send us their "love". They sent invites to zoom meetings so they could "explore the store" as they were safely nestled in their bunkers. Our Team Leaders would walk around the sales floor with their phone in hand to highlight the different parts of their department to our Corporate Champions. From a distance, they picked apart our displays and told us how we could do better. We needed to be better. We were essential. Some of us would follow behind the phone just to secretly flip off the bigwigs. Any sign of conspiracy or displeasure would mean instant termination. The thrill of our disdain being caught was mesmerizing.

During the mass lay off across the country, this retail giant fired over a thousand people for trying to unionize and speak up about the abuse from the company over the past few years. So as far as they knew, we obeyed. What choice did we have? When everyone is getting laid off, we can't just hop into a new career. Many of us had loved ones that no longer worked, and we were stuck adding the title Breadwinner to our roles. We begged for the help of our CEO and our Corporate Champions to be in the stores and actually help. We were scared, we were angry, and we were exhausted. They respond by applying for help with the National Guard.

Their next response to the pandemic was to require masks. But we weren't allowed to confront customers to actually wear them. Still, with this announcement, customers decided to call us employees fascists and any other questionable names they could come up with. We were never allowed to engage with them and took their verbal beatings with silence and humility.

To ease our upset about our new working conditions and the hazard pay expiring, the store started to give us free sandwiches. I looked down at the pretzel roll perfectly toasted hugging ham and Swiss like a grandma hugs her grandchildren and my stomach turned. I couldn't eat this. I couldn't pretend that this was ok. My safety has been traded for a sandwich. I don't think ham will be able to help me breathe if I end up on a breathing tube. I couldn't stomach the idea my wellbeing was being bartered for over lunch meat.

There were homeless people littering our streets due to job loss, loss of access to public services, and loss of family. On the way home, I spotted a man who looked severely hungry. I handed the sandwich to him and he started crying as the warm fresh sandwich hit his hand. There is so much bitterness in the world, I needed to feel like I could bring positivity during this scary time.

When I got home, I put on my teaching hat and logged onto the computers. I had to buy two so we could get through the school year. And no amount of hazard pay or government help could pay me back for that. The school ran out of Chromebooks before I could apply for them- they sold out while their parents were scavenging my shelves and my husband was bartering his severance package. The hours the school district posted for applications were my exact work hours and I couldn't pull away long enough to apply. I tried my best to hide the news tickers from my children as we navigated 6th grade and kindergarten online. Like always, I convinced myself I could handle this.

Kinder was a challenge, I will never understand how to explain what a letter is and why it sounds the way it does. My daughter has ADHD so sitting was incredibly difficult. We took nature walks and I recorded the things we talked about. I drew letters and math equations in the dirt for her to copy. We held living room dance parties to the sounds of ABC'S and other learning songs. If she was retaining anything I would be forever grateful. But on many nights, she would sit on the chair as if it were a swing on her belly. She would scream because the assignment could not be done in nature. This was not how kindergarten should be. She deserved so much better.

Sixth grade was easier. My son understood what school is and how to behave. I am not strong with math but being in school myself (my only options were to accept I would never be seen as human or go back to college and make something of myself) I was able to help him pass. The history lessons created fantastic dinner conversations, and we reminisced about what it would be like to live in the ancient times. We joked about Greek Gods and Goddesses. Science brought STEM into the house and we were able to get the whole family involved. And the Language Arts… it ignited something in me. Something I couldn't put down. I felt this sense of excitement and joy. My son frequently would call me a nerd. I told him the correct term was a cultured bibliophile.

Teaching Language Arts came eerily natural to me. I taught him how to properly write an essay, the importance of an Oxford Comma, and how to analyze texts at a more sophisticated level. I would go to bed thinking about this and wake up realizing that this might be my calling. I knew I always wanted to be part of the education community. My current company used to do incredible things with local communities but lately, it had lost sight of that. I loved teaching my coworkers about the fantastic things my company did and I missed making lessons about food trends and the origins of the foods we craved.

When I came into work one day, the company had added salt to the wound. Shirts were lying across each table that stated "Hero" as if we had a choice. Service industry and anyone else that was deemed "essential" was written out of any and all unemployment help. We were written out of government assistance. We were purposely shoved further into our roles – held hostage by our need to pay bills. Congress knew that if we didn't work, the country would have fallen apart.

During my break I called my community college and changed my degree from Nutrition to English as well as added a few classes. I needed to get out of retail as quickly as possible. Two classes a semester would get me nowhere. I added Full-Time Student to my title. At least this is one I wanted. If anything, the pandemic only added fire under my skin to finally pursue my calling.

Nobody goes into the grocery industry saying they

want to be the calm during the storm of a global health crisis. Nobody takes a job in retail thinking they will be the pawns thrown into the world while an unknown virus causes chaos around them. I took this job eleven years prior just trying to feed my son. I never thought I would still be here. I never thought I would become trapped in a system that lured me in so easily. We were not heroes; we had nowhere else to go. We were essential yet our livelihoods were not prioritized.

THIRTY-NINE

It's Hot and We Can't Take Off Our Clothes

The desert was a faulty hot plate on full blast. Everything the sun touched turned to dust and began to break. Air conditioning units were not immune to this. Units servicing grocery stores were not spared. Our who-knows-how-old air conditioner decided to bite the dust in the height of the forsaken heat wave.

There we stood, working in a sweaty and grumpy kitchen that was nearing 100 degrees (Fahrenheit because…America). Our hats, aprons, and masks were to be worn at all times due to company protocol. The oven at least had no problem keeping its temperature this time of year. But everything else was another story. It was near impossible to keep the food within safe ranges of temperatures and we feared that the meat would spoil before we could cook it. We were constantly nervous about bacteria spawning on our veggies and breads. Potatoes were turning at an alarming rate and even the fresh taters were proposing to go bad by the next day.

In an attempt to be taken seriously about my safety concerns of working in a kitchen this hot, I took the infrared thermometer that was supposed to be used to track our cooler temperatures every three hours and hit several spots in the kitchen with the infrared light. One corner popped up at 99.9 and the screen turned red indicating that the corner wasn't anywhere near the safe zone of food production. I held the thermometer like a smoking gun and pointed it right by the oven and it blipped up as "High"- it didn't even tell me the temperature. It was so hot near the oven and the super sized range the thermometer couldn't even read it. Next stop was the dish pit. 95 degrees there. Maybe the water would finally be hot enough to wash the grease and slime away? Lastly, I put the thermometer right by the tiny freezer. The temperature in front of the door that was constantly being swung open was a cool 89 degrees.

During my temperature escapade, Annie walked into the kitchen. "What the hell are you doin' honey?" Her hand went to her hip as she tucked her gum into her left cheek. It was a funny little thing I noticed she did when she was annoyed.

"Well…the kitchen is sick. It's running a fever and needs to go home." I said with a smirk.

"Is that so? Look. I know it's hot but you guys… you guys need to push through. It's not so bad. Stop your whining and just do your job." She began laughing and walking away. Was she kidding? Was she poking fun? It was hard to tell.

"Yeah, I'll get right on that. Annie, the coolers are all out of temp and my cakes are literally melting. This isn't safe. Our health inspector would shut us down." That caught her attention.

"Say what?" She replied.

"Yeah, these coolers built from wood and Styrofoam can't handle this heat. Funny, you would think porous surfaces would retain temp better." My sarcasm was laid thick with frustration and by this point I wanted her to send me home. My car didn't have AC but my house surely did.

"Quit it. I know it's hot. Just do your best. You gotta fill that case. Pop into the deep freezer in the back. Put some ice in your bra...I don't know!" She was a foot taller than me and sometimes liked to walk up close in a friendly yet intimidating way. This time, I think it was to be intimidating.

"But how can I do my job if my food is spoiling quicker than I can use it? How can I do my job if the butter is melting before I can even put it in the mixer to make buttercream? All I am getting is...sloppy cream." I held out a brick of melting butter towards her. "And don't even suggest I decorate in the cooler, that thing drips like pre-cum. I don't want that nasty cooler water dripping on my cakes." It wasn't even intentional at this point. My mouth just had no filter because of how hot it was.

"Oh, you're just as bad as the boys. Fine. Do whatever." She raised her hands as if they were a white flag and walked out of the kitchen.

It took two weeks for the AC to be looked at and another four weeks before it was fixed. Customers started complaining about how warm the store was. Mini coolers and fridges started failing at an alarming rate due to how hard the systems had to work to stay within safe temperatures. Rumor had it that a few people were diagnosed with heat stroke from working in the 100+ degree kitchen and backstock area slinging heavy boxes. The strain on our hearts from going back and forth between below freezing temps to the sultry heat wave was not lost on us. It was our mission to regulate our body temp while still keeping up with the demands of the business. We were stuffing our shirts with ice and debating what was worse- frostbite, heat exhaustion, or the smell of our deodorants sweating off.

Tempers on all sides were flying. Customers were snapping at us for how uncomfortable the store was. Leadership was extra cranky trying to figure out why we couldn't pull it together. We were all internally fighting with one another because we were the only people we could be mean to without getting fired. We also were getting snippy right back with the customers because they had a choice to shop somewhere else. Our choice was whether or not we wanted to be able to pay our rent. Some people had paid time off to spare and called out until the air conditioning was fixed. Most of us did not have that option.

We began to figure out the precise calculations as to how long our food could handle being in the open air before it needed to be tossed back into the freezer. My cakes were being built literally one partially frozen layer at a time and designs were only put on after the cake had been fully frozen. Thank God that minimal, ombre, and marbled looking cakes were "the trend" when this was going on. It was the only way I could make my mediocre cakes pretty without the buttercream literally dripping off the sides. My cakes stayed up to par with society's standards and that was all that mattered- forget that it took an hour to decorate just one of them.

When the heat became absolutely unbearable, we would take turns sitting in the little freezer. Five minutes in there and you would begin to feel almost human again. Any sweat left on our persons became little itty-bitty ice coolers and clung to us for a few moments after stepping out of the freezer. It was the newest version of a smoke break. We would store our aprons in the freezer trying to create a makeshift ice pack until Leadership busted us. As per food safety regulations, personal items were forbidden to be stored near the food we served. Our water bottles were to only be stored in the designated area by the rotisserie chicken oven. By the afternoon, our drinking water would warm up enough we could have made tea in it because of the proximity to the oven. When nobody was looking, we would place our water bottles in the freezer with the hope of having something cool to drink.

Truth be told, I am pretty sure bras were hidden in that tiny kitchen freezer as well. Girls would go in and be rearranging their shirts walking out. Maybe all those sleepover pranks finally did us a favor- we knew a quick way to cool down without fully taking off our clothes. It was the only way any of us survived that summer.

FORTY

So, You're From California

L et's get this out in the open right now. Nobody cares where you are from unless they ask you. And if they are asking you, it's because they are out of things to say and are avoiding talking about the weather. Small talk is small after all.

Being in a college town meant there were always ample amounts of tourists. Parents would flock to our city to see their precious babies acting like pre-adults in the big kid school. Usually, they were from California because our university was cheaper than the in-state California tuition. During the spring, winter, and fall, our store was stocked full of pretentious parents wanting to brag about their sweet Sally or James that is passing college. It wasn't too hard depending on the degree but the parents who knew that would skip over the fact their Sally was earning her degree in butterfly farming or their James was only passing his color theory classes and not his mathematics. Coming from someone who flunked out of college due to math the first try, I understood the filtered brags. But my mom wasn't telling everyone I was at the top of my class (until one day I truly was).

The Californians always enjoyed making a spectacle about their origins as if we were lucky they graced us with their presence. The conversation would always start with "Well, I'm from California…" in which I would always ask what part because I was coincidentally from there too! Sometimes they struggled to see someone as lowly as me could partake in their state but other times they would think I understood where they came from. In all honesty, I moved at a young age and couldn't really call myself a native Californian anymore- not that I wanted to after dealing with the true Californians. Nobody should associate themselves with that parade. If Florida can have Florida Man, California can have Cali Girl.

The women would always ask us for extraordinary things we couldn't really accommodate. We couldn't create a pop-up bar-b-que. We couldn't create a piano cake. We also couldn't import an item from Italy the way California stores did. It never occurred to them that those stores were probably lying about the pretentious origins of their special requests. Nothing was getting ordered that wasn't already in our order forms. Cali Girl always made sure we knew we were quite the disappointment of a store.

Watching Cali Girl's eyes fade into miserable defeat as they tromped their way into the dilapidated store was a favorite pastime of mine. The last store I worked at offered little to nothing of what their hometown stores offered and it was always a game to see how long it would take before their purchased smiles would falter.

How long would it take for the stink of a decaying store to hit them? The must in the walls was always mixing with the sweet and savory smells of the hot bar. Their noses would go higher with each disappointed step they took. Floppy hats and big sunglasses would ask questions only to remark how "cute" we were for trying.

Nothing beats the woman who mocked me at the bar. She thought it was adorable that my American accent came through when I would say things like *taqueria* and *me gusta cerveza*. "Again! Again!" she would blabber. She would bring her friends in just to show them how horribly I butchered her native language. The syllables would stick inside my mouth like toffee, and it was always difficult to muster the grace to amuse her. After her third visit, I mentioned something about not being her pet. She complained and told Leadership I called her a bitch. To everyone's surprise (including myself) I actually didn't. This woman was angry that I didn't find her as adorable as a toddler playing peek-a-boo. Her wrinkles sagged away from her face trying to not associate with the wicked woman while the Botox fought to hold everything together. Her money couldn't even pay for her face to stay on. There was nothing cute about that. Still, I was promptly chastised and questioned by Leadership for having a customer complain about me despite multiple witnesses stating I never called her such a thing. With these customers, there was always little faith bestowed. They acted as if they could do our jobs better-which I would then suggest they were welcome to perform.

"We're hiring actually, and the bar is pretty low for what they look for, I think you'd pass the screening process." I would retort. Then I would explain how to apply and express how any idiot could get a job there. This wasn't true anymore though. The company implemented a personality quiz that made it seem as if only narcissistic personalities could make it through the first vet.

But alas, I would have people yelling at me over a cake looking "too fluffy" because the whipped cream looked as if it was floating. Maybe they wanted runny cream? Women especially loved glancing at me while they explained how they would have decorated something differently. I would always ask them for some of their tips and tricks on how to do my job- no reply was ever given.

During the early graduation season that always butted up against Christmas, a mother called in for a cake. She introduced herself by explaining she was in fact, from California and was expecting the same exceptional service she experiences in the Valley. After her grand introduction she demanded I create a cake for her daughter dripping with the college's logo and colors. I could not do anything trademarked on the cake and for that, she made sure I understood how lazy and disrespectful I was.

She still ordered a cake that I was to decorate but insisted on the cake being plain. When she said this, it meant plain frosting.

"Just a basic cake. I need smooth sides and when I say smooth I mean it." She hissed through the phone. In addition, she demanded "the cake had to be pitch white-whiter than a virgin's wedding dress". She also proceeded to call the store twice a day for the three weeks leading up to the pick up to make sure I understood her simple request. To add to her insanity, she expected this cake to be fondant smooth. We didn't use fondant. We could get a crisp white out of our buttercream but by then it would be almost overwhipped and the frosting would be light and airy. She couldn't have it all is how I explained it.

On the day she was to pick up her cake she called multiple times asking if it was ready. It was. I had started the cake two days prior. Carefully, I made a crumb coat around it which I normally didn't do for cakes but I knew the cake needed to be perfection on a doily. This crumb layer would ensure there would be no imperfections on this very important dessert. Then, I froze the cake to prevent any more crumbs from establishing themselves. The next day, I created the thinnest layer I could to create an even stronger base. And the day of pickup, I layered the frosting one paper thin layer after another and did the best I could to make it fondant flat. Of course, because it wasn't fondant, it wasn't perfect. But, it was the best I could do given the tools and ingredients I had.

Sure as shit, her floppy hat bounced its way in through the store unfazed by the 50 degree weather. Magically, I was at the cake case shoving it full of my newest creations.

She tilted her obese glasses up and said to me "Barnes. Cake pick up."

"Oh hey, I have your cake, I just put my final touches on it, smoothing it out even more!" I skipped and hopped towards the kitchen where her cake was being stored. The skipping made her nervous. No adult of sound mind skips without a child around. She deserved the nervousness that sprouted from my departure. When I returned with the cake, I handed it to her delicately and decided to walk away before I said something to get me fired. She was not the person I wanted to word vomit all over.

"You. You don't go anywhere until I tell you to." Her

mom voice popped out of nowhere. Actually, now that I think of it, it wasn't a mom voice. It was her voice she used when speaking to those who served her.

"Uhm yeah, I will go. I have many more orders than just your cake but thanks!" I started skipping back towards the Smoothie Bar. It was two hops and boom, my destination was reached.

"How dare you speak to me like that! I need to make sure you didn't do anything...weird or stupid to this cake. I can never trust people like you." She began fiddling with the box. Her manicure and IQ made it difficult to unravel. Out of pure fear of her messing up the cake and having to remake it on the fly, I offered to help. I carefully balanced the boring cake on the display shelf and opened it up for her to assess. "Well, you did it I guess." She sneered.

"Yeah, it's crazy. I know how to do my job!" I skipped my happy heart away for good before she could demand I re-box the cake she had me undress. If she knew so much she would be able to box up the derobed pastry.

It was always the ones from prominent states that acted like the biggest fools. They would always comment about how miniscule our store was or how we didn't have the same array of curried meats as the other stores. We never had enough vegan options either. Our rinky-dinky store was never enough and for whatever reason that reflected directly on those who worked the store. We would be scoffed at and told how we could do better. Some employees took the brunt. Others like me would explain we were just cogs in the corporate machine.

FORTY-ONE

Shoeboxes

_____

It wasn't a rumor. Karl applied for the position of Store Team Leader. Word spread like glitter in a strip club that our favorite nightmare would be back. According to legend, he was married now and his wife was expecting. The story revolved about how this man with a reputation wanted to be closer to family to begin his own. It didn't help that Theo was back in town either. Those two couldn't live far from one another and we were curious when Karl would follow suit.

Corporate was well aware there would be a buzz about the whereabouts of Karl. I wasn't the only one who had a problem with him and we were jostled from dreamland thinking he wouldn't be coming back. As stories from the past and protests filled the air, our regional team had an idea to address our concerns.

They instructed the store to place a shoebox near the time clock. Store Leadership was to leave out ample pieces of scrap paper and we were allowed to write down questions anonymously. We were under the impression the questions we wrote would be asked during the interview process.

Not only were we a store scorned from his brutality years prior, we were also livid Annie was no longer allowed to interview for the position. Company policy stated that if someone was already in the position they were interviewing for, all other candidates had to also hold the title. Annie was an Assistant Store Leader, Karl was already a Store Leader in a different state. Devastation didn't even cover the emotions we felt when we found this information out. It almost sounded like the corporate gremlins had made their choice as to who our new Leader would be and made up rules to nix any competition.

The shoebox was to make us feel like our wrathful voices were heard. Over the box there was a sign stating "Questions for Karl". There were no other candidates running because he knocked all locals out of the race due to his status. Before I could even get a question or two in, there were accusations being tossed into the shoebox. The questions I could see by peeking into the box were as follows: *Have you ever made a woman feel uncomfortable while working for you? What is your policy for Leaders dating team members? How would you handle accusations about your predatory ways? How did you meet your wife? What do you define sexual harassment as?*

To make himself seen, Karl began coming into the store through paid work trips to begin measuring and schmoozing with people. He wanted to seem like he would be an active and supportive Leader but word was getting out quickly. Each time he walked behind me I clenched the knife I used to level the cakes a little tighter. His presence brought back so many memories it was hard to recall the exact feeling I felt when he would brush by me. My co-pilot Mirabelle would watch in curiosity. She wasn't allotted the knowledge of what was flying through my brain when he was near. Each time he came into the store I placed a question into the box.

My questions were: *Have you been accused of predatory behavior? How will you justify your past actions to team members? Have you ever apologized for your actions? What do you consider to be inappropriate interactions with team members? How will you regain trust in the women who used to work for you?*

Ultimately, I stopped myself before I gave away too much of my identity. Plus, the box was getting too full. Annie replaced the shoebox with a bigger box to give us additional room to place what she thought were normal interview questions. When Annie peaked at the questions she was transferring into the new box, he shook her head in concern and disbelief. The accusations were scribbled in a multitude of handwriting and it became obvious to her Karl's behavior was everything I warned her about.

As quickly as the interview happened, it was announced Karl was in fact coming back. He was to be our new boss. My entire soul slinked out of my body when the news hit me. There had to be a solution to this mess.

Immediately I began emailing corporate begging them to transfer me. I explained he did not deserve to lose his job over my history with him but I felt unsafe working with Karl again. I began calling the other two stores in town asking if there were any openings but they said they could not hire me- they couldn't afford another full time employee. In pure desperation, I began begging what was left of our human resources department to speak for me and help me get transferred. I didn't need the whole scene of the #metoo movement but it was vital for my voice to be heard.

Everything was denied. It was explained to me that if I was so uncomfortable I should probably just quit. There was nothing the company could do for me. They claimed they held an investigation but nobody contacted me. Nobody contacted the other five girls who spoke out about their personal experiences with him. We were told to keep our heads down. We were told he was married now so that clearly solved his predatory ways. He had a wife so obviously he respected women. When the human resources person suggested this I hung up on her.

Unfortunately, this is the case for most people in retail. We aren't listened to, and we are so replaceable that companies would rather force us to quit than waste money on an investigation. They would much rather cut costs on products and find ways to ramp up production than to make sure their employees feel safe. We are cogs and when these cogs get squeaky, they try to throw them out.

Annie and Sandy (Mary Anne's replacement) took interest in my pleas. They would pull me aside and ask me directly what happened between Karl and I that upset me so much. Sandy didn't know any of the people I was referring to but Annie did. She had a lightbulb moment when I mentioned Autumn's name. Annie didn't understand why Autumn was demoted until I explained Karl was promoting her while she was literally sucking his dick. Sandy asked me why I had been so quiet for so many years accusing me of making up my experiences. It wasn't anything that needed to be spoken about once he moved. He was no longer in my world.

They were the only two people in my store I truly confided in about the situation. I thought I could trust them.

FORTY-TWO

Let Me See You Tootsie Roll

After Karl came back, he began hustling with his bros. Soon, the Assistant Store Leaders were shuffled around to different stores because the Regional Leader was worried about losing trust in the staff for allowing a known predator to work with his homies. Sal was to be part of store Leadership going forward. What the duct tape store didn't know was Sal was a well known perv as well. Numerous calls to the "anonymous" tip line were phoned in against him yet once again nothing was ever done. I was the only one who had true experience working with him and I chose to stay silent after my concerns were ignored about Karl. Sal was known to lick his lips while watching girls bend over to do their job such as stocking an item on the sales floor or cleaning a display. On top of this, his actions depicted a man who knew he could get away with anything from sexually harassing someone to blatantly being disrespectful to other teams and their products.

Sal and I would get into yelling matches frequently and he often referred to me as the one who would never back down. Sal loved to try to intimidate the girls and acted as if he was this macho man. There was nothing macho about a man who looked like a less deformed version of the Penguin. He was just as round, just as scruffy, and hobbled just like Batman's villain.

Somehow, he was able to convince the younger women his power was sexy enough to vie over. He quickly began racking up "points" by how many women he was sleeping with and then demoting the girls when he had his fill. To avoid any blow black, he began revolving around the store in other Leadership roles until he landed the role of Assistant Store Leader. It was no shock when Sal and Karl quickly became two peas in yet another pod.

Just like the last store, phone calls were pouring into the tip line about his behavior. Thankfully, he never pursued me. My opinion of him was clear and my repu- tation as a narc when it came to sexual harassment superseded me. Usually, Sal would even be mindful about how he treated women around me because he just didn't want to be stuck listening to me gripe about how disgusting he was. A pig rolling in soiled dirt was my favorite insult of mine. He didn't appreciate it.

For whatever reason, he decided to sit at Annie's desk one day. She always had candy for us. It was her attempt to keep our blood sugar up (because regular breaks would just be too much to ask for) and made us feel like she gave a shit about our wellbeing. Every week it would be something different in her small tin bucket and it was fun to see what she would try to appease us with. Snick- ers, Starburst, and Tootsie Rolls were her favorite things to offer.

Sal was lounging in her chair and Kristi, who worked in the grocery department (she was responsible for ordering and refilling the products in the giant bins), walked up to ask him something. I was in the office pretending to watch a mandated training video on a computer from the early 2000's. It was a great way for me to cool down and regain my composure after a customer yelled at me that her cake was "too sweet" and I really should have altered the recipe for her diabetes. Kristi became excited seeing her favorite candy was in the tin this week. Tootsie rolls were apparently her happy place and she was all about it.

"Ooooh! Can I have one?! Just kidding, I know I can." She began to reach her hand in the tin but Sal stopped her.

"Uh, hold up. What do you think you're doing?" My head flipped around as Sal said this. I knew where this was going.

"Yeah? What do I need to do to get one?" Her past abuse began shining through as she softened her tone. She was too young to know she could tell him to go fuck himself and take the entire tin. But, she chose to humor him like a good girl should.

"I need to see you... Tootsie Roll." Sal wasn't the brightest crayon in the box. But, without skipping a beat this girl began dancing what I presumed to be the Tootsie Roll dance. She began swaying her hips and bobbing her arms and head. What I don't think was originally part of the dance was her inching towards him to the point where she was almost on top of him. If a customer had walked in (they often barged through the doors labeled "employees only"), it would have looked like she was giving her boss a lap dance. He granted her a tootsie roll for her performance.

As she walked away with her favorite candy, she began fake gagging. It was clear she felt like she had to give him this dance. Kristi knew if she didn't perform it would be her on the chopping block. When she called the tip-line, the operator took down her information. We waited a few weeks but nothing came of it. If she complained more, they would suggest she apply to a different store but couldn't guarantee her job, her status, or her health insurance. Because of this, she declined to stand up for herself further.

FORTY-THREE

Just a Woman Trying to Do Her Job

E aster was approaching and everyone was in a frenzy. There were quotas to fill and deadlines to hit. Bunny butts and carrots adorned the cakes in my case. I went from being the butt of the joke as a cake decorator to taking full leadership of my own case. A dozen more cakes were adorned with pastel-colored flowers to add a flair to the display without alienating our rather large Jewish population. For this insight, I was praised. Once again, our regional team had forgotten that there are many other holidays and preferences than just the Christian ones.

On Good Friday, our corporate team decided that it was a good time to regroup with my store that was adjusting to our new store Leader- Karl. This was his first holiday at the store in almost 8 years and while he ran much larger stores before this, the Boys Club wanted to check in on the stores. We could be trusted to stock shelves faster than a factory machine during the beginning of a pandemic. We could be trusted to play bodyguard between customers and state legislation about masks. We could be trusted to handle the constant churning of a weak business system with changing technology that would break down consistently. We could be trusted with masking our mental breakdowns with a smile. But we couldn't be trusted to handle a B-List holiday.

My main task was making our company's Signature Cake the day the Boys Club decided to check in on us. When they walked in, I was in the process of creating the simple syrup that is poured between the layers of sponge cake. Fun tip, simple syrup is made up of three ingredients, raspberry jam, piping hot water, and sugar. Due to the sheer frenzy happening in the store from customers piling over one another, product shortages, and the fact that we were only staffed halfway from callouts and mental breakdowns, the ingredients for the simple syrup were sprawled across the department like evidence at a murder scene.

On top of this, every measuring cup I needed was filthy and cleaning them became another task on my list. The dishwashing station in the Smoothie Bar decided to give out once again and left sewage spurting from the sink. It became my job to run them to the back of the store and beg the dishwasher to let me wash them quickly. Thankfully, she and I had struck up a friendship and for some frosting, she let me skip the line.

While I was desperately trying to get my ducks in a row, I was also running custom cake orders from the back walk-in cooler to the hands of hungry and impatient customers. Juggling my time between customers wanting to ask questions about the unclaimed cakes in the cake case, manipulating the many special orders, and navigating my way through the Boys Club as they perused the stores common areas created a frustrating game for me. I felt like Frogger trying to avoid all obstacles.

My workout that day was over 15k steps in a 6-hour period of time. Each step was running back and forth between two parts of the store. Either I was filling "a hole" from cakes selling, bringing up special orders for greedy and pretentious customers, or trying to create a basic simple syrup. On my last trip up to the front to discuss with a guest how I could no longer take special orders (30 cakes was too many for one person to make in a day, 31 would have probably broken me), I was stirring the hot sticky syrup in an almost too small Cambro while leap frogging my way towards the front of the store again. I wasn't looking forward to the customer's furrowed brows of disappointment I was about to witness so I also brought the half made syrup up to illustrate how busy I was.

My trajectory towards the front of the store was quickly flung to a full stop. The entire regional team decided to have a standing chat with Karl and Sal in the middle of a major walkway. Now, this store is small. The building was built before my parents were born and honestly could have been built before my grandparents. The aisles were claustrophobic at best. Eight men standing in a circle discussing end caps and shelving displays put a downer on the shopping experience and my route toward a pissed-off Janice. I politely said "excuse me" but my voice wasn't filled with enough testosterone so it was willingly ignored.

Instead of pitching a fit, I used the moment to take a much-needed breath. This was the most interaction I had allowed myself to have with Karl since he came back. It didn't surprise me that the first response was ignoring me. I quietly listened for two minutes waiting for one of them to notice how much they had blocked the aorta of the store. After a few minutes of observation, Karl noticed me standing next to him. He leaned in with his arms folded to an uncomfortable distance from my face.

"Wanna be part of the conversation with us big boys?" He smirked and winked as he let the words fall from his mouth.

"Huh?" At first, I genuinely didn't hear him, I was relishing in the customers complaining that they had to go down an entirely different aisle to avoid the Boy's Club so they could finish their shopping. The Boys Club was totally oblivious to our customers grumbling. They never heard much if it wasn't a club member- even the paying guests.

"You wanna be part of the conversation?" Still leaning towards me, Karl softened his tone and smiled wider.

"No thanks." I said flatly.

"Then what are you doing? Where are you supposed to be?" He didn't understand that the ring of men was blocking a chunk of the store's walkways making it impossible to navigate through.

"Oh, I'm just a woman trying to do her job, but once again, there's a bunch of men in my way." I stopped stirring my syrup for extra effect. Immediately the men dispersed and I quickly realized that while the statement was true, I couldn't help but think about the hot water I might have just stepped into.

FORTY-FOUR

Good Guys Finish Last

It became clear after two months of working at the duct tape store the killer schedule would be temporary. Freudian slips began to ooze from my direct Leader's mouths and it was clear she and everybody else was unhappy that they hired me. Sandy would wait until two or three people were around to see if I would snapback from her malicious undertones. It was a ploy to write me up. If there were no witnesses, it would be her word against mine and I held better argumentative skills. She was unhappy I had "preferential treatment". Team members weren't feeling like it was an even playing ground. It's true. It wasn't. I had a Monday through Friday job in retail. And, given the nature of my role, I worked mid-morning to mid-evening. I fought hard for my schedule and held out like a girl dangling her virginity in front of a Jock before Danny agreed to my demands.

When Danny left, my protection of a stable schedule was gone. He was the one changing the schedule from the AI designed cluster fuck to the streamlined and perfectly balanced itinerary. Everyone had the shifts they wanted regardless of what the computer said. Everyone was as happy as they could be in retail because of this. Days off were granted without too much grief under Danny and he truly believed that despite our presumed lowly titles, we deserved lives too. For us parents, it helped he had kids suckling at toddlerhood and was also drowning in the ocean of work life balance. Danny understood and did everything he could to make treading water easier for us.

It only took three weeks after Karl's return for him to realize why he didn't see me on Saturdays. He didn't see me on Sunday's because he didn't work them either. My sweet schedule was the little secret between me, Danny, and my old boss who recently transferred to this store, Olivia. They just wanted me to stay happy and to stay with the company. By this point, I could do any job except for meat cutting and was often shuffled around the building to fulfill any of the vacancies that day. But Karl and Sandy were worried that I was getting too big for my britches. They wanted to remind me I was still to report to them and I should be grateful to even have a job through a time when millions of people were being let go.

Days off began to be difficult to take off. Sandy asked me if I would be taking time off in the summer in which I replied "Absolutely! It is my birthday!". A week later, she booked herself a two week camping trip and tried denying my birthday off because they coincided with each other. Her claim was that there would be no cover-age. This was true. I was the coverage. Between budget cuts and people quitting due to fearing for their lives over the COVID19 virus, I was one of the last men standing. This gambit went on for months and by the time spring rolled by Karl, Annie, and Sandy had news for me. When my name was called and I was escorted into the office I knew things were going to change.

There they sat in the dingy yellow tinged room. The monitor in the corner revealed the camera's lackluster quality. Most of the boxes were pure fuzz and I wondered how many vengeful Samaras (the girl from The Ring) could pop out of the TV given the circumstances. How would they act? Would they instantly react as every man for themselves? Or would they be consumed by her presumed revenge in an instant leaving me an exit route? The room was small enough and they were perched oddly close to the monitor.

I chose the chair closest to the door just in case. Maybe a pissed-off ghost wouldn't pop out but an angry woman was about to explode. Tears were already welling in my eyes based on what their intentions were. It was never good when every Leader in the store was in the same room. I was going to be given an ultimatum.

The door closed and I began to tune them out. Their crossed arms were telling me that time was up. My smarts were outsmarted. As the company began pushing for more and more AI, they began realizing some Leaders were fucking with the scheduling and decided that happy and balanced team members were actually the reason why the company was going under. They were bleeding money everywhere and cutting labor to avoid their ultimate demise. We were already exhausted and hanging by a thread. This new AI system was revoking any work-life balance we might have been clinging onto.

While my fearless Leaders droned on about how I took advantage of the system, I began playing with the linoleum with my shoe. It held on strong despite its old age. If only I could pry the corner enough to pop up maybe I could will my voice to overpower theirs. To be frank, by this point, I was tired of constantly having to be two steps above them.

"And exactly who do you think you are prancing around here pretending that you are better than any of us? You need to work when we tell you to work and you will not complain. SOMOR will be creating the schedule and Danny will no longer be able to save you. Olivia will be spoken to about this too. No more special favors. I hate these conversations but you knew this was coming. You will be signing this sheet stating you are available during all operation hours or else we will be having a different conversation." Karl's arms were crossed so hard it looked like he was ready to pop them off. If I signed this, I would never have a weekend again.

"Excuse me? Better than anyone else? I have children. I have seniority. I also have a role that requires me to be here literally every day of the week so what difference does it make? There is no second decorator. Why? Because I'm enough." Pop, the corner of the linoleum began to break free along with my voice. "What? Are you afraid of performing special favors? That is what you are known for. Are you really going to climb up this hill with me Karl?"

"Ok, we are going to have to document any threats." Annie piped in. She knew I was not going to let up.

"And what happens if I don't sign off on this? Other people will still have two days off in a row will they not?" Anger was taking hold of me.

"Well, we're having this conversation with several people." Karl shuffled and moved his arms back to his pockets.

"And who is it? What do you mean? Are the two days

off that this store promised going away too? What about you and Annie's Sunday/Monday weekends? Those must be vanishing too, right?" I spoke clearly and looked Karl dead in the eye.

"So, with your job, it isn't beneficial for the company for us to have you off two days in a row. They need to be split if you even get two days. The way this system works might notice the shift in sales and we may need you for six days." I had to squint because it was clear he was trying to prevent a smile from entering his face. We have been running in circles trying to nip at one another since the first time I spoke to him after his return.

"Because we aren't already doing 30% more sales year over year? Is that not enough for Daddy Warbucks?" My scoff sent them all flailing for a retort. The room became silent and there was not much more they could say. Numbers don't lie and while I was far from perfect, I was crushing the role. "Are we done here with your scare tactics? Are we done trying to convince me to quit?" As I stood up to walk away it was Sandy that spoke up.

"If you don't open your availability to 24/7, you will be demoted to part-time and not guaranteed hours. With how the AI generates the schedule there are no more promises for part time workers. You wouldn't want to lose that now would you?" She glowed as she said this.

As I closed the door so they could have their private pow-wow, I replied "You wouldn't want to lose me either."

FORTY-FIVE

We Should be Called Master Builders

The giant rolling door for the receiving area was threatening to break. For months the people who manned the truck loads coming in and out of the area were notifying Leadership of the impending doom. But, the motto at the store was to wait until the very last second to handle something. We all watched in anticipation as the mid-century metal door slowly turned into a dull and harrowing guillotine.

And then the day happened. That bitch finally broke just like every single one of our souls. How it happened is beyond me. I just got a text saying "yeah, we tried to warn them but... Bessie is broke". It was the only time I was okay with being contacted on my day off. Usually, Sandy would text me asking about special orders that were right in front of her face or asking about things that could really wait until my single day off was finished. There was always something I did wrong. Usually, it was overproduction and the team loathed having to run my cakes to the front- as if it was the biggest burden to bear.

But, if I didn't have them...well... then I clearly wasn't dedicated to my job.

So, when Bella texted me explaining that the door we had been betting on finally broke my only concern was how would we accept orders. I didn't care that it could have careened dangerously right as someone was walking underneath it. If that was the case, that person probably deserved it because there were signs everywhere demanding we secure the chain before walking underneath it. Locking the chain was the only way to secure our vicarious fiend. We all knew old Bessie would fall to her death and none of us wanted to become her victim. There were better ways to go and honestly, we have all seen Final Destination too many times to know not to test our destiny with that beast.

I knew I was walking into a shit show the next day. That was clear because how would a store get its goods if we couldn't open the only door that could squeeze a modern pallet through? We were still deep into the product shortage fiasco of the COVID 19 pandemic and we didn't need yet another hurdle to climb. We were exhausted from the surprises of the companies that would send us everything but what we ordered and we had to constantly find creative ways to utilize the products, sell them, or smuggle them for ourselves.

Before store Leadership remembered that the kitchen was an add-on and used to be the receiving area, they had us break down the pallets so that we could bring the food and goods in through the front door. Cases of brioche and sausage would be piled onto U-boats right in front of the store. Knowing the zip code we resided in, I wouldn't be surprised if word spread that we were a shoplifter's dream. Between the petitioners and the COVID19 testers, it would be a breeze for a vagrant to land their sticky fingers on some macarons as we did our best to do our new jobs.

Customers were disgusted by the inconvenience of walking around us unloading a truck in the middle of an entrance, and it was our responsibility to reckon with them. We were to keep the aisles clear and the doors usable all while breaking down pallets in an unusually hot November. Frozen items like our ice cream and our cakes began melting in the heat. No matter how much teamwork we used, the dream just wasn't working. It was a losing battle. Plus, the delivery trucks took up the entire parking lot while we unloaded. It was in fact, "getting real" in our parking lot between the truck drivers not wanting to drive in the close quarters and customers being trapped behind the trucks, or not able to park at all. Tensions were soaring through the theoretical roof.

And then one of them, Annie or Karl, realized that the kitchen had a door that would roll up and accept deliveries. The kitchen was actually an add-on, an afterthought, and the area used to be the receiving area for the original store. In between creating cakes delicately decorated with holiday cheer, I was to dust and clean off the cobwebs that were sitting on the chain since before I was born. As a team, we cleared the way and moved our pots and pans storage area that secured the door into the receiving area. This door was more perilous than the last one. She had no mercy and would slam shut at the wrong vibration. We were told that her chain would be permanently padlocked during delivery hours to avoid any workman's comp situations.

This door was inches from our packaging storage and only a few feet from the food production area of the kitchen. Dust began swirling into the kitchen and would settle anywhere and everywhere. Does anyone want a buttercream cake with the essence of dust? It is the newest trend on TikTok.

Not only were we dealing with our personal dust storms every ten minutes, but there was also no way in hell an entire pallet could make it down the ramp and through the kitchen door correctly. The bones of the store were from before the 50s and nothing was ready for our super-sized appetites. It took three people to steady each pallet to bring them down the itty bitty yet steep ramp and another three people to steady the load as it was vicariously balanced over every pitfall in the floor.

It was quickly realized that we were in the same predicament as before. Our pallets would need to have been broken down immediately before the product could go any further. It was hard enough to squeeze them through the front doors and it was impossible to squeeze them through the single door that led us out of the kitchen. But, there was one solution.

The Styrofoam walk-in cooler wall could be removed. It was more than just an emergency exit, it was a way to pretend the store was functioning normally! We carefully unhinged it from the wall and escorted the pallets from the kitchen into the walk-in cooler and into the receiving area. This was a tight act as the door to the cooler opened up towards the ramp and it was a rather sharp turn to get the pallet in the correct position so that it could be pushed through the cooler. My station was at the juncture between the ramp and the cooler door. Anytime I offered to help, the boys would proclaim that they had it all under control. When one of the guys got too cocky and decided they could do this job on their own, I was the one who ended up with bruises and lackluster stories as to how I got them. It isn't very fun explaining that a guy lost control of a pallet. Sometimes,

I wish I could have come up with something more interesting for my injuries.

As the days went on, it was clear the real receiving door wouldn't be fixed anytime soon. Instead of allowing the Styrofoam to crumble from constantly being detached and reattached with each load, my coworker Mirabelle and I devised a plan to create a sticky and safe way to perch the wall back up between loads. We suggested creating a Velcro-like situation and it saved us from not only losing our receiving area but also losing our walk-in cooler that was already constantly threatening to be out of temp. Store Leadership took credit for the idea, it wasn't something I needed on my resume so I let it slide.

But the dust tumbling in through our new receiving door was still an issue. Mirabelle and I began siphoning signs used for advertisements around the store and created a mini wall around us to help keep the integrity of our products. Nobody is eating cake to get extra iron so why would they start to do so now? While we placed them thoughtfully and effectively, there was no way to keep the dust out of our area. We began to take the plastic coverings for the speed racks and taped them into mini tents to protect us and our products from the dust.

Frustrated, Sal began to try to convince us to not set up our tents. He was worried about the loss of labor due to this time consuming activity. Every day we would put them up, and every day he would take them down. Sal suggested we were overreacting to the situation and felt that there was no contamination despite the pebbles found on my station. He suggested that we needed to remember our place and I retorted with "We belong in the kitchen like the good women we are. Oh wait... we already are!"

It took a few months for the real receiving door to be fixed. Apparently, the door was so old they no longer made parts for it so it had to be custom-made. During a good year that would take time, but during a time of labor and product shortages, it took for-ev-er. Building a new tent became my daily routine and watching Sal tear it down was just part of it. Removing the Styrofoam wall and lugging one load after another through the pitted walk-in cooler became everyone's workout when it was our turn to help. When the door was finally replaced we didn't know what to do with ourselves and we relished in the fact that we no longer needed to be master builders building little metal and plastic forts in the kitchen as part of our daily duties.

As time has passed, there were more blurbs of not-so-mini fixes we had to figure out. For a month the kitchen sink would spray like a whale if the faucet was touched wrong. To fix this while we waited for the company to approve the fix, we decided to keep the faucet running constantly and Jerry-Rigged the faucet with tape and rubber bands so that nobody would be able to stop it. This was the best solution we could think of because the lever was falling off the faucet and it was the only sink we could use for the dishes. To make ourselves feel better about the constant rush of water, we would talk about how there were always dishes to be washed.

Another instance of us having to become creative was when the wheels of the U-Boats would pop off. These were designed to only last a few years. Between the wear and tear of the daily loading and unloading, they should have lasted much longer but because of the poor condition of the floor, they would wear down much faster. It would also be a surprise when a wheel would pop off and you would be sitting there desperately holding up one end of the fully loaded contraption. If you let go, everything would tumble. If you held on attempting to keep the balance, you were likely to get an intense full-body workout. Tart shells and macaroni would go flying when your strength gave out and it would be you that was blamed for the loss of product.

To fix this, one person would hold the U-Boat while another person would wedge the wheel back into place. To make us feel like we fixed the actual problem, a third person would then guide the U-Boat to safety (the sales floor was always smooth as a baby's butt and the safest place for these dilapidated carts). We would attempt to wrap the achy joint with tape but it never worked for long. We tried super gluing it as a last resort but it never held due to the moist conditions of the walk in coolers. Brute force was to be the only solution for this one. It's why our biceps were so strong!

But, there was more than just wobbly U boats and faulty kitchen sinks. The glass inside of the cake case didn't actually fit the shelves. They were hand-me-downs from other stores and we were expected to "make it work". I noticed that if I washed the shelves but didn't let them dry all the way the sanitizer water would become sticky. The stickiness would help prevent the shelves from shifting while we were loading or unloading cakes. On the occasion that that didn't work, I would simply tape them to the shelves and hope that Leadership didn't notice the mess. This is also why I began lining each shelf with gold boards. They were there for a reason. We needed to shine that pig.

When the piping for the Hot Bar would go down, we would do our best to wrap the lines with cloth and then tape them together. There was always something that needed fixing. What did we expect from a store that was as old as my great grandparents? We were able to trap coolant and antifreeze with our wrap jobs using duct tape and old rags. If we slipped and forgot to refill the water wells of the hot bar they would dry out. The inside of the bar would corrode and become unusable. I won't say someone did this on purpose, but there happened to be only two people scheduled between the day and night shifts for two weeks with no relief in sight when the hot bar well ended up becoming bone dry and ultimately corroding. That sucker couldn't be used for four months and it was the most glorious four months of our culinary lives. No longer did we need to monitor who put their dentures in the mac n cheese, what kid might have sneezed all over the over steamed broccoli, and no longer were we burning our hands on the pre-cooked food we would heat up in the steamers that would give us a forceful daily facial.

I think the scariest incident of trying to piece together a major part of the store was when the freezer door handle broke. You could not push the release button from the inside because of this break and you also had to pry the door open from the front because the handle would fall off every time you breathed on it. We were told that we still had to use the death trap for our freezing needs because it was our only major freezer. Even those of us who weren't religious began praying every time we went into the freezer. We would bundle up with two jackets, hats, and gloves in case we got trapped. Sal and Annie would tell us there was a reason why they placed an extra ax in the freezer- we could hack our way out if we did get trapped.

One of my coworkers had a brilliant fix. I would love to know who it was but the truth is I don't. They had created a fully functional handle out of a sales hanger. Somehow, this sales hanger was looped exactly where it needed to be and it fit perfectly in the old door handle frame. This magician of a person slipped the retail hanger through the holes of the broken handle and rigged it so it could function as a normal latch. You could lift it up and pop! The door would open. You could even push open the door from the inside of the freezer by hitting the release button. Freezing to death in the back of a grocery store quite possibly could be one of the worst ways to go and this underground vigilante saved us from having to be remembered as the one who was found frozen stiff.

Towards the end of my time there, the roof in the kitchen gave up on its valiant pursuit and caved in. It collapsed because the hood for the rotisserie didn't work. The giant oven would frequently slip out of place and end up filling the kitchen with hot, humid, oily air. When I suggested that construction was never part of the skill set I was wanting to attain, nor was it part of my job, it was communicated that my role was to do whatever was asked and if I had cared about my team, I would need to step up to the plate. Instead of helping, I turned into the paparazzi. I began photographing everything around me. Watching my team spend time fixing a roof that was out of code baffled me. We were not contractors. We were not trained for this and the safety concerns mounted as the slick hot rotisserie air wrapped around my teammates determined bodies.

This was something I just couldn't get behind. The broken tile lathered our water bottles with out of code foam. No doubt there was asbestos hiding amongst the shrapnel. Karl suggested that it was our fault for not constantly making sure the rotisserie oven wasn't directly underneath the vent. We felt that it was his fault that the vent didn't actually work right and that the oven on wheels could not be put into "brake mode". He instructed that we were to piece together the ceiling tile so that we could operate in the kitchen without fearing more of the fluffy insulation falling down.

Fearful of their jobs, a few of my coworkers quickly grabbed a ladder, glue and promptly began putting the puzzle pieces together of what was once a properly fitting roof tile. It took them their entire shift to almost get it right. But so much was lost as the tile continued to crumble that it became Humpty Dumpty and no matter that nearly all of the kitchen staff was working together, they just couldn't put it back together again. For weeks, the insulation would crumble into our kitchen until the roof could be fixed professionally. For weeks, the steam from the rotisserie oven would create more swollen ceiling tiles that would threaten to burst. When it became clear that the tiles would not be replaced soon, we went back to our roots and patched the holes with cardboard and duct tape.

FORTY-SIX

Dumpster Divers

E veryone's gotta eat and sometimes, food in a
grocery store dumpster is the best possible place.
When times are rough and people can't afford basic
necessities, they look for creative ways to make ends
meet. Really, who would pass up free food if they were
hungry? And who am I to judge someone who is so
desperate for a meal that they would dive into a dumpster filled with an eternity of unknown surprises? These
dumpsters were beacons of hope for some.

I didn't mind adding to the ever-growing food
pyramid in those giant bins but sometimes I wondered if
the food that was tossed could have been donated like the
other products. Food that was untouched would be
plopped into a trash bag and flung head-first into a giant
bin of freebees. This happened daily and word had absolutely spread to the less fortunate communities.

Many times, my coworkers and I would be mindlessly throwing our waste into an industrial-sized bin and
pop! A human would jump up from inside the metal
sarcophagus and usually be just as scared as we were. It

would be us vs. them but we were both frozen like a deer in headlights. Our fear would overcome both parties which made the situation difficult to move away from.

To avoid the surprise encounters we began banging on the side of the bin before unloading our garbage into it because we wanted to at least be warned if a human was foraging for a meal. That way, we could give them some decency and they would also not scare the piss out of us unsuspecting wage-earners. The divers would usually know what times to avoid the area because they were always afraid we would call the cops on them. Phoning the Blue Boys for something as simple as a desperately hungry person needing a bite was the lowest priority on my list. Watching a cop come way too late to arrest someone for being hungry was never of interest to me either. The real crime, however, was allowing so much food to go to waste. Yes, the company would donate hundreds of items each week to the community food bank. All of the items that were about to go bad would find themselves smashed into the plastic bins for volunteers to wheel away.

Yes, the company would encourage us to find creative ways to utilize products that were threatening to go bad. We would really try but it was difficult to come up with creative uses when we were forbidden to veer from the mandated recipes. Sometimes, we would help make some products disappear ourselves. My favorite thing to do was to hoard a package of the smoked cheese dip until the very last day and then oops! I guess we need to sample some! Danny and I would devour half the container before sampling it out to customers.

But, depending on what side of town the store was on, the divers would want much more than just a simple bite to eat. At my last store that was in a wretched part of town we were frequented by addicts. Homeless, hungry, and in need of their next fix they would wait for our discards like a lion ready to take its prey down. It was one man's luckiest unlucky day ever the day my cake case was finally replaced.

At the edge of our dock laid a beacon of hope for this man. The case was older than your dad's best aged Scotch and was oozing with promises of copper and metal. Leadership had hauled it to the back and scheduled a "bulky pick up" the next week. Despite my concerns of this case attracting the wrong attention, little thought was put into the situation. They had taped a printed sign that stated "broken" on it and called it a day. It didn't take even two days before that case shattered on a guy who wanted to harvest the precious metals lurking underneath the surface.

Out of nowhere we heard a giant crash and the sound of glass shattering reverberated along the side of the building. I quickly ran to the rolling door that was wide open in the kitchen and several of my Leaders ran up behind me trying to figure out what had happened.

There we saw a man in a wife beater bloodied and cursing up a storm. I immediately understood the situation. He didn't understand that the sign which read "broken" was a warning that the hinges didn't hold the glass up. I knew one day it would shatter but had hoped it was in the store and caused a commotion. I wanted so badly for the company to take my safety seriously even if that meant risking my health. Instead, the moment was wasted on a junkie trying to steal metal and copper from the glass door of doom.

Quickly, we began closing the make-shift receiving door that led straight into the kitchen and made sure that the door leading to our "boneyard" (this is the place all our junk was left to rot) was locked. Thankfully, nobody was out there trying to sneak in a break or a phone call because we were not about to let anybody in. The man had begun to stomp around the building cursing and yelling. It was another hour before he vacated the premises. Shattered pieces of glass were all that remained of the Final Destination style dome that I once propped up daily. My beloved glass case had an honest attempt at murder and failed (much to the company's relief). The door was made from safety glass so the shards that hit him must have been defects from old age. The rest of the glass lay scattered across the parking lot the way windshields are strewn across the street after an accident.

Junkies and homeless folk weren't the only ones who frequented our dumpsters though. Between inflation, lack of raises, and well… the need to be able to afford alcohol or weed to survive this job, we were constantly broke. My coworkers would luster over the newly tossed macarons- spoiled out due to them expiring in the freezer. They would drool over loaves of bread and hot bar treats. Sometimes, their eyes would bug out of their skulls waiting for me to scan out a cake or scone.

Shamelessly, they too would dive right on into the dumpsters after work and then gloat about the dinner they created for themselves. They wouldn't dare just leave work with their hands full of product. Even though it was all considered garbage, dozens of people had been fired previously for siphoning away spoiled goods instead of throwing them away. This is not an old practice, when I worked at a locally owned fast food restaurant the owner suggested he would rather watch his hundred dollar bills burn rather than donate his leftover bagels to charity.

Many of the culprits stealing perfectly old food were my friends just desperate to feed their families. Many of them assumed that if it was already spoiled, scanned out, and supposed to be dumped it should be fine to be brought home. In a country where overproduction was a serious issue, these thieves were technically doing the environment a favor.

Sometimes, my sticky-fingered coworkers' fridges and pantries were stocked better than mine. Sometimes, they would offer their services to us folk who were too scared to get caught. Sometimes, they would argue that they really did purchase the goods they consumed. All the time, most of us turned a blind eye and just thought *I really gotta do that sometime.*

FORTY-SEVEN

Never Again

"Those cameras don't even work." It was word vomit, but it was spewed at the right time. Karl's body froze and I could visibly see him stiffening up as he lifted his head. For a second, he stayed frozen. His next move had to be meticulous. I just revealed that his threats about firing the next person who was caught nibbling on wasted food were weak. The accusations that we were mocking him couldn't be caught on camera but Karl liked touting as if he could see our satire through the screens. He couldn't prove any of his ill conceived accusations and now he knew that we knew.

"They work just fine. I see everything." He doubled down, threatening again to fire someone on the spot who defected against his commands. The truth was that no cameras truly worked in the store. The electrical lines in the building couldn't support newer cameras and ours were on the way out. Nothing but fuzz was coming through on those suckers. The only reason why I knew they didn't work was that I had seen the false surveillance. During the many conversations in the

Leader's offices, I could visibly see that the cameras constantly went offline, they showed little to no picture and if they were human eyes, they would be deemed legally blind.

I think my words stung a little more than if they came from anyone else. He tried to pretend the history we shared didn't exist. And I had been waiting to prove to him that it was me that finally had the upper hand. My protests and outcries may have fallen on deaf ears about him coming back to the store, but my intentions stayed noble. He would never have power over me again. He would never be able to bully me nor trap me in a small office again.

This was the first time I allowed myself to show these cards. I have been stockpiling them since I was pulled into his office after begging the human resource team to transfer me so I did not have to confront him. In that little office he accused me of a smear campaign. Then, to add kindle to my rage, he openly threatened to retaliate against me about my accusations.

Annie was the one who summoned me into the office. I looked up at Sandy who was across from me packaging donuts for the weekend. They both acted as if it was a normal talk that was about to happen. Sandy suggested that it was to talk about the schematic for the weekend, how Karl wanted to see the cakes displayed. Annie suggested that she had no clue what Karl wanted to talk to me about.

My heart sank in my stomach as I followed Annie into the small office. Their stories should have matched. Neither of them were good at lying and it was obvious the conversation I was about to have would not be one I wanted. Each step I took walking towards the tiny office, I could feel the cold sweat of confrontation budding.

This talk was going to be the showdown I begged the company to spare me from. *Here we go...* my thoughts trailed into a mindless black hole as Annie closed the door behind her. She knew. She was to be the female representative to prevent further allegations.

"I praise you! You have no right to say those things about me." Karl began the conversation acting as if he was doing me favors and I was biting the hand that fed me. I stood silently. Once again, the #metoo movement left me out of the equation of equality and representation. It didn't protect all of us. If there was no limelight and no publicity, harassment survivors still were not being heard. "I had to explain to my wife, I have a baby on the way, a baby! And you say those awful things about me?" He slunk into his chair and crossed his arms, flexing his biceps that boasted his dated tattoo. His spiked hair was at full attention waiting for my response.

What was the point of talking if my voice would be silenced once more? He took advantage of a single mom, then when I denied him he stopped giving me raises, stopped promoting me- his supposed prized possession at the time. He sabotaged my livelihood more times than I could count and yet I stayed loyal out of fear of not being able to provide for my small family. Though this time, he couldn't call me unenthusiastic, he couldn't tell me I was too emotional, he couldn't tell me I didn't understand the nature of the job.

"Well, good. You should explain to your wife. I truly hope you have changed." I tried to look unphased, but I knew my expression was betraying me. Tears of frustration and anger welled up but I didn't want them to start rolling, I've already cried too many times because of this idiot.

"Do I make you uncomfortable? Because if you keep

saying that I am this horrible person I can make sure that you can never transfer to another store again. I will never show you praise, I will never support you. I will never give you a recommendation to anyone who asks inside or outside the company. Your career no matter what profession you think you could do will be over." He sputtered and I knew that his buddies at other stores already knew. They were once all Leaders under the same roof. My career with the company was already over after being passed up multiple times due to my negligence of returning the under-table favors he fervently proposed. Interviews began with Leadership asking me why after ten interviews I hadn't landed a Leadership role. It was never an easy explanation without sounding petty.

Despite the perceived unawareness of the situation, our regional teams and human resources knew when he hit on me. I turned to them when it happened and that's when I found out all the Leaders knew each other from childhood. They knew when he told me I had to go to the Team Build where he insisted we go to a horror flick and snuggled next to me. They knew that he put his arm around me and when I flicked it away he put his hand on my leg suggesting he would comfort me during the film. They knew when he started dating and promoting my coworker whom he directly managed.

They knew and they did nothing until it was too late.

They knew and were doing the same exact thing to other girls in the store. The news of my outcry wasn't anything new. It's why they wouldn't let me transfer stores. There were too many secrets nestled into the furrows of my brows. There were too many secrets us girls were keeping in fear of losing our jobs in the middle of a possible recession. If the company kept us together maybe we wouldn't spill the beans to people at other stores. Maybe we would learn our place and shut up.

"Two hot girls in a small room? Do you remember saying that to me and your ex-girlfriend? Does your wife know you have a history of dating girls you were managing?" Silence. He sat forward in his chair contemplating his next response. Karl's wife did know because she was also his direct employee when they met. The happy couple began dating just like he and Autumn did- his new love was managed by him when they shared their first smooch. It didn't matter how much he denied the behavior, we both knew he said those things. He also knew that I had more arsenal and everyone in the room could tell I was holding back. And now the token witness Annie knew I was telling the truth. His body language said everything Annie was wondering about, he was guilty. But she too needed to stay in the game and protect herself so she stayed silent.

Karl claimed there was an intense investigation after outcries beyond the things I personally experienced were filling up the box meant for interview questions. Nobody was asking what they love about the company. There were no questions about the intentions of how they would handle a store that was held together by duct tape and lackadaisical wishes. Nobody was worried about whether or not our new Leader liked the local scene. There were no intentions of connecting with this person. We all became fearful and began speaking out. Still, nothing was truly done and I was left sitting in an office alone with my predator. He was demanding answers as to why I would slander him in such a way. I reminded him it wasn't slander if it was the truth.

What was concerning me though was the betrayal of Sandy and Annie. They were the only two people in the store to know what had happened. I didn't dare talk to anyone else about the situation because I promised Human Resources I would not play the game of Telephone with my coworkers. Not only did I not want things to get out of hand, I hated the idea of so much attention. I didn't want to be stuck answering questions with answers that still harmed my mental health. Whether it was Sandy, Annie, the regional team, or Human Resources who swore to keep my identity safe it was hard to tell who ultimately betrayed me. But someone leaked my trauma. Someone didn't protect me and I was stuck in an office being confronted by my monster. He would not reign over me again and I was to make sure of that.

So, when I revealed his bluff to everyone in the kitchen, it was a deeper jab than revoking the bit of power he held at the store level. It highlighted that once again he was not to be trusted- that his rhetoric should never be listened to. His authority slipped a little bit as he slinked silently out of the kitchen knowing his empty threats of instantly firing someone were mute.

FORTY-EIGHT

A Guy Walks into a Juice Bar

E verybody has heard the joke by now, but it is worth telling for this next adventure. A vegan, an Atheist, and a CrossFitter walks into a bar. I know this because they would always tell me immediately. But when a chauvinist walks in, you don't have to be told, you can smell him a mile away.

The store's sliding glass doors slid open as he waltzed in holding his trophy baby in the car seat. It was his way of telling the world that he can get laid and ejaculate enough to impregnate a woman. The smell of Axe and multiple hair products swallowed any other senses I may have had. My eyes teared up as he walked closer, not because of his jaunty waltz but his odor was gut-wrenchingly strong.

While his stature and appearance stated that he was clearly middle-aged, his swagger suggested that he still thought he was a frat boi coming from a party- possibly doing the walk of shame. He began giving me his order, talking to me as if I should already know it. Turns out, he's a regular and couldn't tell any of us apart. He really did think we all looked the same. I was simply covering a break for my co-worker. She needed to pee and God forbid she leave her station unattended for three minutes to relieve herself. As he was walking towards me, Aria slipped back into her station unbeknownst to me.

"Oh hey you." He interrupted my greeting. With this, my attention turned to my now relieved coworker. But, did he really think she cared about him with that line? Did he think she gave a shit if he knew her name?

"Hey," She half replied. For someone as talkative as she was this was an oddly short response. Her pigtails trailed along her face. Her dark eyeliner threatened to melt as she fumed with annoyance.

"Hey I've been thinking about something and I am not sure how to say it correctly, but figured you two are the perfect ones to test my theory on." He began to lean on the counter as if it was a bar downtown. I could feel Aria roll her eyes behind me.

"You should probably perfect it before you say it." I wrote the code for his drink on a slip of paper and handed it to him so he could pay for his smoothie at the registers.

"Nah, I want to tell you my theory. It's a good one." His smirk said it all. He was about to walk into a deep, dark, and soggy trench. "As a man, I notice a lot of things." He began leaning harder on the too high counter as if he was hitting on a chick with the word *slut* written on her forehead. He took a breath and put down the carseat holding his son onto the antiquated linoleum floor.

"Women are really amazing creatures. You are beautiful and fierce, I mean think about lionesses and other female animals out there. You guys don't fuck around." He began sprawling his unsolicited opinion onto us.

"Keep going." We responded in unison. This isn't going to end well and we were fully invested in how badly this fucker was going to crash and burn.

"So, women, you guys are fierce and far superior when it comes to living and caretaking and stuff but intellectually? Far inferior." Ouch. These lionesses were about ready to pounce.

"Seriously? That's what you felt you could say to us? Yeah, going forward I highly suggest you keep that thought to yourself. And yes, I did just do you a favor by reminding you to shut your mouth. Maybe you should have taken my original advice." I snapped and put his cup down. There was no way in hell I would willingly make him his smoothie.

"Ah see" He said as he peeked at his cooing baby. "See? You are so intellectually inferior you didn't understand I just complimented you."

"Look, I could tell why you were single before you spoke, but now, I know you will never find a relationship." I sputtered. I knew I shouldn't have engaged, but he just degraded the two biggest feminists in the store. It hurt him a little more than expected and he glanced at me confused. He didn't know his ex also frequented the store and had already told us about his stained laundry.

"Enlighten us then." Aria suggested as she crossed her arms. "I'm too intellectually inferior to understand."

"Well, you guys just get yourselves into the most stupid situations with men, and endanger yourselves so easily it is hard to prove you're smarter than us. You're a whole other species man." The man scoffed as he said this last line.

"Is that what your ex feels about having a baby with you?" I lashed. Maybe he didn't understand the degrading comment. He was the mistake- not the baby.

"If you like, we can show you how stupid women could get." Aria peered over my shoulder as she spoke.

"See? You women are so hot headed, You don't know where to stop." His smile grew anxiously and we stretched our bodies to look taller.

"I have brass knuckles in my car, I actually have a few other things in there too. Still wanna see how stupid a girl can get?" Aria's threats were not empty. Immediately he began to backtrack. His stance got taller as he realized he may get jumped in a grocery store by two baristas. We. Don't. Fuck. Around.

"Uhm, oh uhm, see? That's what I mean. I mean no that's not it. Uhm forget I said anything." The back and forth went on for a few more minutes.

While he battled my coworker, I grabbed his cup. Does he really want to see how inferior women are? Well, he should get a dose of his own medicine. Slowly, I began filling his cup with the contents of the smoothie he ordered. I put everything in the blender while Aria occupied him with more instances as to how we could portray our obvious hot headedness.

"Hey, can you help me? I need something from the back." I shouted to her. Immediately she understood what I was doing and told him we have some stupid girl stuff going on and to excuse us as we walked into the dish area nestled in a corner out of sight. The blender full of the newly blended ingredients never left my hand as we disappeared from his view.

We sat there talking and laughing at how stupid he was. She popped her head out for dramatic effect. Did this guy really think pissing off two people who directly handle his food was a good idea? Obviously, we didn't add or subtract anything to his drink- I wouldn't dare. But, I wanted him to think I did. So, after two full minutes, we came back out giggling and shaking the blender. I blended his drink to perfection for a second time and handed it to him.

"Should I be concerned?" He said. "I have my baby boy with me, is this safe to give to him?" The man either had a heart or was willing to quite literally poison his baby boy to prove a point.

"Aren't I too stupid to do anything? After all, us women are pretty intellectually inferior" I said as I walked away. Aria was doubled over because it was clear we just scared the bejesus out of the suave wanna-be frat boi.

Frat Boi's response was to quietly take his drink away and say nothing more.

The Leader On Duty was convinced that he could kick the customer out for his discriminatory behavior. He wanted to ban the Frat Boi but Karl, Sal, and Annie decided that us ladies should have "taken the compliment". We were to address him with respect and diligently serve him further perpetuating Frat Boi's idea we were beneath him. This company was so afraid of losing a few dollars that we were expected to take the emotional and verbal beatings of all customers without hesitation.

Their decision wasn't going to fly with any of us. Everytime our new frenemy came into the store, Aria would look him dead in the eye and exclaim "Nope!" and promptly walk away.

FORTY-NINE

Inventory

I f you are a retail or restaurant worker I give you full permission to skip this paragraph and just go onto the next. You already know what I mean when I say "inventory". For those of you who have never worked in either role listen up. The end of the month is an annoying little prick. Us employees are tasked with counting every Goddamned item in the entire store (or restaurant). When the store closes you best believe we are gearing up to pull all-nighters. If the count is wrong we could be in huge trouble. This is because fluctuating numbers meant either someone wasn't using the right amount of product or stealing. We had to make sure to scan out the spoilage perfectly throughout the month or else it would be our names on the chopping block of shame. We had to note every time we took a bite out of something to "sample" it. If there was a product that spilled, it best be counted, and we better have a solid reason as to why we spilled it.

There was once a girl who had bumped into one of the many cracks in the floor just right (okay, this wasn't hard to do because the floor was more turbulent than a teenager's acne riddled face) and ultimately lost an entire speed rack of pumpkin pies two days before Thanksgiving. They splattered like a victim in a slasher film. So, when it was inventory time, we knew that every single item needed to be accounted for and it was vital nothing was counted until 4 pm to help get more product out of the backstock area and onto the sales floor. After that, the backstock could be counted. It was only after operating hours every single item on the sales floor would be accounted for. This is why towards the end of the month the shelves start to look bare. Retailers need to meet budget goals and account for labor that will be used up when employees are working and sales cannot happen.

During the height of COVID my Leader Sandy refused the vaccine. She was convinced it messed with her menstrual cycle and created deformities in pregnancies. What did she care? She was a lesbian who would tout how she never wanted babies. But, learn from my mistake, don't let that type of word vomit come out of your mouth. Anyway, she was gone for several months "with COVID" leaving me and my favorite doormat of a coworker to figure out how to run the team with zero experience and zero pay raise. When she was due to return, she called out. She called out for seven days in a row. Usually, this means the team member would be terminated for failure to return to duty but for an unresolved reason, she was spared because she promised to be back in time to count inventory.

Inventory day strolled around and between medical emergencies, COVID, childcare issues, and lack of people I was the only one to show up on that fateful day. Sandy claimed she was still too sick to work. There was no grace given to me for the lack of employees; I needed to hold up the duties of the team. I was to run the Smoothie Bar and Bakery while also counting our precious goods. I got 15k steps in by noon and there was no end in sight. Not to mention the Culinary department had a few callouts and the only person to show up had just started training. Once again, after being told I was not allowed to train new hires, I was in fact training newbies.

When I was approached to lead inventory, I told them sure under one condition- I would not stay past 7:30 pm. My children would have been home alone since 1 pm and while my now tween son was a very capable babysitter, it was wrong to expect him to facilitate both his education and his sisters for hours on end especially with little to no notice.

In my groove, I didn't notice my husband texting me. He was managing a restaurant downtown and was sending me pictures. Being a foodie, I figured it was just food porn. But it wasn't. I still wish it was.

Text one: *Hey, I thought Casey was sick with COVID?*

Text Two: *Who is she with? Maybe she is better but Sandy isn't?*

Text Three: *Should I go over there and say hello to them? Maybe it could score you some points since I'm cool with Casey and she is Sandy's girl?*

Text Four: *Look, I know you're incredibly busy, sorry, nothing is urgent.*

He began sending me pictures of the several women relishing a girl's night. And lo and behold... Sandy was right next to Casey.

I responded: *That's Sandy right next to her. Here I am pulling a 14-hour day while our babies are home and she is "too sick" to work. Yet, she's clearly enjoying some girl time?! If they are still there please make sure to tell them I say hello.*

He responded: *Are you sure that's a good idea?*

His second response: *Nvm, decided to say hello. Her face dropped. Wish you saw it. Please show Karl and Annie the picture of your boss that is just so ill and totally fucked you.*

My hands were shaking too much to hold my phone while I processed this revelation. I decided it was in everybody's best interest to put the phone down. Here I am, working myself to the bone for a company that couldn't even pay me hazard pay for more than a couple months. I get reprimanded and written up when my kids get sick but she can just go out on the town when she is supposed to be working? My thoughts began to spin out of control, not able to put the newfound fact down.

Karl walked into the kitchen as I was trying to grapple with how to approach him about the situation. Breathlessly, my words spewed the news about Sandy's whereabouts. His response was that her life was her business. I asked why I was never granted the same kindness. I asked why it was okay to blow off work for a few cocktails and not okay to need to care for my sick children- forget about myself. When my daughter was discovered to have lice 30 minutes before my shift started I received a third write-up over it- but Sandy was allowed to gallivant around town even though she claimed she was sick. I have worked with 104-degree fevers because of the repercussions of my calling out for the day. Karl doubled down to remind me that nobody likes a narc, and it would be in my best interest to let the horse die.

The next week it was found that my count was off. It was me who got into trouble. Forget that I stayed for double the amount of time I should have. Forget the fact that I was running multiple venues. It was always about the numbers and tattle tailing was not acceptable.

FIFTY

The Box of Sadness

If you hadn't cried yet, you hadn't officially committed yourself to the job. It was common practice for someone to be hiding in the walk-in cooler just sobbing their eyes out. I have been known to waltz in there from time to time too. Whether it was the lack of being able to handle life's emergencies because we would literally lose our jobs, feeling ill and not being able to afford to call out, management belittling you and berating you, or customers just being flat out dicks and forgetting you are a human being with feelings, there were ample reasons to lose your shit and end up sobbing for your mommy in the giant refrigerator. Sometimes I would try to hide in there and burrow myself between the moveable racks overflowing with food. It always ended up with either scaring the complete shit out of someone (usually my boss Danny before he moved) or me walking out of that sucker with bloodshot eyes and casting an awkward silence into the room.

I would wait for the newbies to break down before I decided to give them the warm welcome they deserved. I would tell them "welcome to the business, it will be okay" the second their eyes became leaky with despair while showing them the best places to cry. Usually, part of the initiation would mean sneaking them a snack too because who wouldn't want to emotionally eat when you are being berated in a million-dollar fixer-upper? Their eyes would become a mix of confusion and gratitude as I would sit with them and talk about what made them cry. Normally, it was the pressure of the gig and the fact that customers would rather see us as robots and burnouts rather than active citizens in our community.

One day, a box showed up in the kitchen. It was a brand-new speed rack! Talk about Christmas in July! We had been demanding a new set of racks for a year by this point because the wheels on the old ones were literally falling off. Chunks of the wheels were missing on every rack we owned. Erosion due to the rocky ground was named as the culprit.

It was up to us to decide which rack would be replaced. The Bakery team and Culinary team bickered over who deserved the shiny new toy. On one hand, we were both wheeling out goods continuously. We could share. But, sharing means that you care, and sharing also would lead to fights over who's asparagus juice was left on the rack and spilled onto chocolate chip cookies. Ultimately, we decided on an on/off basis. Some days it would belong to the bakery, others it would be used by the culinary personnel. The day was always made better when I got to hang out with my new friend The Speed Rack.

The box our plaything came in was left in the kitchen for us to break down and dispose of. It was the height of an adult and it was wide enough to fit even our burliest of guys in it. There was a slot at the top reminiscent of a window you would see at a speakeasy. We had to cut the rack out of it due to the size and our incision left a cool little door in the box for us to easily slip in and out of.

The temptation was rising in the kitchen, who wouldn't want to play with the giant box? It ultimately turned into our little fort. Someone had written "The Sadness Box" on the top and we all knew it was our new favorite place to go and cry. It was much more comfortable than the walk in and more soothing because if you were in there, everybody knew to leave you alone. I definitely loved to hide in there just to get a moment of solace.

It was a revolving door of us using the makeshift fort. There was just something magical and soothing about being able to slip into a cardboard box and allowing a very real feeling to wash over you in privacy. Some would tell us to save our feelings for lunch but unless you magically had an invisibility cloak, you were never left alone during your lunchtime.

Customers had free access to the "break room" because the public bathrooms were right next to our tiny area. They would oftentimes ignore the sign suggesting that nobody but team members were welcome and would barge in demanding we find them their precious sprouted bread. Leadership would come in looking for one person after another for problems that could have absolutely waited thirty minutes while we enjoyed our sack lunches we brought in. Supervisors, Trainors, and other team members would pop in and borage you with questions about products. And when you were in the bathroom, chances are a junkie would be banging on the door until you finally finished relieving yourself and emerged from their safe haven.

So, this box, this stupid cardboard box was the best

thing that could happen to us. It was the only place nobody dared to bother us. It was our hug when we needed it most.

Leadership didn't like it. It was an obstruction in the kitchen. It was against regulation. It was childish and just proved they hired a bunch of adult babies. Maybe the adult baby thing wasn't too far off, the job was hard and we were constantly burnt out. Karl made sure that we took our refuge down and explained to us through his angry teeth that he felt like we were mocking him. For the first time we weren't but why not poke the bear? He took away our comfort fort!

FIFTY-ONE

What's That Smell?

Sharps boxes were banned pretty early in my career. These are the orange boxes you might see in a doctor's office or some establishments to safely dispose of medical needles. When they are in a grocery store, they are usually used by diabetics who need a safe place to throw away their insulin shots. Unfortunately, these boxes attracted desperate addicts needing needles to use their drug of choice. Junkies were eager to "use the bathroom" and then have what sounded like a huge blowout fight with the sharps box as they would pry the contaminated needles from the locked containers.

It was always like clockwork. The guy or gal would come in looking like they haven't seen a meal in weeks. They would plead that they needed to use the restroom and that they were simply on a road trip. They were absolutely tripping but it wasn't the good ol' American experience we think of. After us reluctantly giving them the key, they would hole themselves up into the bathroom and perform whatever ritual they needed to get their high. Then, they would begin to holler and shout.

They would sit there and bang bang bang on the sharps box. We would always hear the defining moment when the box was torn off the wall exposing everyone to whatever pathogens lived on those needles.

Depending on who was working, we would begin to take bets on how long it would take these vagrants to get what they wanted. Being incredibly young and naïve, I lost multiple times and had to purchase many energy drinks as payment. Nobody was disappointed when those boxes disappeared- except our neighborhood addicts. My wallet was particularly satisfied that I would no longer be shelling out each time someone broke into the box.

Still, they always found a way to make the very public bathrooms useful to their addictions. The problem was so bad Leadership put digital locks on both bathroom doors. They were protected with a four-digit code that would change weekly. The catch? We were expected to give the code to anyone who asked and simply monitor their use. This didn't seem like much of a solution and as time passed, Leadership realized giving the code to any Bill or Bob that walked through the double doors was just as good as not having a code at all. Soon enough, we were expected to memorize a new code every day and constantly drop what we were doing to let Susan or Sally into the bathroom. It wasn't easy denying people the facilities so oftentimes Leadership would cave and just let in anybody as long as someone promised to monitor them.

Not only were our bathrooms the new wave Opium Bar, but they were also extremely outdated. There were only two toilets for the entire store. Apparently, the city had grandfathered the building into compliance because of the sheer age of the superstructure. Honestly this shouldn't have been surprising because the building itself was grandfathered into every single code and ordinance. Nothing in the store was "up to code" according to modern safety standards but because it was considered historic, she was able to still stand tall. For perspective, this store had two toilets. A new building of the same size and same occupancy would be required to have at least six porcelain thrones. The lack of a proper amount of places to urinate became extremely problematic during the holidays.

There would be days when the lines to the bathroom and the cash registers would become intertwined like teenage lovers. Sloppy and unorganized, customers and team members would struggle to figure out which line they belonged in and how to move forward with their desires.

We were not to use paid time to wait around for the bathroom to become vacant. Yet, there would be times when a full thirty-minute lunch would go by and the line would barely move. Between slow customers and people confusing our bathrooms for a personal masturbatory, injection site, and the occasional pity party pit stop, the line would barely budge. We would be expected to hold our bodily functions for hours on end. Many of us said "Fuck that" and would wait to urinate on company time because we were not Amazon and refused to wear Depends during our shifts. I was one who would wait it out and allow myself such niceties as relieving myself.

This would become tricky at times but the only other alternative would be to piss myself- and what would they do if I needed to go home and change? How would they explain that to Human Resources (or what was supposed to be Human Resources since most of them were laid off by this point)? Anytime someone in Leadership gave me a hard time, I would mention that if I became infected with a UTI because of holding in my pee it would be covered under Workman's Comp. I would remind them that I would happily pee in the middle of the sales floor if they would prefer a scene. Or better yet, go home for the day under paid leave due to incontinence. They didn't like when I started on that bandwagon because everyone else jumped on it too.

What holiday this story belongs to is blurry at best. All I remember was that my bladder was threatening to burst and it was imperative I waited for the bathroom. Both restrooms had been occupied for well over 45 minutes, but I couldn't risk walking away. The slightest shift of balance could have sent me into a bladder malfunction. Even standing still was becoming sketchy.

So when the person opened up the door after using the loo, I didn't think to look if I would bring someone like that around my family. I didn't think to sniff the bathroom like we were trained to do before closing and locking the door. I didn't think about the fact that I never heard a toilet flush and rather heard rustling with the fan and toilet seat. The fan was a favorite place for them to stash their drugs- once a baggie fell on one of my coworkers while she was peeing! She was convinced it was a ghost but we all knew better.

Anyways, I raced into the bathroom. It was such a high priority I began unzipping my jeans while I began to fiddle with the finicky door lock. This was a vital skill to have so that your frantic dash to the porcelain throne would be successful. No other thoughts were streaming through my head despite the many warning signs. Maybe in my desperation, I didn't want to acknowledge the truth.

When I was midstream it hit me. There were swirls

of smoke in the air. The inevitable smell of burning plastic, chemicals, and... my head began to become light. Lighter and lighter my mind floated upwards towards the fan. My heart caught onto the game and began beating loudly and quickly. Suddenly, I wasn't just pissing like a racehorse...I was physically reenacting one.

The amount of crack smoke that filled the bathroom was obscene and dangerous. It lingered in the air as it swarmed around my unsuspecting body. No doubt the guy before me was tweaked out of his mind. Yet, he didn't even seem phased by the amount he ingested. I popped out of the bathroom feeling crazed and like I needed to tear apart the building. Not only was I enraged that I was in this situation- but I was also high as fuck.

My newly promoted Leader Olivia began laughing hysterically when I approached her and said "Oh shit! You are fucked up! I didn't know you like to play hard-ball. Is that why you never come to our late-night drink fests?"

"This isn't funny, I feel horrible. My head and heart are pounding, and I feel like I am going to pass out. It was the bathroom on the right-hand side. That fucking tweaker hot-boxed me." I kicked her out of her chair in the office and she immediately realized her joke was lost and out of line. She told Karl right away and his response was that we knew what to do. He was uninterested in my demise and more interested in giving the cute new cashier a tour around the building so she would feel prepared for her role. She was his newest hire and it was clear the cycle would be starting again.

Olivia and I got the giant box fan the store purchased for these very instances. The world was woozy and wavy as my head pounded with each step I took. Nausea was kicking in but it was important to stay strong and make sure we secured the bathroom so we could air it out properly. Nobody should feel the way I did at that moment. We positioned the fan so that the door was propped open allowing the giant fan force fresh air into the molested bathroom. This was such a common occurrence that we had a sign printed and laminated stating that the bathroom was in need of attention and to not move the fan. Olivia taped the sign up and suggested I sat back down in the office until I felt better. Sending me home would have done no good- I was in no condition to drive.

I wasn't the only one who experienced this. Our bathrooms being downed by illegal substances were the norm by the end of my time with the company. There would be days when both bathrooms would be down because of how prevalent the drug use was. The store had to invest in a second fan to battle the beast. It always took a good two hours or so to air out the bathrooms. The situation would leave many customers and employees on edge that the only bathrooms in the entire strip mall were out of order. Those were the days I was grateful that Lacy (a dear coworker) lived in the apartments behind the store and would let some of us use her bathroom when desperate measures were needed.

FIFTY-TWO

Put a Glove on It

The trope is no joke. Management sitting around checking their emails for hours while the employees are left scrambling to make ends meet was something that happened almost daily. There were some token Leaders who busted their ass just as much if not more than we did, I had a few of those angels during my career. They were the true M.V.P.'s. But, they weren't the ones getting promoted into Store Leadership positions. They didn't set themselves apart from us hourly folk well enough and were often passed up for that reason.

In the midst of not being able to hire decent humans to work because many people didn't feel safe to work in such a public setting during a worldwide pandemic, us team members were constantly on the move. We were drowning in the chaos of retail. Numerous times I would pass by the Leader's office and overhear their laughter while snacks were being shared (they sampled just as much as we did). Mumbling obscenities under my breath was the norm as I raced past the office door to serve multiple customers at once.

My never-ending to-do list was encroaching, and it was pivotal I left work on time that day. They didn't want me hitting overtime, but they also didn't want me to leave without making sure my section of the store was stocked perfectly. It became routine for only two of us to be working in my department for the entire day and between the Smoothie Bar and the Patiserie side, completing each assignment was my Mount Everest. Each task began to pile on and I was tired of being the Jackass carrying the weight of my team towards the top of the mountain. The other girls felt the same. We were the mules and if we knew better, we were to just keep our heads down. No raises, praises, or promotions were looming as a reward for our hard work so why were we carrying all of this weight?

Being fed up one day, I grabbed a couple boxes of the blue single use gloves we were to wear when handling food. My feet marched me into the Team Leader's office. Annie and Sal were sitting there presumably shooting the shit. I am sure if they were asked, they would have sworn on the company's failing stock that their conversation was vital to the success of the business. They most certainly would have added something about how they were discussing an extremely important and confidential email upper management always seemed to possess. Their work was so important and so pressing they didn't bother to close the door nor put away their snacks.

In a fury, I tossed the boxes on their desks. Annie's box of hand condoms was first. Her eyes grew wide and her mouth dropped a tad as the box fell clumsily on her desk. Sal luckily caught onto my gig and caught his box of freshly opened wrappers. Their eyebrows furrowed. How dare I treat them in such an undignified way! Didn't I know how to speak to my superiors? Usually, this is how the conversation went. My reply would always circle around the idea that if they truly were superior and of higher standing than me, I wouldn't have to ask for help more than once. They would be able to see that a team run by two people would need at least an extra hand. On a good day, this team needed four bodies to operate without a hitch. In my humble opinion, these Leaders were no better than I was. We were equally in the slums as long as we called the same company our employer.

"Prove to me you deserve your roles." I spat at them as they stared at the boxes dumbfounded. It wasn't the way I should have asked for help but I was halfway out the door when Annie began with her retort that never touched my ears.

Five minutes later, Sal and Annie came into the kitchen. I was able to organize two different stations for them to work on during the short interval between my demands and their response. A U Boat was waiting for Sal. Sal's new job was to stock the department salesfloor. My soul could not handle a conversation with him and was not willing to even breathe the same air as he did. The giant cart was stocked in the order of how things needed to go and I had previously written down the shelf life on each box. All he had to do was stock and tag the overly priced sweets. Annie's station was set up too. I had placed the brownies that needed to be taken out of their bulk packaging and placed into their new smaller packaging on the table. To make things easier, each of the four types of brownies were labeled with the number written on the plastic wrap of how many containers needed to be packed for each flavor. Next to her was placed a black cart so she could stock them in their special area when she was finished.

Instead of reprimanding me, Annie asked me if I was okay. Tears began to stream down my face, and I angrily explained there wasn't a single person in the store that was okay. We were all drowning. We were exhausted. We were tired of being invisible to Leadership and it was time they stepped up and jumped into the mosh pit of our store rather than sitting comfortably in the bleachers. The word vomit spewed for a few minutes and afterwards I felt numb, embarrassed, and empty. The poisons of my employment situation had exited my body in a violent and pathetic fit.

Sometimes I think back on the conversation and wonder if she was sincere when she apologized and swore she understood what I was saying. She had to play the game too. This company ran a Boy's Club, and she was the token female sprinkled into the sundae of Leadership. At the time I didn't care for her apology but looking back, I think she meant it. She was a smart cookie and deep down had a heart. Annie just had to protect herself just the same as anyone else.

This open conversation graduated to other things. We spoke about our kids and lives outside of the crumbling walls. She even gave me props- admitting I was really doing all the things and getting very little in return. She promised I would reap the rewards. Deep down in our hearts we both knew the rewards would start when I left the business. Annie even acknowledged how she struggled being a present parent because of how demanding retail was. She was married to her job and missed out on many milestones because of it. Out of my entire time knowing her, it was probably the sincerest moments I had ever had with her.

But then she finished packaging the brownies and it was time to label the diabetes inducing morsels. Have you ever seen *I Love Lucy?* The episode where she goes to See's Candy was basically playing out in the kitchen like it did however many years ago on American televisions.

Due to the monotony of labeling our products, my body had memorized the speed of the tags being printed. Print. Tear. Slap. Print. Tear. Slap. My movements were methodic and meditative. It soothed me to do this part. The sound of the machine's soft buzzing was hypnotic and often I would find I had labeled 30 plastic containers without even realizing what I was doing. It was a five minute Zen situation. For Annie though, it was anything but.

The PLU was typed into the machine and the number of labels she needed were typed in for her as well. All she had to do was press "start" and snag the tags as they printed. She began hootin' and hollerin' over how fast the tags were being spat out of the machine. Because the machines acted as if they were on AOL Dial-Up, by the time it registered she had pressed *cancel* a hundred times, her entire hand was wound up in unusable sticky tags. If I had a dollar for every tag that found itself wrapped around her finger, I would have made more money than I actually brought home. Because of this snafu, the machine became jammed. A jammed printer was a daily occurrence so it wasn't anything that concerned us kitchen folk. The tape enjoyed wrapping itself around the roller on the inside of the label machine- it too feared our customers and did anything it could to avoid its fate.

"Oh, don't worry, I got it." Was my response to her perplexed grimace as she realized the machine was jammed. To her, it was another service call. To me, it was just another day. "It gets jammed all the time."

"I'm sorry Boo, I thought I was going to be helping

but what in God's name do you do to keep up with that thing?" My smirk and giggle couldn't be repressed. It was an episode of UnderCover Boss yet her disguise was nothing but ignorance. "And what do you think you're doing with that knife?" Her hand went straight to her hip and her lips pursed. She didn't even think about the fact she would need to change her gloves because she touched her clothing.

"This? This is how we get things unstuck because this marvelous company can't seem to give us proper equipment" I squeezed the paring knife into the machine and delicately cut the tape. Slowly, layer by layer, I lifted the problem out of my way. Might as well put a scalpel in my hand... it's the same thing, right?

"No Boo, that's how you *break* the machine. I'll call in a service order." She began to reach for her phone.

"And wait for someone to take five days to do what I'm doing right now? No, thank you. And this machine isn't messed up because we unstick it, it's messed up because it's cheap as shit." Who was supposed to be tagging these brownies again?

"Well, it looks like you don't need me anymore." Annie began to turn away. She probably had e-mails to write about how insubordinate I was.

"Oh no, I need you. Aria needs her break and these still need to be stocked." I won't say it was me, but I won't deny it either. Someone pushed the brownie cart aggressively toward my fearless Leader.

"That's what you're here for." She flung her words at me as if they were boogers.

"Yes, would you like to take care of the cakes being picked up today and the pastries in the oven? It will take me two minutes to write down each item and explain how much time is left for them. There's only five types in there right now." I began to pull the parchment paper closer to me. If a list was to be made I needed to start making it.

"Oh you, always needing something. Fine. I'll find someone else willing to do your job." She scoffed and walked out. That was when our sincere conversation flew out the window. Was she playing me to get me to bend to her will? Or, was our conversation about juggling motherhood and retail the only genuine conversation I would ever have with her?

FIFTY-THREE

Tinkle Jar Victim

"Oh my God. Oh my God. Oh my God." His squeal could be heard the second he swung open the door to the industrial sized back room. "Oh my God. That was not apple cider vinegar." His face was twisted in a grimace that looked permanent. I never cared for Jack. Despite being on the panel that hired him, the second day he worked it was clear we made a mistake. Before any real information about his circumstance was revealed, it was mighty fun to watch him squirm. Nobody took his whining seriously because it was commonplace for him to get squeamish. This guy had no stomach and found himself working on the wrong side of town for thin skin.

"Well then what was it?" Someone piped up. My head was still bowed over my current task of shifting items from the shipping pallet to the U Boats for proper storage. It was better to just mind my own business. Ears perked, I was able to eavesdrop for a moment.

"It. Was. Piss. Piss!" He choked out the words as if he was trying to spit the waste matter off of his hands.

"Wait. What?" Now that was too far. I didn't like the guy but piss was a whole other monster. What was more unfortunate was the fact most of my coworkers weren't even phased. Of course, some whacko left piss in a jar. Between the hippies and the homeless, it was hard to decipher the mental illness when it walked into the store. We were in an area that battled mental instability, economic collapse, drug addiction of epic proportions, and of course pretentious hippies. Everyone looked unstable and homeless. It took a trained eye to interpret who was what.

"It's urine. I can smell it. It reeks. Oh my God, I have piss on my hands." He was trying to push his way to the bathroom. There was a line of three people waiting to relieve themselves and it was clear one of our daily patrons was using the bathroom as a safe place to alter their reality. Jack would need to wait his turn.

We would have offered him the kitchen sink and thrown caution to the wind with all the food safety violations, but the sink was currently broken and the nearest one was across the store in view of the public. We were all in agreement this incident needed to stay under wraps.

"Where was it?" Curious eyes began to pop up. Mine were included. This spectacle couldn't be ignored.

"The wine department. Someone put the jar behind a bottle of wine and I went to stock the wine and boom. Piss." His disgust was growing the more he thought about it.

Heads began to pop out of different crevices of the store and suddenly, either everyone was on break or nobody was. It was hard to tell. But we gathered around the back room ready for an emergency huddle- except Store Leadership was not welcomed. They wouldn't be able to do much. Maybe they would offer to check the faulty cameras but what would come of it? The culprit had left long ago and there was no telling if or when they would strike again.

Sure enough, the strikes kept coming. For six months people were finding jars of piss in their departments. Holes in shelves would be filled with the gift of urine. U-Boats would knock over jars of it as they were rushed to the sales floor in desperate need of the freshly delivered product. Jars were found in the walk-ins. They were found near the Food Bank Donation bins. Customers were either blind to it or magically never found the odd gifts. I sometimes giggle to myself thinking about their reactions- they already struggled to hear the word "no". They already struggled with the store's musty aroma and the way we polished our dilapidated joke of a store. It was our turd and we were told to be proud of it. But, there was just no way to eloquently explain why jars of human waste were being found across the market.

Rumors spread about how it had to be a disgruntled employee. Or maybe it was a former employee- it was hard to know but it made sense with how many people had left the company throughout the year. Some suggested it was a homeless person who was mentally ill. There was enough public anger and insanity sifting through the store that any scenario could have played out as well. To add to this conspiracy, it was usually the Leaders and Team Members who were disliked the most finding the jars. The attacks seemed pointed and intentional. Nobody could accept this yet the rumors flew to new heights when we realized who was finding the disgusting tokens of admiration.

Jar after jar, the unpleasant gifts continued to be placed delicately throughout the store. The mischief maker was well disguised and well aware of when certain areas of the store were being watched and when. And just when we felt like we were getting closer to answers, the droppings would stop. We would take a deep breath in gratitude that we no longer had to be nervous about grabbing a jar filled with a disgusting surprise. But sure enough, the jars showed their smelly selves once again.

We learned to be on guard most of the time. Leadership was on edge because they knew they should have been next. If it was an employee, they were convinced the jars of piss would probably be upgraded to warm shit smeared across their desks. A guilty conscience speaks volumes does it not? No such thing ever happened. For this reason alone, it couldn't have been a former or current worker.

The only area that hadn't been hit after six months was mine. I thought I was immune. My attitude was usually veiled enough to stave off customer complaints. Sometimes, I would slip but it was usually to someone who would rather sue me than urinate into a jar. My guard was only half up because of this.

It was business as usual for me. My exhausted body dragged the speed rack from one end of the store to another. I was only half paying attention because the massive amounts of caffeine I siphoned hadn't kicked in yet. The fluorescent lights were the Sirens above me singing hymns that one day I would break free from this place. The linoleum glided underneath me as if it was the Styx River leading me to Hades himself. Calm and collected, the store led me to my destiny- the cake case.

Usually, there would be some form of trash sitting near my display case. No biggie, people couldn't use basic problem-solving skills and needed to throw their trash away and at that very moment- how could they possibly walk two feet to the nearest waste receptacle? As I approached the display of sweets, my mind began focusing on the cakes needing to be grabbed. My concentration was broken by something sitting on the top of my pretty little diabetic nightmare of a display.

There it was, the usual trash. An apple juice bottle was perched perfectly on the top of my display case-mostly full. The juice sat there longingly waiting for its owner to snag it. The fullness of it told me that it had to belong to someone. They must have forgotten to grab it after they went to help a customer, clean something up, or take the department temps so it would be one thing off my Honey Do List.

In slow motion, my hand began to reach for the bottle. My heart was yelling "Nooooo" but my body was already hitting peak inertia. Newton's Law was in progress. There was no stopping and instead of my heart coming to an abrupt halt, it began to prance directly out of my chest. And then suddenly, I felt the warmth of the bottle and every hair on my body found itself standing straight up in perfect unison. I was the next victim.

Quickly and without thinking, I chucked the bottle as hard as I could into the trash. Thankfully, this bottle was dry on the outside. Many others were not so lucky and I had to say extra effort of making sure the urine made it into the bottle with a tiny hole was appreciated. The biohazard nestled deep into the trashcan and was buried by a flurry of paper towels from washing my hands raw.

After my incident, the jars were placed several more times. Each time the culprit struck my curiosity of who it was grew. The drop offs were happening so often again it became the new joke. Chupacabra was left to the wayside and the odd noises and random items literally flying off the shelves became old news. We were obsessed with the gruesome situation. If we could, we would have printed news articles to hang around the store. The headings would have read something like *New Tinkle Jar Victim Identified in the Meat Department.*

Just like Jack the Ripper, our newfound friend disappeared overnight. The jars of piss suddenly stopped appearing for good. If it was a disgruntled employee, they moved on to bigger things. If it was a homeless person, they were either dead or in jail. Either way, we never looked at apple juice or apple cider vinegar the same.

FIFTY-FOUR

Freedom Rings

Two weeks before the Fourth of July Roe V Wade was overturned. My girl-powered team was devastated. We began sharing countless stories about how we had to face the question of whether or not we were to get an abortion. This frustrated Karl and he kept reminding us to "keep political talk out of the kitchen". We never actually mentioned politics, just thoughts about how abortion is basic medical care. We spoke about our anatomy not policies. It only proved our point that our voices needed to be heard and it was time for us to begin talking- really talking. As a nation and as a team, we were tired of being silent. We were exhausted from the male-dominated system that touted the idea our bodies were to be governed over and shamed.

Lacy began making jewelry as a way to cope with the mounting pressures of the lingering pandemic and the pressing concerns for women's rights. She would come to work with perfectly crafted earrings, necklaces, and custom rings. It drew a lot of attention because we were eager to shop small and only spend our money on local women-owned businesses. Four days before our nation's birthday, she came in wearing the most beautiful and thought-out earrings I had ever seen.

She was adorned with black hangers dangling from her ears. When asked, she said she had ordered a bunch of Barbie hangers as a way to hang her new jewelry neatly. The only reason why she made the hanger earrings was to see how well they held up and to make sure they could handle any sort of weight. As our conversation continued, our eyes grew large with excitement. A plan was devised. We have found a way for our voices to be quietly heard.

On the morning of the Fourth, my cake case was decked out in red, white, and blue. Cakes were dressed neatly with buttercream frosting and there was no detail missed. Beers and firecrackers were displayed effortlessly throughout the store allowing our customers to feel the true American Spirit riddled with capitalism and bad eating habits. Like always, I checked my case for missing cakes before clocking in. This was a terrible habit I never learned how to break. There were gaping holes but it was already planned and my arsenal of cakes were ready for action.

As I strolled towards the back I noticed there wasn't anybody on the sales floor. This was odd because it was eight am on the day of our blessed country's birthday. It was an all hands on deck holiday yet there were no hands… and a lot of empty deck. Thankfully I snapped out of my thoughtstream as soon as I attempted to swing the door to the employee area because at the very moment I was trying to slip through, I noticed there were several people standing in the way. I knocked as a courtesy but then quickly realized why they were all standing there. Because of how lost I was in thought, I didn't hear the slightly muffled screams from Karl.

"And don't you ever think about bringing in outside food or drink! What do our customers think when they see this? Hmm? Do you think they feel you have confidence in our products? Does it tell them that they should spend their money elsewhere? Does your behavior tell them that it is okay to not spend your money at this company? How would you feel if someone was walking around eating a McDonald's Happy Meal while working at Olive Garden? Come on! You are embarrassing as team members. You are completely indignant! If you think you can waltz right over me, well, you've got another thing coming. The next person I see carrying a cup or food from another establishment... the next time I see this... it will be an immediate final. I could have you all replaced by tomorrow if I wanted. No more outside food or drinks!" He was in one of his rages and customers could hear him screaming at us. Squeezing myself through the door made it impossible for customers to ignore the spectacle.

A passerby popped her head in to make sure us team members were okay before I could even get a glimpse of Karl's mouth twisted with anguish. I slipped by Karl, clocked in, and sipped my Starbucks quietly as I snuck through my coworkers. If it wasn't for that random customer doing a welfare check, I probably would have been roped into the manic speech and been used as an example for bringing in contraband. Nothing like an irate store Leader on the day of Freedom.

As the day continued, Karl was starting to notice something about the outfits my team was wearing. Through my conversation with Lacy, we decided to spread the word that every woman in the store should wear all black on July 4th and wear the earrings Lacy made out of the Barbie hangers she just bulk purchased. Over half of the women in the store agreed and we were all dressed head to toe in black and wore our statement earrings while serving customers red-handed. Our fingers were stained red from the red food coloring she splattered on the earring holders.

Karl was walking around the store in a panic and carefully observed our wardrobe. He couldn't truly cite us on this, and we were technically doing nothing wrong according to our Retail Bible. It said we could not cause disruption, but it never said anything about a silent protest for women's reproductive health rights. It never said anything about us organizing against a new political era. It did say that if we organize and try to unionize we would be fired. But we weren't there to throw over good ol' You-Know-Who, we were here to state that hangers were the only sign of freedom a woman had anymore.

"Where did you get those earrings?" Karl inquired. To this day, I have no clue why he asked me. He knew better than to ask the one person who consistently challenged him. I was not afraid of him anymore. Karl should have realized that I knew I didn't have to answer him nor did I need to explain myself. There would be no clean-cut throw your coworker under the bus answers spilling from my mouth. And I certainly wasn't about to tell him it was my idea.

"Oh, a local artist made them! I love them. They are light and hang onto my ears easily." I smirked as his smile faded. It wasn't the answer he wanted and he realized I would rather get written up than bleed out the name of my ally.

The rest of the day us girls were heavily enjoying ourselves. Many of our customers understood the statement we were making with our black outfits and hangers dripping from our ears. It was hard to stay silent due to the sheer pride of our silent protest. When customers "got it" and praised us, we would proudly relish in our moment of power.

Karl must have gotten some cardio in while he struggled to figure out who provided the earrings, what they meant, and how to write 75% of the store up without catching the eye of the Corporate Champions. He dashed from one team to another, squinting and glaring at us. Trying to figure out who was the culprit and why we chose to organize in such a way. Yet, he couldn't. He popped behind the olive bar, the salad bar, coolers, anything he could to peek at us and eavesdrop thinking we were going to openly talk about our protest. He was more active in the store than we had ever seen him be. Karl was being driven insane trying to gather evidence. Most of us naturally wore a lot of black and usually when one person found a new jewelry artist, we all jumped on board. So while we were absolutely protesting, it was difficult for him to prove it.

It was another instance to confirm he did not control us and we would find a way to remind him that we were free individuals.

July 5th rolled around and there was a printed sign by the time clock. It read *Under no circumstances should large jewelry be worn during work. Large earrings that dangle are not to be worn.* The Retail Bible never discussed earrings. Before my shift even started, someone had already ripped the page about dress code out and highlighted that earrings were in fact, not banned from employee attire. This was stapled to Karl's note anonymously.

FIFTY-FIVE

Pass the Roach

No matter what store I worked at, there would be an influx of insects infesting the building during the summer and winter months. It was the perfect storm of extreme weather and shitty pipes, old buildings, and well... the promise of food. In my last store, it was a nightmare. If you get queasy with bugs you would not survive the summer and winter months in the kitchens my company provided. The summer months were the worst because not only would you have to deter roaches, but you would also become tasked with deterring flies, mice, and the occasional bird or rodent (a bunny once found itself in our kitchen).

Hot summer days meant perfect breeding grounds for flies and there was no amount of food-safe deterrent that could keep them at bay. On our resumes, we should have really written down "fly ninja" as a special skill. Twisting up the cleaning towels and snapping them to kill our prey like high school boys in a locker room became an everyday achievement. The walls in the kitchen were lined with post-its filled with tally marks of how many flies we killed. Just like cops, we swore there were no incentives. Yet, at the end of the month, we grew more competitive trying to earn the coveted contraband coffee we would win from a local cafe. Obviously, Leadership was not included in this competition or else it would have been a $5 gift card to the store- so we could buy a partial lunch.

Customers would complain about the infestation. This was the only instance where the customer was right. It was disgusting and embarrassing to be boasting our high food standards while there was a ball of flies openly gnawing at our vegan mac n cheese. Maybe it was all the extra protein from fly legs that made the food healthy? Or we could think of it as a workout for our immune systems. Not only are you purchasing your fresh pepperoni pizza, but you are also gaining antibodies!

And just like flies, if you saw one roach you knew there were hundreds that weren't visible. They really loved the crappy sewage systems in the store and were always found near the drains. My last summer at the company was the worst to date. The store was infected by the parasite and they were becoming ballsy. Those fuckers would run out of the sugar and onto the salesfloor in broad daylight. Many times I would find myself stomping on one stealthily while speaking to a customer about cereal. I had to keep my chill and act like their precious breakfast story was the lead singer of my attention. These roaches were fast, they were big, and they could fly.

Upon sighting them, most of the girls I worked with would screech and hurl themselves as far away from them as possible leaving the boys to kill them and clean them up. They would willingly fling themselves into the trope of being a damsel in distress.

As for me, I killed the roaches. It was satisfying feeling them squish beneath my feet. The hard shell and their nougat-like filling spilling out like a Cadbury Egg were fascinating to me. It was interesting to me watching how their body would squirm and yet be shattered or even cut in half. But I would rarely clean them up. The dead carcass was made to be a warning for the other bugs- a sort of medieval *No Trespassing* sign.

In one day, I had killed 15 of them. Which meant there were probably at least 500 more creeping around the building unseen. I began a tally in permanent marker on the wall of how many were slaughtered by my wrath. There was no need for a label. We all knew. Annie couldn't figure out what the tally meant but it was because she was rarely in the kitchen. Leadership figured we were just being whiny when we complained about the insects. Maybe the writing needed to be literally on the wall. While it wasn't ideal to be caught defacing the mid-century property, I was willing to take the hit for the team to get our voices heard.

As the tally began to climb higher, my team began to realize it was me who was creating it. They also realized it was for the amount of roaches that I was responsible for killing. When the lightbulb went off in their heads, the boys began doing the same. They just knew better than to fuck with my tally so they began their own. In one day we collectively added another 16 tally's onto the wall. I would like to think that these tally's live on and are a warning to my successors. Hopefully, they notice the foreboding tallies and are just as obsessed with them as Olfgen was with the writing in her armoire in Hand-maid's Tale.

Another record was broken late in the season. Twenty-three of them. What were we going to do with twenty-three roaches? If they were cannabis, we would have had a grand ol' party. But, they were the OG roaches and we were tired of looking at them in our garbage cans. That is when Brendan, one of the line cooks, and I exchanged glances. We knew exactly what to do.

Our secret needed to stay under wraps because there was an imposter among us and we still didn't know who it was. There was a dustpan everyone hated and we knew nobody would seek it out so we took it and hid it in the walk-in cooler. Anytime someone told us of a new kill, we politely offered to sweep it up. As the tallies grew on the wall, the dustpan began to fill with the dead.

"Bring Out Your Dead!" I would chant as I whisked around the kitchen sweeping up the murdered roaches. My job was part one of the mission. I worked days and was under close watch by Leadership. It was well known I was the defector of the group and they wanted so badly to catch me in the act. Thankfully, Brendan worked most nights- when Leadership usually had already gone home. He was tasked with the second part of the job.

Just before closing, he would do a "final sweep". The dustpan would emerge from its shelter in the giant fridge. He would offer to sweep the Team Leader's office. Because of the ancient wiring, cameras could not be installed in the office and the ones monitoring outside of the room pretending to witness who went into the office were fuzzy at best. Plus, the front office was a hub for many things. His intentions would be safe as he would slip into the enemy's realm every night.

This is when our plan would come to fruition. When nobody was looking, he would shove the roaches that weren't oozing their yellow guts under Karl's locked door. He would shove them using different amounts of strength to make it look natural. Every now and then, Karl or Annie would leave their door unlocked on accident and Brendan would place the roaches around the offices with precision. Some were to be found immediately, some were to be found much later.

It puzzled them every single day. Karl began deep cleaning his office. He began asking us if we noticed an issue with roaches and we all said it was getting out of control. Our fearless Leader began researching new ways to deter and kill them. Annie and Karl just could not figure out why there were so many dead roaches in their offices. Their lunches were no longer taken in their private quarters and the candy Annie would offer to sweeten us up disappeared to hopefully deter the roaches from crawling near her desk. No matter their efforts, the roaches kept coming.

For months, it drove Karl mad. He would stay perplexed as to how this was happening. Why were they so attracted to his office? Why would they only sometimes show up in Annie and Sal's? Sometimes I wish I stuck around long enough to continue their confusion. I don't know when they figured it out...or if they ever did.

FIFTY-SIX

I Quit

I t took several years to make it through the resume screening process. Many employers looked over my skills as a retail employee and suggested that they were not transferable to their companies. Hiring Leaders would tell me to look within my field and to provide a better understanding of the roles I was applying for. Clearly, they weren't seeing my potential. As my college degree inched closer every day, I began to worry my academic achievements would be overshadowed by my decade-long career in retail.

Content writing companies would suggest I didn't know how to identify a customer base. If I couldn't identify a customer base, then how would I grow it? But what they didn't understand was that retail was molding yourself to and curating an intriguing monologue to a revolving door of different types of customers. My job was to identify the needs of each customer and be ready to pitch a sale to steer them towards whatever item I was pushing that week. Maybe it wasn't a written word campaign, but it was absolutely a form of communication and advertising. The companies I was applying to would tout about how communication was a vital part of the role and without proper experience, I was surely going to flounder in the positions offered.

They didn't take into consideration that retail is sales and my job as a content writer would be easier than what I was already doing. Communication, customer retention, and growing the client base was at the heart of my role in grocery retail. At least with their jobs I would have a target audience that I could aim at comfortably.

When I applied for Human Resources positions, they would tell me I needed experience in employee relations. These companies perceived my lack of experience in an office as a lack of understanding of the human nature part of the job. They also thought that I wouldn't have the wherewithal to speak on public platforms and communicate effectively due to my "low" status. Recruiters would suggest that my job didn't suffice as proper communication experience because I was not working in employee relations directly.

Basically, I had no true experience in the field and companies were at a pivotal era in their hiring where they were able to choose candidates with tenure over fresh meat. Companies scrutinized me and assumed my problem-solving skills were not at par due to the paper descriptions of my roles.

These same companies were convinced I lacked the ability to prioritize tasks. They questioned my time management skills and worried I wouldn't be able to juggle multiple projects at a time. A common misconception is that retail workers are given tasks and we are to complete them like mindless robots in the order in which they are written. This is not the case for any company. Even assembly line workers need to prioritize their tasks.

Analyzing evolving weekly schedules and then organizing, planning, and executing "important" training modules for 30+ people each week was not credited as enough experience in time management nor was it acceptable experience for Leadership skills. Neither was my ability to take a mile long list and conquer every goal set out before me without fail. My accomplishment of beating year over year sales by over 30% each year was not impressive to many of my application viewers. By the time I was applying for jobs, I was able to perform four to five tasks at a time.

It became clear my experience working with the public was not enough. My experience working in constantly evolving conditions wasn't enough. My status as a hero who could conquer all things such as global pandemics was only relevant if I stayed in my genre as a retail employee. I stocked the shelves while everyone thought their Amazon boxes were going to kill them. I calmed down customers and coworkers from nervous breakdowns. And at night, I would help my kids through their schooling and then work on my own. Putting this all down on paper I wonder how any of us made it through. We were not doctors, therapists, or even mediators yet we were flung into emergency situation after emergency situation. Due to this, we learned skills every day that would benefit any career.

But none of that mattered. On paper, I was someone who was destined for a life of hourly wages. It began to feel as if I should stay in my lane and never hope for anything above what was offered to me. Businesses couldn't wrap their minds around the idea that I was capable of anything beyond the perceived confines of stalking shelves. I was capable of organizing learning opportunities, commanding a team, problem solving techniques, mass communication, and organizing events.

And then an opportunity came. A dear friend of mine connected me to a resume writer, Natalie, who saw my potential. Natalie saw my budding future and urged me to see it in myself again. She created a resume that properly highlighted every skill I possessed in a seemingly unskilled type of career. This incredible human reminded me I was capable and ready to take on a role outside of retail.

And then the moment came. A job I desperately wanted was available in educational research- hosted by a dream company. In my mind, I was nowhere near qualified, and my resume lacked many prerequisites. I had been sent more rejection emails than I could ever count, and felt hesitant to hear another dismissal. Natalie urged me to apply with my new resume. Everything I had accomplished was on this one document and it was begging to be sent out. She was confident my potential would now be seen.

I thought about it for a while. I was afraid. And yet, what was another rejection but a reminder that this world is a cruel and dark place? Maybe sending in the resume was a subconscious self deprecating attempt at reminding myself that I was never leaving the company. I was destined for a world of piss-filled jars, customers yelling at me for prices I have no control over, and a turbulent schedule that would siphon me out of my role as a present parent. But, I applied anyway due to the amount of encouragement from my coworkers and Natalie.

Already accepting defeat, I wasn't ready for the phone call that came. My skill set was recognized. I was to be interviewed and they wanted to talk to me sooner than later. The position had a strict starting date and it was creeping closer and closer. Despite the deadline, the hiring team made it inherently clear one of the reasons why they were still looking for a candidate was because they were refusing to settle. This would not be an easy interview.

A week later, the interview was to be held. I was scheduled despite my attempt to get the day off. Thankfully, the hiring Leader who was hosting the interview was accommodating. We agreed to do the interview via Zoom and I covered up my grease stained company work shirt with a cheap blazer I had purchased a few years ago. Purchasing the blazer was my way of sending out my intentions into the universe to leave the world of retail. If I bought it, maybe the opportunity would come. It sat in my closet for three years wishing for the day it would be used. I don't know who was more excited- me or the blazer when I dusted it off and promised it would be put to good use.

The day of the interview came quickly. I walked into the industrial-sized kitchen with my laptop in hand and my old friend draped over my shoulders.

"What are you doing with that?" Annie asked me as she was walking out of the office.

"Oh, I have an interview today. I will be taking my lunch early." Her smile dropped. Was she happy she potentially didn't have to deal with me anymore? Was she nervous because her top player was making it obvious she was leaving? Either way, it was my goal to get out of retail no matter what toes I needed to step on.

"Oh, yeah that's fine." As if any other answer would have been acceptable. Of course, it was fine.

The minutes crept towards me as if they were a thief in the night. Vomit swelled inside my throat just long enough for me to panic. My hands grew sweaty and cold (is this where I talk about Mom's Spaghetti?). It was time to interview. Every bone in my body told me I wasn't ready. From the massive amounts of rejection emails and straight up ghosting from previous companies I was convinced that I was simply wasting everyone's time. Shakily, my finger pressed my employee ID into the time clock for my early lunch and decided to press forward with the interview.

I pranced out to the parking lot thinking the morning rush had subsided. This was terrible thinking- it was the summer and there was no such thing as a rush. Customers were a steady stream lazy from the early morning heat. As my Zoom meeting was encroaching, a large truck pulled to the front of the store. To make sure I understood they were in the parking spot near me, the driver revved his engine a few times before he got out. Fear slunk into my soul thinking about how this engine could tank my interview. He had to turn off his truck right? Nobody was wasting gas right now. I thought, but the engine never subsided. Still, this was the quietest place I could interview. Warily, I began to log into the meeting.

The monster truck purred like a loud cat as the mini conference began. The hiring manager was hurling questions my way as his confidant was clearly being pulled out of vacation mode to meet with me. Guilt and imposter syndrome danced around the table I was sitting at. Would they notice I was scared shitless? Did they know this was my last shot at a job I could possibly enjoy? Their questions stumbled over the roar of my new jet engine friend and they thankfully had a sense of humor about the situation.

Multiple times, I was stumped by their questions. My

words puddled at their feet in a murky stutter that I just couldn't mop up easily. This was not the career I had studied for and I began to become nervous I was possibly setting myself up for failure. This company was well known by the community as the best of the best. The lead boss had a major pull in the realm of education. Only the best were hired by the team I was speaking to. By the time we had finished the interview my heart had broken. There was just no way I pulled this off. My jet engine frenemy fled the scene and I was left to sit in my own silence.

Three hours and a panic attack later, I received a phone call. They offered me the position. My phone slipped out of my hand and my jaw dropped further than the Mariana Trench. I didn't know how to respond but I knew that the answer was yes, I would accept. The caveat was that I knew nothing about the profession and needed to learn quickly. This was fine. I wasn't too terrified of that part. A special skill of mine was to pick up new knowledge quickly and for some reason I enjoyed putting myself in sink or swim situations.

The other caveat was that I had to start nearly immediately. There was no time to waste and the clock was ticking. A two weeks notice couldn't be entertained and I was expected to cut ties with the company in a not so great way. After my shift was over and I was berated by another customer for not having sugar free pastries, it became clear to me that this bridge was intended to be burnt down.

Soon after the paperwork was signed with my new company, I had made my mind up on how I would go. If I couldn't leave on good terms, I would make sure I left in a style that was fitting for who I was and how the grocery retailer had treated me for so many years.

My car made a pit stop on the early summer morning of my departure. I stood tall and walked into a donut shop. I wanted to make sure Karl, Annie, and Sal knew I didn't care about the emergency "store meeting" a few weeks prior about outside food and drink. If I brought some in though, what would he be able to do anyways? Fire me? The best would be a final write-up. Plus, I was quitting anyway.

I watched as the donut shop employee stuffed the box full of donuts. She was trying to make small talk but I was too giddy and nervous to reply. For over a decade I had dreamt of this day and it was finally here. I always joked about causing a scene when I left. Everybody thought I was too chicken shit to do it. Yet, here I was standing in the middle of a donut shop purchasing donuts I knew better than to bring into the building.

The car ride to the store was filled with excited nerves. I decided to take my time to calm myself before my big entrance and got my tire pressure checked. I stopped to get a coffee from a local coffee shop across the way. My lollygagging needed to come to an end. Today was a day of triumph- I was to leave on my own terms. As a last attempt to prolong the announcement, I wrote a note to my store on the inside of the donut box. And then it was the moment I had been waiting for for so many years. I waltzed into the store for the last time.

Customers side-eyed me while I entered the building with the donut box wide open. I told my coworkers to meet me in the back so they could read what I had written on the lid. The bright colors of the donuts lit up the muted walls that surrounded us. Donuts adorned with gummy worms and googly eyes pierced through the depression that perpetually lingered in the store's air. Gasps and laughter began to fill the store on that fateful morning. Cheers were being shouted and well wishes were pushed towards me as I clocked in for my final shift.

Store Leadership didn't know how to respond. Usually, people who want to leave on bad terms will cuss them out and stomp their feet. I was still making a spectacle of myself but I wasn't violent. In fact, I was the opposite of violent. I was offering donuts of marginalized peace. They were my tattered and stained white flag. By the time my shift was over that day, I was spoken to by Annie about how she didn't think I would be the type of person to leave like this. My response was something along the lines of how they clearly have never taken me seriously.

When my final shift was over, I left the empty box open as a reminder of how the company had left me-empty and depleted. Plus, Karl wasn't there that day and it was imperative that he saw the empty box waiting for him at my station with the note still scribbled on the lid-*see ya on the flip side, I quit.* I hoped to see some of my friends on the other side, they didn't deserve the world we were in. But as for me, I had finally quit.

CPSIA information can be obtained
at www.ICGtesting.com
Printed in the USA
BVHW040800250723
667766BV00006B/77